The Absent Heart

*a novel inspired by the letters of
Robert Louis Stevenson*

ALI BACON

Praise for The Absent Heart

'Stylish and lyrical, a vivid evocation of these people and their milieu. Had me reading at 3am.'
Catherine Czerkawska, author of *The Jewel, The Amber Heart*

'An uplifting, at times heart-breaking, novel of three people whose existence became central to each other and the misunderstandings and jealousies that this engendered.

Meticulously researched, beautifully written, a glorious book.'
Sarah Bourne, author of *Ella's War, The Exile*

'This gorgeous story about love and devotion imagines Frances Sitwell's life trying to balance her relationships with the two men she loved. This story is a testament to the strength of women. I loved it.'
Jane Anderson, author of *The Girl Who Fled the Painting, The Paintress*

'I was carried away by this achingly beautiful love story. I knew little of Stevenson before and delighted in learning more about him in this lovingly crafted novel. A triumph.'
Rachael Gray, author of *The Elderwick Mysteries* series.

*'Absences are a good influence in love
and keep it bright and delicate'*
Robert Louis Stevenson

'Sir, more than kisses, letters mingle souls…'
To Sir Henry Wotton, John Donne

Published by Linen Press, London 2025
8 Maltings Lodge
Corney Reach Way
London W4 2TT
www.linen-press.com

A CIP catalogue record for this book is available from the British Library.

Cover art: Arcangel
Typeset by Zebedee
Printed and bound by Lightning Source
ISBN 978-1-0683417-7-9

Dedicated to the memory of Charles Lowe, 1849-1931,
native of Brechin in Angus, graduate of Edinburgh
University, writer for *The Times* newspaper
and acquaintance of Robert Louis Stevenson.
Also to his surviving third, fourth and fifth generation
cousins, Dorothy, Morag, Keith, Steve, Ellie,
Lizzie, Callum, Max and Zoe.

Acknowledgments

As ever, many people helped bring this book into being. Thanks go, first of all, to the community of Stevenson scholars who welcomed me to their midst and provided encouragement at many steps along the way. Jeremy Hodges, Stevenson biographer and secretary of the Robert Louis Stevenson Club, provided support from the outset and made detailed comments on an early draft, while Richard Drury, Robert Louis Abrahamson, Mafalda Cipollone and participants of the RLS Conference 2022 in Bordeaux offered advice and useful information. Wes Rogers from Hamilton, Australia, came late to my inbox but contributed a wealth of information about the real Frances Sitwell and her family.

However, perhaps my biggest debt of gratitude goes to writer, researcher and all-round creative Jude Jablonski of Milwaukee. After a chance encounter at an online event, our long-distance conversations sustained me through the ups and downs of several drafts and continues to this day. I have her to thank for both friendship and unabated enthusiasm for *The Absent Heart* in all its incarnations.

Fellow writers of Just Write Bristol have played as big a part as always and novelist Catherine Czerkawska provided insight at a critical stage.

Huge appreciation too, to Lynn Michell for accepting my second offering of historical fiction and ensuring it came up to scratch, also to her band of Linen Press interns for enthusiastic support.

And the usual suspect! Thanks to my sister Dorothy for being the Suffolk connection and husband Geoff for accompanying me on research trips, (except to France, where Penny Morse endured a record-breaking heat-wave, for which I can only apologise!) Thanks to daughter Ellie for her interest and design input. I hope all of you feel the outcome was worth the energy expended.

Historical notes are at the end of the book. Any errors of fact or judgement are my own.

About the Author

After graduating from St Andrews University, Ali moved to the South West of England where her writing is still strongly influenced by her Scottish roots. Following her first contemporary novel, *A Kettle of Fish*, she wrote *In the Blink of an Eye* (Linen Press, 2018) which reimagines the life of an early Edinburgh photographer and was listed in the ASLS best Scottish books of that year. She has had a number of short story successes (Evesham Short Story Prize, Bristol Short Story Prize, Local Writer) and regularly takes part in literary events. She conceived *The Absent Heart* through a family connection to the writer R. L. Stevenson.

A Meeting

Cockfield Rectory, Suffolk, 1873
Frances was susceptible to shadows, to seeing things from
the corner of her eye which disappeared when she looked
more closely. That's what made it so astonishing when
the movement she glimpsed through the window turned
out to be real. She was in the drawing room with a book
on her lap, but the words skittered across the page in a
meaningless dance. She sighed and laid the book aside.
Maud, her friend and hostess, was hemming pillowcases.
The mantle clock chimed a silver note and outside a flicker
of light shivered between the poplars. There it was again,
the shiver, the shift in the atmosphere. Someone was
emerging from the tree-line; long-legged, stick thin, an
angular frame clothed in a soft flapping jacket, a face
obscured by a straw hat. A real person. This time she was
not mistaken.

She trawled through the mist of that morning's
conversation. 'Oh,' she said to Maud. 'Could this be your
cousin, do you think?'

Maud didn't turn to look but bit off her cotton sewing-
thread with an efficient snap. 'He's not due until six. But
Lou's movements are rarely predictable.'

Outside, the young man stopped, spent a few moments
gazing back at the way he had come, then made a leisurely
turn towards the house. As he walked, he skipped and

kicked at small obstacles on the gravel path like a child playing hopscotch. By contrast, the tune he whistled was in a minor key.

Frances closed her eyes and tried to place the melody. When she opened them, he was opposite the window but evidently couldn't see her, because his gaze scanned first the billowing sky, then the massed greenery of the garden, lighting on the spot where the pond winked between the trees. He smiled and she felt his surprise. *Here's something new.*

Frances's son, Bertie, was playing a solitary game on the rug. He jumped up and ran to the window where the new arrival came closer and pulled faces through the glass so that the boy laughed and grimaced in reply.

Maud got to her feet and a few minutes later brought her cousin into the room. 'Lou, this is my dear friend, Mrs Sitwell.'

He had hazel eyes set wide apart and an air of expectancy. He blinked like a woodland creature waking from sleep, alert to each change of the air. Having ascertained things were to his liking, he came forward, brushed his dusty lapels and dropped to one knee in front of her. '*Madame*, Robert Louis Stevenson, *à votre service.*'

He was being deliberately comical and she very much wanted to laugh, except she'd forgotten how. Instead, she put her hand to her mouth, then touched his shoulder to bring him to his feet. He caught her hand and kissed it and the shock made her snatch her fingers away.

Bertie couldn't contain himself. 'Come and see the garden, there's a boat and an island!'

Louis was being dragged outside. 'You and I, we'll talk later, won't we?'

A knot gathered in her chest. She didn't talk. She had forgotten how.

Louis and Bertie disappeared down the hall. She could hear them chatting like old chums and from the window saw them emerge into the garden. She and Maud looked out to where Louis was steadying the boat in the shallow water, the sun full on his face. He was pale-skinned, neither handsome nor displeasing, his features still settling to their final form.

Maud sighed. 'I had forgotten what a fidget he is. Never still for a minute. Don't let him annoy you.'

Not long after, he was back, a languid shadow in the doorway. Maud had left the room. His eyes glinted. 'Your son has gone off to have his tea. I'm not disturbing you?'

She shook her head.

He motioned to the Chesterfield. 'May I sit?'

She nodded and he folded himself next to her, a complication of arms and legs. His eyes were too large for his face, the slim-fingered hands moved in a broken rhythm as he spoke. His hair, growing long at the temples, hung forward. He brushed it back with both hands, then placed them on his knees and stared at them in fierce concentration.

'Thank you for playing with Bertie,' she said. 'He needs company. Badly.'

'I had a lonely childhood too,' he said, 'I know how it feels.'

The knot in her chest was starting to unravel.

He raised his eyes. 'I can't help thinking we have things to say to each other,' he said, 'I don't know what, or why.'

He grasped her wrist, asking for help or offering, she didn't know which. She looked at the hand and felt its weight. Since the loss of Freddie, no one had touched her. No one had dared.

The knot was undone. When she tried to speak, her mouth was shapeless. She barely felt his arm around her shoulder but a voice was crooning close to her ear, 'There, there.'

When she had collected herself, she apologised for her tears.

His smile was wide. 'Nothing like a good greet,' he said. 'My childhood nurse did the same for me many a time.' He took his arm from around her.

It was her turn to offer comfort. 'Tell me about your nurse, about your childhood. Tell me everything.'

He heaved a great sigh and his story tumbled out. 'I've used my parents badly. I tried to be honest, I offended them. I'll never be forgiven.'

She understood none of this. 'A good father will always forgive.'

He shook his head. 'He has run out of forgiveness. His patience is at an end.'

Her hand was on his shoulder and he took it and gripped it fiercely, so hard he was crushing her fingers. She prised them away as gently as she could.

He groaned. 'Now I've hurt you!'

'Only a little.'

He slid to the floor, raised her hand to his lips and kissed it several times like a puppy demanding affection. 'Just give me a skelp and send me upstairs. We won't speak of my troubles again. Now you must hold *my* hand so tightly it hurts.' He placed her fingers around his, 'No, tighter!'

This time she didn't hold back her laughter. 'Louis Stevenson, wherever did you come from?'

His eyes were mischievous. 'I came from Waverley Station, a badly-wrapped parcel flung on the train, or maybe I was sent by Heaven.'

He rested back against her skirt. His eyes were closed as he spoke. 'Can I stay here?'

The boy needed consolation. She imagined the softness of his hair if she were to lay her hands on his head. The imprint of his body on her legs was warm and solid. She allowed her thoughts to drift. Outside, the surface of the pond was unruffled, its shallow waters held no danger. This village, the house, its garden, this was her place of safety.

PART ONE

Sanctuary

I hope you are well today, and le chapelain did not trouble you.

Robert Louis Stevenson to Frances Sitwell,
1st September 1873[*]

[*] Booth, B.A. & Mehew, E. (eds.) (1994-5). The Letters of Robert Louis Stevenson. New Haven/London: Yale University Press, Vol.1, p.288.

1.

Minster, Kent, 1868
As Albert heaved himself off the bed and began to dress, Frances turned to look the other way. *Don't catch his eye.* Daylight was creeping around the curtain. Her face looked back at her from the wardrobe mirror, a pale smudge, accusing her of cowardice. Albert's morning fumbling had come to nothing and it was best not to remind him of his failure. The more he feared impotence the rougher he became, as if violence would instigate desire, which in his case it sometimes did. Better to let him pretend there had been some satisfaction than have him prod himself to life and try again. The bruises from his last attempt on her were only just beginning to fade.

Later, she stood at the vicarage window and watched him stride down the path and out of the gate, eager to catch the London train. His coat was brushed, his bristled neck a plump cushion between the white half-circle of his dog collar and the rim of his black hat. His head was cocked a little to one side, unmistakable pleasure in the set of his shoulders. He was as glad to be leaving as she was pleased to see him go, but for her the inrush of relief would be short-lived.

Of all the places she had expected to end up, the Island of Thanet was not one of them, but this is where marriage had finally brought her, a chalky plain with neither estuary nor open sea in sight. Would things have been different if she had been washed up on a real island with speckled seas and breezy cliff-top paths, instead of this flat landscape where the dismal hedge blocked out a low horizon?

She sat down at the table where the previous day she had begun a letter. *Dear Mother.* Her pen refused to go beyond the salutation. It was ten years since they had seen each other, twelve since Susan had invited Albert Sitwell to their Dublin home where she liked to show off her daughters at musical evenings. Frances had inherited her mother's dark hair and strong profile, and had recently acquired a deep bosom, enhanced by a slender waist which defied demure corseting. Her father called her his handsome filly. Young men's eyes came to rest on her then slid away, disconcerted by such conspicuous femininity. She sometimes looked at her sister, Suka, freckled and gangly, with something like envy.

Only Albert Sitwell, a little older and unabashed, whirled her into a dance. 'You're the most beautiful woman I have laid eyes on,' he whispered in her ear.

She shook him off, but he was handsome and lively and she wanted to be loved, even if there was whiskey on his breath.

He was given a living in Stepney. 'There are worse things to be than a vicar's wife,' her mother said. 'And London, think of it!'

Frances thought of it daily, a place of books and writers. Even more than in Dublin, a woman could be part of it. And she had reached womanhood. She felt the pull of its current; to be of one flesh, to procreate children. Her family moved to Australia. She chose Albert.

She laid her letter aside. In the upstairs playroom, Freddie and Bertie were squabbling. She went to scold them, then stopped at the door. They were wrestling together, a bundle of laughter, fair heads almost indistinguishable. She separated them in her mind, Bertie eternally playful, Freddie, a little older but needing to be coaxed into his brother's boisterous games. She went to ruffle their hair, tickling their warm necks to keep them laughing. The sound drove the shadows from the low-ceilinged room. Her sons were the only part of her life with Albert that she couldn't regret. Freddie would soon be nine, Bertie eight already. Soon they would go off to school. How she would miss them.

Downstairs she wrote her letter; Albert and the children were well; the weather was dispiriting, she amused herself as best she could. There was no point in complaining. If her marriage, embarked on with such hope, had become a prison cell, it was up to her to scour the walls and find a chink of light.

She thought of Albert's jaunty departure. His position in the church gave him the use of a house in Bayswater. This is where he ran off to with such enthusiasm. Frances was never invited but it was time to stake her claim on a life beyond this almost-island. She called to the boys to get ready for a trip, an adventure, she called it.

The house in Chepstow Place was smaller by far than the vicarage, but as she got the boys down from the carriage its aspect pleased her. It was painted white. It sat neatly between its neighbours. She wrinkled her nose. The odour from the Thames was unavoidable, but it reminded her of Dublin and the possibilities she had glimpsed as she danced in her mother's sitting room.

The Irish housekeeper, big boned with hooded eyes, was surprised to see her.

'Himself is bringing visitors back. Men of the cloth. I've prepared afternoon tea.'

Frances stood firm and the woman, grumbling a call to the maid of all work, said she would find them luncheon. As the boys wolfed down the cold cuts, Frances looked out to a walled garden which trapped the late April sun in its farthest corner.

'I'll take the boys outside, then we won't be in the way.'

The garden was not only small but unkempt, the patch of grass yellowed, with a whiff of cats. A single apple tree was blighted by a canker. She would tell Albert to get it seen to, to make this somewhere the boys could play. Soon after she heard voices from inside. Two men in cassocks and dog collars came through the French doors, deep in conversation. Albert was behind them, encouraging them onwards. In these surroundings she saw him as others would, the red-rimmed eyes, the cheeks jowly and threaded with broken veins, his bright devilment disfigured by dissipation.

He strode up and leaned over her, his voice flecked with irritation. His cassock smelled of a cooked lunch eaten elsewhere. 'Did you have to come today? Can't you see I'm busy?'

More visitors were drifting from the house. She was his wife. These were his sons. 'Perhaps you should introduce me?'

He didn't reply and Frances got up from the rug to take the boys inside, wondering which part of the house she might find free of vicars, until she was stopped by someone coming to greet her. Like the others, he was in clerical robes, but his face was weather beaten, the corners of his pale blue eyes sharpened by crows' feet.

'Mrs Sitwell, I presume? Don't let us deprive you of your garden,' he said.

Albert introduced Professor Babington, an archaeologist and rector of a rural parish near Cambridge. He was also, they had just discovered, related to Albert by marriage.

Frances forced a smile. How much might a relative, however mild his looks, have in common with her husband? Babington, however, had other ideas. He waved Albert away. 'Look after your other guests, Sitwell.' She liked his authority. 'And what interests do you have, apart from your family and your garden?' he asked.

Frances was under sudden interrogation. Freddie flopped amongst his books. Bertie was clinging to her skirts. She brushed a strand of hair from her forehead. 'I've only just arrived. The vicarage is in Thanet. I thought we needed a change.'

'Ah, the temptation of the city. Both stimulating and tiring, I find.'

'Minster is rather dull. I'm hoping to see some concerts. I love music. Otherwise, my greatest pleasure is to read.'

Babington gave her answer due consideration. 'Yes, reading is such a solace,' he said. 'As is writing, I find.'

This straw, thrown down so casually, caught her unawares. 'I always meant to write.'

A raised eyebrow, but who could read and not think about putting words on a page?

'I teach the boys myself,' she said to Babington. 'Somehow there hasn't been time.'

He nodded. 'Children, such a blessing!' he said.

She loved her children, they also sapped her energy and her will-power. Bertie's damp fingers were curled round hers. 'Mama, can we have tea?'

She was tempted to shake him off and see what else the rector had to say, but he had done his duty with the wife of his host. He inclined his head. 'Lovely to have met you, Mrs Sitwell. Don't let me keep you.'

She took the boys inside, both disappointed and relieved. Babington was an uncomfortable reminder of what she had failed to do. She watched him from the window, at the centre of a small group, not the loudest but the most emphatic, quietly confident of the point he had made, the vicar's wife entirely forgotten.

That night she woke to find Albert looming over her, the first time in months. When she made to get up, he flung her down like dough on a floured board and entered her with pulverising force. When she cried out, he put his hand over her mouth. She bit him and he laughed as he sucked the blood.

She arranged for an extra bed to be put in the room and a curtain to be hung between the two. It was a meagre protection, but although he could have torn it aside he never did. Before the boys were born they had lived in India. Some nights, she knew he left their bed and padded to the servants' quarters. She had felt no anger, only relief. Who knew where he found his pleasure in London?

They lived to the outside world as man and wife, they gave occasional dinner parties at which Albert was amusing and urbane. She wasn't sure how long she could live like this, until a letter arrived, not from Australia but with a Suffolk postmark. The country rector had remembered her after all.

2.

Maud Babington was younger than her husband, straight-backed and with a shrewd smile. Her eyes flickered over Frances and came to rest on the boys. Dismissing the carriage driver, she stepped forward and reached out a hand to each of them. 'You must be Freddie and Bertie. What a long journey you've had. Shall we see if Cook has been baking?'

The boys made short work of the slices of plum cake set on the square kitchen table, then Maud shooed them into the garden, telling them to go anywhere within its boundary, and took Frances into the main part of the house.

'The boys can have the top room. Let me show you to yours.'

On the way, they passed a light-filled drawing room looking out to a wide lawn, and a dining room with tall narrow windows. Maud motioned to a closed door. Churchill's study. He likes to call it the library. He'll be back tomorrow.' Maud was clearly accustomed to being alone.

Upstairs she showed Frances to a small guest room. 'I didn't think you would need much space. The view here is nicer.'

The window overlooked the garden, some of it with formal planting, the rest left almost wild. She could hear the boys, somewhere out of sight, calling to each other.

Maud read her unspoken thoughts. 'They're quite safe. Children love hiding in the shrubbery. There's a marshy area but I asked for it to be fenced off before you arrived.'

Frances's bag had been brought up. Above the felted green of the garden trees, she had an uninterrupted view of the Suffolk sky, puffed with fanciful clouds.

She and Maud stood together by the window.

'I hope you'll enjoy being here,' Maud said. 'I believe your home is not a happy place.' At Frances's silence, she touched her arm lightly and added. 'I'm sorry, we need not mention it again.'

Frances smiled her gratitude. This was all she wanted, for Albert not to be mentioned, as if he didn't exist. 'You must tell me about yourself,' she said.

A quizzical smile. Maud Babington wasn't used to being asked but she was ready to confide. Her family were mostly on the South Coast. She alluded briefly to her childlessness. 'Some things are not meant to be.'

When the door had closed behind Maud, Frances lay down on the counterpane and let her eyes follow the cornice of entwined leaves. She hadn't just found sanctuary; a cornerstone of friendship had been laid.

Outside, Freddie was calling. 'Mama, where are you? Come and see what we've found.' Maud's answer was indistinct. Frances roused herself and went to the window. 'Wait for me!'

When she came back to her room it was still light. To the side of the window there was a writing desk. The inkwell was dry but she opened the small drawer to find a full bottle of ink and a few sheets of paper.

She settled herself on the hard wooden chair where guests were not expected to linger. It was an enjoyable discomfort and she could accustom herself. She ran her hand over the desk to feel the worn grain of the wood, its varnish dulled but mellow, like the skin of an apple left in store through the winter.

It was the first of many visits. Each time she arrived under the sentinel trees of the rectory and felt the gravel of the drive give beneath her feet, Frances felt a sense of re-awakening, of rediscovering the woman she might have been. As soon as she was alone, she would peek into the drawing room, sidle over to the piano and raise the lid to play a soft arpeggio, a celebration of freedom.

On other days, she would settle straight away at the writing desk. She began by writing a journal, her impressions of the rectory and its surroundings in different seasons. When the boys started at Marlborough, she came to Suffolk alone and wrote book reviews modelled on those she found in the London magazines left lying around the house by the bookish rector. Between visits, she began to slip away from Chepstow Place in the afternoon to the London Library, imagining the writers who had been there before her.

'We have another guest tonight,' Maud said one Saturday over breakfast. It was autumn, more than a year since Frances had been visiting Suffolk. 'A Cambridge don, a Trinity man, quite the rising star.'

The rectory was Frances's private paradise. The last thing she wanted was to share it with a stranger. 'Oh, Maud, I'm entirely out of the habit of meeting new people. Especially those of scintillating intellect.'

Maud laughed. 'I doubt Colvin is one to scintillate. Rather the opposite.'

Frances shook her head but Maud was insistent. 'My dear, you'd be doing us a favour. I have failed absolutely to put Sidney Colvin at his ease and Churchill says he needs drawing from his shell. You're so well read and, I mean, just look at you!'

Frances knew that her looks had faded in the last few years. She had become careless about brushing her hair the recommended number of times or of presenting herself in a light that might arouse Albert, or anger him, depending on his mood. Maud's teasing sent her upstairs where she was surprised by the face that looked back at her. Her skin had regained its creamy suppleness. She unpinned her hair and picked up the brush. She had sloughed the effects of Albert and his switchback moods. She had no wish to 'turn heads' as people used to say of her, but Cockfield had given her back to herself, not in the gaiety of her girlhood but as a woman, a woman with a future, if only she knew what it was.

Churchill's study was dominated by the huge oak desk where a tray of sherry glasses was perched on a worryingly unstable pile of papers. As Frances and Maud came in, the visitor, slim and straight-backed, his back to the door, was in mid-flow. The voice was light, a tenor in pitch. 'But can we trust this Schliemann fellow? He hardly has the credentials.'

Churchill caught his arm. 'Ah, the ladies have arrived. May I introduce our dear friend, Mrs Sitwell?'

The visitor stammered a greeting and flushed a noticeable red, apparently stranded between ancient Troy and the social niceties of Suffolk.

'Mrs Sitwell,' in front of the visitor Babington was formal, 'This is my good friend Sidney Colvin, a scholar and a writer who will soon be known well beyond the lawns and spires of Cambridge.'

Poor Colvin looked more embarrassed still at this unlooked-for praise. *No wonder Maud has asked for Frances's help.* She held out her hand which, to her surprise, he did not shake but bent over with exaggerated courtesy. He might be a rising star, in his twenties Frances guessed, but he had the air of an older man.

She acknowledged this gesture with a nod and withdrew her hand. 'Please don't let us interrupt your discussion. The discovery of Troy is such a fascinating prospect, a combination of reality with myth, don't you think?'

Now he was not so much embarrassed as startled, presumably unaccustomed to women offering an opinion. He composed himself and smiled. 'Perhaps that is Schliemann's gift to us, to separate one from the other.'

In the room, the sense of relief was tangible. The man could speak after all, albeit with a slight burr in the *sepawate.* Frances risked another question. 'And what are your other areas of interest?'

With a blink and a gulp, he went on. 'I write about painting, but English letters are my real love. Principally p-p-poetry.'

Here they were thankfully on more solid ground. 'I find prose easier to approach,' she said. 'I am in awe of poets but sometimes uncertain of what they are telling me.'

'So many people are afraid of poetry,' he said, 'of misunderstanding its meaning, but understanding is less important than feeling the poet's intent.'

Frances liked his sudden fluency. He was earnest, but also sincere. 'So, who would you say are today's greatest poets?' she asked.

This unleashed a flood of names. Rossetti, he said, was

his current favourite and he was lucky enough to have attended some of his soirees.

'You put Rosetti over Tennyson?'

'Tennyson is the master,' Colvin was quick to reply, 'some say past-master. Rossetti has yet to find his peak but it may well be higher.' He took a breath as if to go on then stopped himself. 'Do you have a favourite poet, or poem, Mrs Sitwell?'

As a girl she had loved *Shalott,* but she didn't want to disappoint him with a glib answer. 'I would have to think about it.'

Colvin smiled. 'An answer shouldn't be rushed. I look forward to the results of your deliberations.'

The gong sounded and Maud practically clapped her hands in delight. 'The great poets, what an excellent topic for dinner!' she said.

Babington, who had been hovering with the sherry decanter, replaced it on the desk. 'Colvin, why don't you accompany Mrs Sitwell?'

Frances was caught off guard. It required courage to offer her arm to a stranger, but it would be ridiculous to draw away and Colvin complied with a hesitant respect. He was as nonplussed as she was. They somehow surmounted the awkward moment and progressed, arm on arm, down the corridor. If only she could draw him from his shell. She dropped her voice. 'Can I guess, you're a poet?'

He shook his head. 'Sadly, no. My talents are for analysis and criticism. As far as poetry goes, I'm content to wallow in the words of others.' He seemed to regret this choice of words. 'I mean...'

'Wallowing – why not? We all like to wallow now and then.'

As they sat down to eat, Frances felt some sympathy for the man Maud thought difficult. He had a sensitive nature. It wouldn't surprise her if, despite his denial, he tried his hand at poetry, scribbling in the privacy of his college rooms, tossing his efforts into the wastebasket when they didn't meet the standard he expected of others. Quiet but impassioned, shy but also verbose, Colvin was something of a curiosity. As they sat to the table, she watched his neat hands make a minute change to the placing of his cutlery. He proved a well-mannered and deferential dinner companion who thanked her for her company. It was impossible to see beyond or beneath his fastidious, slightly ascetic exterior. What he might think of her was an absolute mystery.

3.

Next day they all attended the village church where Churchill Babington took the service. While the congregation had filed out Frances lingered amongst the pews, where next to her Sidney Colvin launched into a history of the church, pointing out the remnants of medieval England and the dilapidated state of the misericords. He was free of the awkwardness he had shown the previous evening.

She thanked him for enlightening her.

'Knowledge is not a thing to keep to oneself,' he said.

'You're not a regular church-goer?'

'I'm not much of a believer, but I enjoy the music and the architecture. The works of man, I suppose, rather than God.'

She couldn't resist adding, 'Although done in God's name.'

He was silent, either unwilling to argue or unable to disagree. Frances thought the matter laid to rest but as they began their walk back to the rectory he spoke while looking down at his shoes.

'Talking of God, or gods, you're reminding me of last night. Before dinner, before I went to Babington's study, I caught sight of you. Of course I didn't know it was you, at the front door, looking out into the garden.'

She had walked through the shrubbery before changing, enjoying those last moments of solitude before meeting the newcomer.

He looked up at her shyly. 'It was a moment of pure enchantment. You were standing against the light, a silhouette, so perfect a picture. I had you down as a nymph or a goddess.'

She had forgotten she could have this effect, more surprised at his confiding it and needed to lighten the moment. 'And this was before the sherry?'

He accepted her teasing. 'Indeed. Although I'd spent the afternoon reading poetry. The effect can be similar.'

She felt herself soften towards Sidney Colvin, a man who got tipsy on poetry.

When the men had left for Cambridge, Maud came to find her in her room.

'I think you made quite an impression,' Maud said.

Frances shook her head. She and Colvin had managed a few intelligent conversations. It was still a relief to see him go.

Maud was standing behind her at her desk. 'Frances, if you want to gain some independence – and I think you do, you will need friends, beyond us here at Cockfield I mean.'

Frances contemplated the clouds as they rearranged themselves above the shrubbery. She had agreed to help Maud out with Colvin. She hadn't seen there was some other stratagem.

Maud went on. 'Sidney is always grateful for invitations. Surely you can each benefit from some new company.'

If, in the confines of life with Albert, she nursed occasional fantasies of a lover, he did not take the form of mild-mannered Mr Colvin. Still, Frances remembered the sense of possibility she glimpsed the day she arrived at Cockfield. Could her happiness lie at the door of a shy Cambridge academic? His manners were impeccable. She had a lot to gain from his conversation, his culture, the circle of friends he hinted at.

'He is very learned. I enjoyed his conversation.'

'Well, he clearly worships the ground you walk on,' Maud said. 'And you will always be safe with Sidney.'

For all his talk of goddesses, she did not want or need to be revered. But she thought of what he had told her about an archaeological dig in Greece, of pulling shards of pottery from the earth, brushing off the soil, observing their beauty, delivering them to a museum for safe-keeping. She had every desire to be treasured and preserved, most of all to be safe.

In the coming weeks, her visits to Cockfield coincided more and more with those of Sidney Colvin. She learned his childhood had been spent close-by on the family estate which he spoke of with great nostalgia, an estate gambled away by an uncle, leaving him and his widowed mother all but destitute. From London acquaintances, she discovered he had a growing reputation as a fierce literary and artistic critic with an increasing number of publications to his name. As for the friends, Ruskin, Rossetti and Morris, he dropped their names into the conversation with the same unaffected grace he employed to flick pebbles into a muddy pool that had formed in Maud's garden.

She eventually confided her ambitions to write.

'Really?' His expressive eyebrows shot a warning, but she persisted. She didn't aspire to be the next George Eliot. She simply wanted an occupation, perhaps an income other than what Albert allowed. He inclined his head in apology and explained the difficulties of finding publishers, but he did not dismiss her ambition. She knew several languages. Would she consider translation?

Translation was a respectable task but surely not on a par with original writing. As a compromise she agreed to try her hand at travelogue, a piece on Germany, where she had spent part of her childhood. When it was completed, Sidney helped her polish the prose and she sent it to several magazines, none of whom showed any interest.

'You must keep trying,' Sidney said.

His encouragement was a blessing. Her writing desk became a place of contentment and a vital part of the *possibilities* which hovered like rainbows on the Suffolk horizon. On winter evenings she became more closely acquainted with the piano downstairs and could soon play all of the music which had lain neglected, Maud said, for years.

The following summer, Maud had the boggy area of the garden made into an ornamental pond and was persuaded by the boys to acquire a tiny rowing boat. The day the boat arrived was cool with a grey sky but the boys threw themselves into the tub and pushed themselves off, waving in glee. 'Look at us!'

'Sit down Bertie,' Frances called, 'You'll capsize!' although the brackish water was barely up to their knees.

Tiring of the new adventure they brought the boat in and jumped out, splashing Frances's shoes as they passed.

'Hide and seek,' yelled Freddie, 'Come and find us!'

She lifted her dress and set off into the shrubbery where the foliage nudged her shoulders and she found herself in the half-dark, quite alone. She worked her way between the laurel leaves and the wall of the house, her fingers exploring brick and moss. The path, usually firm and dry, was soft under her feet from recent heavy rain, the air green and heavy. Turning a corner, she came into a small clearing and almost fell over Sidney Colvin, standing against the wall, his head bent over a slim book. In his other hand he held a pencil.

'Mr Colvin! What are you doing here?' Missing him by the pond, she had assumed him to be out on some errand.

For a second he looked quite blank. 'Ah, nothing, I mean only...'

'I'm sorry. You wanted some peace and quiet.'

He was hiding. she understood, from her and from the boys. He was never at ease with them.

'I'm not much of a playmate, I'm afraid.' The sheepish smile suited him. 'As a child I had few friends of my own age.'

'Don't worry. I prefer books to boats too.'

He offered her his arm. Somewhere amongst the trees a pigeon cooed and with it a feeling crept over her of the deepest contentment. She could happily have sat at Sidney Colvin's feet while he explained some point of prose style or prosody. 'I'm so lucky to have you as a friend.'

He shook his head. 'The good fortune is all mine.'

In the distance the boys were howling through the farther reaches of the garden. 'I should go after them,' Frances said, but neither of them moved. 'What were you reading?'

He held up the book, open at the page. 'I like my poetry to echo my surroundings. It's Marvel. *Fair Quiet, have I found thee here...*' he read on, to *'Society is all but rude, To this delicious solitude..*

'Oh yes!' Frances said. '*Delicious solitude!*'

Sidney Colvin was brimming with enthusiasm. 'Listen to this,' he said.

Yet it creates, transcending these,
Far other worlds, and other seas;
Annihilating all that's made
To a green thought in a green shade.

His head dipped towards her and she felt a whiff of hair-balm, the brush of dry lips on her cheek.

She recoiled. He was a trusted friend, she could be the same to him or a precious piece of porcelain, an ethereal nymph if need be. She wasn't ready for more.

He sprang away from her. 'My mistake, forgive me.'

She was penitent. Her reaction was uncalled for 'No, not at all, it's just…'

The kiss was chaste, only the surroundings made it feel otherwise. She smoothed her skirt and pulled her wrap around her. Could she accept his friendship and still refuse him any intimacy? To take away the need for words, she returned his kiss lightly, on the cheek.

'Frances, your happiness is all I desire,' he said. 'You know that, don't you?

And I will look after you, always.'

She accepted the affection wrapped up in his shy formality. 'Thank you, Sidney,' she said. 'That means a great deal.'

With her hand still on his arm she guided him out of the clearing, through the trees, towards the sound of voices.

4.

Rue Monçeau, Paris,
11th September, 1869
My Darling Frannie,
This is a brief note in response to your many pages
– who knew how much you could write! Believe me
I do appreciate your letter and your pleas for help
even if I was astonished you asked for my advice. I
may be your older sister but I have never felt myself
to be the wiser. But I do quite see we have only each
other in the whole of Europe and so I will do my
best with my advice.

I'll be honest that I never much liked Albert Sitwell
and although I hoped for your happiness, I doubted
it would come from him. Matthieu and myself may
have had our problems but he is a dear man and
none of our troubles are of his making.

You have met a kind and wonderful man who
shows you the respect Albert denies you. If you have
no desire to give yourself to him, that is surely for
the best. Unless he becomes importunate (and from
what you say this seems unlikely) you may continue
in chaste friendship and have some respite from
Albert's uncouth behaviour. As you say, you have
little to hope for in your marriage. Women like you
– and one assumes they are many – find escape

where they can. You must rejoice you have found yours.

M. has recently returned from Panama and is in very poor health – we each have our crosses to bear! – otherwise I would be hastening to England to see your Mr Colvin and shake his gentlemanly hand.

Please greet him from me.

Your loving sister,

Suka

Writing down her dilemma had been enough for Frances to solve it. She must simply live the life given to her, or rather the two lives, lived in parallel, like the tracks of the railway that never met. She didn't suspect that one day the points might be wrongly set and trains that should have passed each other in safety would ultimately collide.

One Friday evening in late October, on her way back to Chepstow Place, it was raining and as a cart lurched past, she held herself back from the curb, watching the muddy rainwater course along the gutter. It was hard to picture Sidney in the metropolis. Was he taking sherry at his gentleman's club, or visiting one of his good friends? She imagined their conversation, cultured, civilised, respectfully argumentative, while she had only Albert's cold disdain to look forward to.

Albert was often delayed by church meetings or journeys from Minster, and so she was surprised to see him seated when she entered their small dining room. The room faced the back of the house and was shielded from the noise of the street. The heavy curtains were drawn and the gas light threw into relief his increasingly heavy jaw.

'Well this is nice,' isn't it?' he said, spreading his hands across the Irish linen cloth.

Since any geniality was usually a joke at her expense, Frances smiled but said nothing as the housekeeper brought in a tureen of her customary brown soup and laid it before Albert.

He ladled some into a bowl and passed it to her. 'Of course we may be dining together more often from now on.'

Frances met his eye, indicating an enquiry.

'I have a new curate in Thanet,' he said. 'He's very competent. He'll take care of services from now on and so I can spend more time here.'

Frances felt the silence thicken until she could bear it no longer. More strained suppers, more of Albert's febrile temper, not to mention Mrs O'Leary's terrible food. 'In that case,' she laid her spoon to rest in the bowl and glanced to check the dining room door was closed, 'I hope you'll look for a new cook, because this soup is completely tasteless and I'm sure the stew will be no different.' The air was cleared. It brought some relief to focus on domestic arrangements.

Albert's gaze was level. 'I beg to differ. Irish Stew is Mrs O'Leary's speciality.'

On cue, the housekeeper reappeared and removed the soup, returning with platefuls of meat and a dish of vegetables, for which Albert thanked her effusively.

They ate for some minutes in silence broken only by the hiss of gas and a gust of raindrops against the window. Then, from his jacket pocket, Albert took the silver toothpick he favoured and worked it methodically around his teeth, a habit Frances had begged him not to indulge at the table.

'Besides,' he said, as if they were deep in a conversation, 'you spend so little time here these days, does it really matter?'

Since she had begun visiting Suffolk, Albert had given no sign of objecting. She suspected he preferred having the house to himself. 'I still like to think the house is run properly. Would you invite guests to a supper like this?'

'I generally prefer to eat out with company. But feel free to invite whom you please. I'm sure your Trinity man would eat whatever you laid before him, perhaps out of the palm of your hand.'

The Trinity man. She was relieved he hadn't spoken Sidney's name, imagining it on Albert's lips, removed like a fishbone and set fastidiously aside on his plate. Poor innocent Sidney, but Albert hadn't finished. He was enjoying her discomfiture. 'Colbert, is it? Or Colvin? Hasn't a penny to his name, I hear, so he might like a hot meal.'

Without raising her eyes, she watched Albert covertly, alert to any movement that would bring him around the table to put his hand across her face. He remained seated: a reply was expected.

'I met Mr Colvin in Suffolk, at your cousin's house. He is a regular visitor there, as am I. What he does in London is his business.'

Albert's mouth twitched – in anger or amusement, she couldn't tell. 'Suffolk, yes. I'm sure there is much fun to be had amongst the hay wains.'

The idea was so ridiculous she put her hand to her mouth to suppress a laugh. Tumbling in hay? Nothing could be less like Sidney. Except the laugh died in her throat. What proof could she advance that no such thing took place? They spent hours together at Cockfield, many of them alone. Maud encouraged their friendship and gave it room to grow.

Albert was another matter. 'You disgust me,' she said. 'You tar everyone with your sordid imagination. Sidney,

Mr Colvin...' She corrected herself too late. She had let go of caution and his name was written in the air in letters a mile high, '...is a man of impeccable propriety, a good friend, no more than that.'

Albert laid down the toothpick and ran his tongue around his teeth with a kind of relish, as if she had just described a torrid affair, perhaps what he had hoped for.

'An excellent protestation of innocence my dear, but you should be careful. Even what happens in the country gets around. People do love to gossip.'

Conversations about poetry, a single kiss, barely returned. For these she was to be punished and she cowered at the thought. It had been a long time since Albert had forced himself on her, but that could change in an instant. She got up to leave the table, to leave the house if necessary, but Albert rose too, laying his hands on her shoulders, his breath reeking of undercooked onions.

'Get off!' she turned her face away and tried desperately to shake him off.

His grip tightened. 'You are my wife and I won't be made a fool of. You need to learn a lesson, my dear.'

Somehow in the struggle he was behind her with his arm around her waist. His manhood nudged at her skirt. Her breath was constricted. She struggled to speak. 'Let me go. You are *not* made a fool of. Can't you understand?'

He loosened his grip and she broke away, gasping for breath.

He was waving his arms in mockery. 'Only friends,' he squeaked, aping her objection. 'Well, that says a great deal.' His face had darkened. She wondered how much he had drunk before coming to supper. 'I can't bear to look at you. Such a beauty. Such a waste. When we married you were never so cold.'

'And you were never so cruel.'

His only response was to go to the sideboard and help himself to pears and a cold posset whose gelatinous lumps Frances watched fall from the spoon. She was dismissed but she didn't move. Something had been started that needed to find its conclusion.

He sat down at the table with his pudding. 'Well make up your mind, Madam. You cannot have me and your donnish chum.'

Frances's fingers found the edge of the table, a solid certainty in a world tipped on its side. 'What did you just say?'

Albert ignored her. 'As for denying me my conjugal rights, in other circumstances it could be grounds for divorce.'

He fell silent. He had gone farther than he intended, just as she had let Sidney's name tumble from her lips. Perhaps it was meant to be. The possibility of not being Albert's wife flew around the room. Pandora's box was open; hope had reappeared.

'Divorce?' She barely knew what it entailed. 'If I were given that choice I would jump at the chance.'

He tried to laugh it off. 'You can't get rid of me so easily. I'm a churchman, I can't divorce.'

From Albert's manner, fiddling with his napkin, rearranging the unused cutlery, she suspected things were not so simple. Maybe even he was tired of their broken marriage. Ways and means might be found, if she could drag out of him what they might be. She wouldn't let this go. She sat down again, not in submission but with purpose. They were warring nations: she must set out her terms.

'We have no affection for each other. I don't sleep with you except when forced. You have a housekeeper to cook and clean and no doubt you have other ways of satisfying your... needs. I crave only books and lovers of books around me. Why would you want me?'

Albert's voice was tired. 'I sometimes wonder, but you are the mother...'

She cut him off. 'The boys are at school. You rarely see them even in the holidays and if you wish to, you may. I can make arrangements. Surely it would be easier to pay me an allowance than to have me here under your feet?'

'An allowance? Why should you enjoy yourself at my expense?'

She had no means of her own. Her family was scattered, unable to help. 'How else can I live?'

The rain outside had relented. The carriage clock ticked towards eight. He sighed and pushed his plate aside. He wanted his freedom too, but how much?

'I will pay for the boys. No more and no less.'

She closed her eyes and felt blood that had stilled in her veins resume its journey of life. Her hands and feet, her bosom and the core of her being belonged to her again. The walls of her prison had fallen, she could step outside, but she felt no joy, only sadness at years gone to waste.

She would leave nothing to chance, there must be no misunderstanding. 'So we'll separate. We'll live apart.'

He wiped his mouth on his napkin and crumpled it onto the table.

'I'll look into the procedures.'

She nodded her agreement but she wouldn't thank him. It was a mercy for them both.

He stood up and for a moment she thought they might shake hands, but he was ringing for Mrs O'Leary to clear away. 'Ecclesiastical separation,' having hit on the words he brandished them with evident satisfaction. 'You won't be able to remarry, you realise, not in my lifetime.'

Albert thought he was having the last laugh, but Sidney was her saviour, not her lover, and even if she were totally free, he had no means of supporting a wife. Marriage was the last thing on her mind.

Upstairs she stood by the window and looked out over the dark rooftops. She wasn't sure how she would manage the practicalities, but her freedom from Albert was everything and with Sidney's help, she would find a way.

Just out of sight, the river rolled along through London to the marshlands of Kent, taking with it the flotsam and jetsam of human society, some washed up by the tide on its bespeckled banks. She had been truthful with Albert except for one thing. She was not cold. She was still young and full of desire. Some days it was an ache that longed for a lover's hand on her cheek, a dear head against her breast.

<h1 style="text-align:center">5.</h1>

The process of separation, begun the next day, would run into years, involving complex machinations amongst bishops and proctors whose job it was to establish if there had been any culpability on Frances's part. To her and Sidney this was no more than inconvenience. There was no wrong-doing to be proved. For the sake of propriety, they avoided going about together in town but his friends became her friends and she received a warm welcome in all of the drawing rooms where Sidney had prepared the way. 'How lovely to meet you at last,' they said, the writers, the craftsmen, their beautiful talented wives. 'We've heard so much about you.'

She felt herself unfurl in their company like a tree coming into unexpected bloom. Should she wear her hair more loosely, like Janey Morris? she said to Sidney. Should she try those billowing gowns?

'Please no! You're not like them, thank goodness!'

She was only joking. To be outré, to be talked about, was the last thing either of them wanted.

Sidney was blooming too. He had a small book published on the depiction of children in art and he was a regular contributor to *Encyclopedia Britannica*, all of which supplemented his meagre income from teaching and editing. Ironically his trips to Cockfield were less frequent, their meetings all the more appreciated.

In the Spring of '73, they were invited to spend a few days at North End, the new home of Edward and Georgiana Burne-Jones. Sidney was in Cambridge, contesting for a new professorship. He was too busy to leave, he wrote, but Frances should go to North End. She would enjoy it.

Georgiana wrote to Frances too, telling her that their house was 'a breath of the country' and with Edward busy with a new portrait she would welcome Frances's company. Frances was happy to accept, to feel a part of Sidney's life even when he was absent.

Georgiana (*call me Georgie, please*) welcomed her at the door and led her to a morning room looking out over the garden. Glancing into rooms they passed on the way, Frances could see some were ornately decorated and furnished in the arts and crafts style, while others were bleakly plain, presumably still to be given the Burne-Jones treatment. The effect was disconcerting, like a gallery still in the making. Used to the unfussiness of Cockfield, Frances found it disconcerting, not a house in which to feel at home.

Georgie, a pretty brunette with doe-like eyes, seemed less at ease than when Frances had met her in London. As Frances accepted tea she strode around the room, staring out to the garden then bringing her attention back to Frances with some difficulty. Was she waiting for someone else?

'Does your husband work elsewhere?' Frances asked.

A flicker of concern crossed Georgie's face. 'Yes, very often. He has a commission at the moment, a portrait which seems to be taking forever.' Georgie recommenced her pacing. Frances remembered hearing about the sitter, a Greek girl. 'Let's walk in the garden,' Georgie said. 'Nanny can bring Margaret to join us.'

Georgie's daughter was barely three but a good-tempered addition to the company. Frances got down to play on the grass with her and was rewarded with the sunniest of smiles. The boys had grown so quickly. 'How lovely to have a daughter!'

Out here Georgie was more relaxed. 'Yes, I am blessed, we both are.' Their son Philip was at school with Freddie and they talked for a while about the boys.

'Mr Colvin is such a lovely man,' Georgie said out of nowhere, as if Sidney was about to arrive, or waiting for them in the morning room. 'You'll marry one day, I'm sure.'

Georgie was being kind. Frances and Sidney's general circumstances were well-known, the details less so. 'Marriage won't be possible, not in the foreseeable future, but we are happy as we are.'

A breeze stirred the trees along the perimeter of the garden. Frances wished ardently that Sidney was here in the country house which didn't feel quite right. She missed his arm under hers, his gentlemanly warmth, the feel of him beside her. When he pecked her cheek in welcome or farewell, she was no longer repelled. Sometimes he joked. 'No proctors watching?' which made her laugh. She had thought she could never marry Sidney, but she had been wrong. She could ask no more of a husband than good company and constant devotion.

Georgie was talking about the Slade professorship for which Sidney was being considered.

'Yes, he's very excited he might be on a par with Ruskin.' The famous critic was Slade Professor at Oxford

'I'm sure he is, considering their history!' Georgie saw Frances's blank look. 'Didn't you know? The families were neighbours for a while. Ruskin took a whole pack of boys under his wing, as a kind of tutor I suppose. Your Mr Colvin was one of them. I have the impression he was quite smitten with the great man.'

Frances was surprised to have been in the dark about this part of Sidney's youth. 'He's certainly a huge fan of Ruskin. You'd think he was some kind of saint.'

Georgie hooted with laughter. 'I think sainthood is well out of reach. At least it should be.'

Frances had no interest in Ruskin's notorious private life, but after four years of Sidney's company, perhaps she didn't know him quite as well as she thought she did. His quiet manner did conceal some great passions. She would have to investigate his youthful adoration, find out if there were other saints at whose shrines he had worshiped.

Edward Burne-Jones joined them at dinner. 'Mrs Sitwell,' he said, 'I'm so pleased you could come.' The artist was all smiles. He was similar in age to Sidney but his eyes were more shrewd than soulful, the grin naturally affectionate. Perhaps faces were sometimes dealt out wrongly. In some heavenly error, Sidney had been made to look like an artist, Burne-Jones like a cheeky schoolboy.

'And so nice that you got back in time,' his wife said with a tartness he chose to ignore.

'I hope my wife has been making you feel at home.'

'Very much so, you have a beautiful house.' She could have added *spoiled a little by your bickering*. If all dining rooms were riven by these covert arguments, perhaps she would not marry after all. 'I'm hoping Georgie will show me her woodcuts. I've heard they are delicious, I mean very accomplished.'

She had meant the food was delicious but really, something in the air was disrupting her powers of speech.

'They are very competent,' said Burne-Jones. 'We should have some of them framed, shouldn't we, dear?'

Wife, husband and visitor withdrew together and, in the darkly beautiful sitting room, Burne-Jones's narrow eyes were tired, the lines around his mouth too deep for a man of his years.

'It's a wonderful room,' Frances said to him. 'Your handiwork, I'm sure. And yours, Georgie.'

Burne-Jones didn't seem to hear, as if he had run out of polite conversation.

'I hear you're working on a portrait.'

In the second before he answered she saw that she had rekindled something best left to die of its own accord.

The artist roused himself to respond. 'Portraiture is always useful to an artist. Brings in the necessary.' The answer was oblique and the flame subsided. 'But it can be a great pleasure. Would it be very rude of me to ask if you might sit for me some time?'

Frances was astonished. She was so different from the wives, the famous pre-Raphaelite models. And she'd had no sense of Burne-Jones seeing her with an artist's eye.

Georgiana leapt in 'Oh yes, you must,' she said to Frances. 'You have a wonderful profile. The men are always talking about you.'

Did Burne-Jones mean it, or was she a pawn in their domestic feud, a distraction from his present sitter? She didn't want to be an object of gossip, but an artist's model was an object of beauty.

'I'm very honoured,' she said. 'If arrangements can be made, yes, of course.'

It would be years before any sitting took place. By then Frances knew like everyone else how Edward Burne-Jones had been in an affair with the Greek sitter, and how

Georgie was more often with Morris than at home in North End.

Next morning, she was woken by a ringing at the front door. Her first thought (fuelled by hope, last night had been a trial) was that Sidney had taken it into his head to come after all. She rose and opened the curtain just enough to see a uniformed boy directly beneath her, conversing with the housekeeper who was pushed aside by Georgie, still in her nightdress, a shawl pulled around her shoulders. The voices were indistinct. A telegram. Surely not bad news. Georgie was a dear.

Frances was about to retreat from the window so as not to pry on a difficult moment when Georgie turned and looked up towards her. Seeing Frances's face, her hand went straight to her mouth and she shook her head as if to say, 'Don't come down, never come down. This is something you don't want to know.'

6.

On that bright, deceiving, spring day, while she gossiped with Georgie and planned her future, Freddie, the playful and studious son, had taken ill at school. Suffering, they thought, from a simple cold, his fever rose and he quickly and unexpectedly deteriorated. He slipped away later that night. The school sent a message to Chepstow Place, but Albert was not at home. Frances never asked where he was or why. It took until morning to find him, and for him to deduce her whereabouts and send the telegram.

Georgie helped a numb and disbelieving Frances onto a coach which took her to Marlborough. The country outside passed by, drained of colour, until she closed her eyes, hoping this was a terrible dream from which she would wake. When she opened them, nothing had changed.

At the school, Albert, white-faced, helped her down, patting her arm awkwardly. 'You don't need to see him,' he said.

'But I do. I must.'

Only the sight of his face, turned to cold and unfamiliar wax, could convince her he had gone. Her life, she thought, should have ended with his, but he had left and she was still here. She could not go on, and yet this moment gave lie to that desire. She *was* going on. For her, there would be no ending.

Bertie, at Marlborough with his brother, had been told nothing. He was taken from his classes, brought to his parents, and they took him home. 'Is it a holiday?' he said as the carriage rocked under them. 'Where's Freddie? Isn't he coming?'

'Hush,' Albert said while Frances stared out of the window. His voice was tight. 'Freddie…can't be here. You must be brave.'

Bertie failed to understand and Frances couldn't bear to enlighten him.

At home, the boy was petulant. 'When is Freddie coming back? Who's giving him supper? When can I go back to school?'

Frances gripped the back of a chair, wishing that the fabric on her palm was not so real, her sitting room not bathed in its usual afternoon light. To tell Bertie, to watch his face as he comprehended the truth, was beyond her, and so she left it to Albert.

'Sit down, Bertie,' Albert said. 'Your brother took ill in the night, he grew worse and nothing could be done. He died early this morning. He isn't in any pain. He's with God. We must all be brave.'

Bertie's pitiful, 'I don't understand' needed a response. Frances roused herself and took him to the armchair where she cradled him on her lap and rocked him like a baby, clinging to his life force as if it might bring Freddie back.

Bertie struggled free. 'Let me go, Mama!' and ran off crying.

She remembered none of the rest of the day until Bertie's bedtime, when she followed him upstairs, to keep him company she said, but really to lie in the neighbouring bed, desperate to reclaim the smell and feel of Freddie.

But she was deceiving herself, the sheets had been changed long since.

In the morning, she woke from a fitful sleep to a spring morning made dark by grief. Leaving the curtains closed, she splashed her face with water and rubbed it until it was raw. She could erase neither grief nor guilt. She had been wrong to plan a life with Sidney. Intent on her own happiness, she had been careless of her son's safety.

In the evening, Albert said, 'We had better arrange things, I suppose.'

She was grateful for his practical knowledge. He ordered black-edged announcement cards which he filled in and posted.

'Do you want to send any?' he asked.

Albert would contact the Babingtons. They would tell Sidney. She had no idea where he was.

The funeral took place in Minster. She would have liked Freddie to have been buried in the city, but she had no strength to argue with Albert's choice of his parish church in Thanet. She returned as quickly as was decent to Chepstow Place.

Two days later, Maud was standing in Frances's sitting room, searching for things to say, finding none. Frances could not help her.

Bertie, still at home, was lining up his collection of soldiers on the carpet, knocking them down one at a time and patiently standing them up. 'Freddie is gone, you know,' he said to Maud. The boy's understanding of death was a recent and unnerving acquisition.

Maud caught her breath. Bertie would soon be back at school. Frances agreed it was better for him but dreaded his going.

'What shall I do? I don't know what to do,' she asked Maud when Bertie was out of earshot.

Maud sat down and stroked her hand. 'Don't forget you have Sidney. He is beside himself. He wants desperately to see you but thought it best to wait. He doesn't want to intrude.'

Intrude made no sense, as though the death of her son were merely a matter of manners.

'That's not what I meant. I have no occupation.'

Maud was at a loss. 'You have your writing, and Bertie…'

Bertie would soon be gone. She did not have it in her to pick up a pen.

Maud rushed to fill the silence, telling her how Sidney had won his professorship. 'Slade Professor, imagine, he is still so young, although Ruskin for some reason was not in favour.'

These names, Slade, Ruskin, were from some other world. Sidney had never been close to the boys. If he had truly cared, he would have come.

By the end of May, the apple blossom in the garden had fallen, leaving the hard green buds of nascent fruit. Albert – he was grieving too, she knew – had not taken to the bottle but had thrown himself into his work, a remedy which Frances envied him. Maud came to call most weeks, her sole link to a world beyond the house and the depths of her grief.

'My dear,' Maud said to her on her next visit, 'You're very pale and thin. You can't go on like this. You're spending too much time alone.'

Frances had some sewing on her lap. It was not the solitude which affected her. She drew it around herself like a cloak, or more likely a shell which hardened as the weeks went by. The inactivity was harder to bear. She had no heart for the park or the library. She had picked up a garden trowel and scrabbled in the border only to think of Freddie in another patch of earth.

'I visit Freddie every week. Sometimes I spend the night in Minster.'

Maud was vexed. 'Visiting Freddie's grave is not enough, not at all, and there's nothing else for you in Thanet. You've said so yourself. It will do you no good. You need company and conversation. Next time I'll bring Sidney with me.'

Sidney had written several times. She had not replied. He was a shadow on the edge of her consciousness. Like Maud, he wanted to help, but his good intentions made no difference.

Frances's silence made Maud change tack. 'I have a better idea,' she said. 'You must come to us, you and Bertie of course.'

Removing herself, leaving Freddie, arranging a journey. It was too much to contemplate.

'Think of Bertie. He'll need company in the holidays.'

She might deny herself but she couldn't deny her son. She agreed.

In the weeks that fell between, she began to picture Cockfield with its wide sky and garden greenery. Maud and Churchill would be kind. She could sit at her desk by the widow. The solitude there might be more forgiving. She didn't think of it as a way back to Sidney. With Freddie's death, a curtain had fallen swiftly and silently, cutting her off from that hope of happiness.

Cockfield Rectory,
June 29th, 1873
My Dearest Frances,
I can't tell you how delighted we are that you have agreed to come to visit us next month.
I'm afraid I must intimate one slight change of plan. My Aunt Maggie has written from Edinburgh asking if I can give temporary sanctuary to her son for July and August. With my other sister and her husband coming too, we shall be a houseful for a while, but I could hardly refuse. The boy has had such a dramatic falling out with his father (this is very much their style) that a period of separation is required.

I'm sure my cousin will be no trouble. In fact, he has aspirations to be a writer, and maybe if you are feeling stronger you will be able to give him some guidance. Above all, he is an amiable young man whom no one could dislike. His full name is Robert Lewis Stevenson, but with typical contrariness the boy has adopted the French form 'Louis' while retaining the English pronunciation. Why am I telling you this? The family knows him simply as Lou.

Until next month,
Your affectionate friend,
Maud Babington

PART TWO

Fall from Grace

I have been living in Cockfield gardens all morning; coming and going in the shrubberies and leaning a long while over the gate. Every place is sacred....
Robert Louis Stevenson to Frances Sitwell,
October 1873[*]

[*] Booth, B.A. & Mehew, E. (eds.) (1994-5). *The Letters of Robert Louis Stevenson*. New Haven/London: Yale University Press. Vol.1, p.338

7.

Maud had been right. Cockfield could not assuage her grief, but its country air was a balm and its sunlit, book-filled rooms a sign that some things didn't change. The other guests sensed she wasn't ready for society and let her keep herself to herself. Then Louis Stevenson arrived, and in a single afternoon his gauche innocence made a nonsense of her silent suffering. As they wept together, he dismantled the barrier she had built around herself and her sadness rolled away like the stone from a tomb. Her son had gone and with him her old life, but she must seek out a future and embrace what she found there. Most of all, she shouldn't be afraid to laugh.

Meanwhile Louis was working his magic on the rest of the company. Everyone was entranced by him. Over dinner he set out how he was studying hard to improve his style and make a career of writing. Frances watched him charm the room. When his eyes flicked over her, she knew the afternoon was as much in his mind as it was in hers. For that moment of release, she would always be grateful.

Bertie had also fallen under his spell. The following morning, venturing out before breakfast, she came around the edge of the house to find Louis and her son running on a lawn spangled with dew, making patterns in the grass with their feet which Louis stepped around with cat-like grace. After a wave of welcome, he picked up a stick from the other side of the path and used it to refine the design. 'Look Bert, will we draw a map?' The boy preened himself on Bert, his new friend speaking to him man to man.

Frances retired to the stone seat, turning her face to the sun, feeling her limbs stretch and loosen, letting the voices drift around her until the gong sounded for breakfast. They went back in through the morning room where Frances kicked off her sodden shoes and Louis gave her his arm to keep her from overbalancing. She lifted the hem of her dress which was dark with dew and wrung its edge.

Louis yanked at Bertie's sleeve to stop him stepping on the polished floor. 'No you don't! Let's get those dirty shoes off!'

Maud was passing as they tumbled over the threshold. 'You're all up early today.' Then looking at Frances more closely she added, 'I think early rising suits you.'

Later that day, Maud found errands for Bertie to do in the village, seeming to understand Frances and Louis could benefit from each other's company.

The afternoon was still but sunless as they walked down the lane to the church. The fields were ready for harvesting, gold under a pewter sky.

In the graveyard, Louis wandered amongst the headstones, then sat down on the low wall and put his head in his hands, still in anguish over his battles with the father he loved but failed to comprehend, although the cause of their latest falling-out was clear enough. Louis, having discovered the rationality of the new sciences and the necessity for a man to exercise his intellect, had declared himself an atheist. His father, a stout upholder of the Scottish faith, was outraged. Louis must drop the stance he had come to in all sincerity or give up hope of reconciliation.

Frances knelt down and put her hands on his shoulders, still slumped in despair. 'You mustn't take it so hard. Families have their disagreements. You will be a worthy son.'

He returned her gesture, making a double bridge of hands between them. 'You absolve me from my sin. You're my mother confessor!'

With a laugh, she pushed him gently away. 'You're being ridiculous!'

'It's true! Only you can save me!'

How this sat with a lapsed member of the Scottish church, she had no idea. Deep in the earth, the bones of the faithful must be exuding some sense of the Almighty.

They stood up and she told him about her troubles with Albert, something she rarely talked about. With Louis there was no shame or embarrassment.

He touched her face and she didn't back away. 'You're a jewel, a peerie jewel,' he said. 'He must be a brute.'

She was awash with relief. She too had needed forgiveness. Any niggling doubt she had over disobeying Albert and pressing for separation crept away to die amongst the mossy gravestones. She laid her cheek on the shoulder of Louis's velvet coat, brushed by his fine hair. She asked him why he was growing it long.

'I was a sickly child. I still am. My mother thinks it keeps me warm in winter.'

She raised her head but they were still almost touching each other. There was a frank affection in his eyes that made her catch her breath. His emotions ran so close to the surface. Feeling herself on a cliff edge, she groped for a hand-hold.

'I can see how wrapped up you are in your writing,' she said. 'You must show it to me. Maybe I can help.'

That evening, he presented her with a sheaf of papers which she carried off to her room. As she sat at her desk, lifting the top sheet, she braced herself. He was young and his university studies were in mathematics and law. She would be kind but give any necessary criticism, just as Sidney had done for her. She brushed away the memory of that kindness (had she been too harsh recently?) to focus on Louis. There would be solecisms and clichés in his efforts, perhaps nothing to praise. She rehearsed the words she would use to deliver the blow.

After a few pages, she turned back and started again, reading for interest and for pleasure. His words were unashamedly derivative, copying the style of any number of famous writers, but they held that same bewitching brew of confidence and innocence she had seen in Louis himself.

Next day, she congratulated him and said he should use this time to write more. 'I learned my craft here, at Cockfield. It's a perfect opportunity.'

He bit his lip, as if memorising what she had said. 'Yes. Time is what I need. Time, encouragement, advice. Thank you.'

Maud's other guests had gone, but every evening at dinner, Louis expounded on his need to write. His childhood of books and reading had catapulted him into the world of letters. 'I've learned about many things: lighthouses, engineering, law-courts, but words are the source of all knowledge, our only conduit for the human imagination. How can they not be our best asset, the most valuable thing we can give to the world?'

Churchill Babington prompted him for his achievements in writing so far. On this Louis had less to say. Aside from a few short treatises on Scottish history, he had little proof of the talent he simply knew he had *or could have with effort*. 'I need to learn,' he said. 'A teacher would be such a help, but who can teach the writer unless other writers? I'm so very lucky Mrs Sitwell is here to help.'

Frances laid down her fork. She knew her limitations. 'You need other teachers and writers, better than me.'

'No lack of those in Cambridge,' Churchill said.

A silence fell on the table. The prime candidate's name, still unspoken, sat on Frances's shoulder like a bird chirping for attention.

'Why don't we ask Mr Colvin?' she said, since this was what was expected.

Maud was enthusiastic. 'You must write to him straight away and ask him. Is he in Cambridge, do we know?'

Churchill chimed in. 'Colvin? I saw him just the other day on Trumpington Street.'

'Then I'll write to him,' Frances said, 'I've seen Louis's work. It's well worth his attention.'

Louis was on his feet, hands on his lapels, ready for a new oration. 'Do you mean Professor Sidney Colvin? I was reading him in *The Fortnightly* only the other day. He is the new man of English letters!' In his gesturing Louis succeeded in tipping the salt pot over the table so that some hasty clearing up was required by him and Maud.

'He is our very good friend,' Babington said, 'Mrs Sitwell's particularly,' although this was largely lost in the general furore.

Louis bowed to them all in turn. 'My dearest friends, you not only offer me a welcome but also keep the best possible company for a writer. If there is a God in Heaven he is on my side after all.' Serious or jesting, Louis always held centre stage.

Frances let her thoughts come to rest on Sidney. Freddie's death had been a stone cast into a pool, its dark ripples still spreading over the surface. For a few days her grief had been laid aside. And yet that could never be. Sidney would bring them all down to earth.

8.

With Sidney due to arrive, Frances was filled with apprehension. Since Freddie's death, she'd kept him at arm's length and yet all the time she'd been fending him off, another part of her had wanted nothing more than his gentle smile, the comfort of his arm on hers. What must Sidney think of her? Would his affection have cooled?

Louis had been asking her questions. 'What's he like? Is he very strict?'

Frances opened her mouth to say no, never, not with me, but how would Sidney seem to a student, however eager? 'I know him as a friend, not a teacher, but I'm sure he would never be harsh.'

On the day of his arrival, the weather was terribly hot but Louis announced he would go to Bury to meet the train.

'Take the carriage,' Maud advised.

'No, no, if we walk we'll have a chance to get to know each other,' Louis said.

It was late afternoon when the men arrived at the rectory. Louis was pale with exertion but his face alight. Frances found the courage to let her eyes rest on Sidney, who chose that moment to waft his hat in front of his face.

Maud was in fussing mode. 'Sidney how lovely to see

you! What on earth has taken you so long? Was the train held up?'

Louis saved Sidney, apparently tongue-tied, from having to answer. 'Blame me, blame me! I brought him the long way round and took a wrong turning. We were halfway to Melford before I realised. But what a fine walk we had. We talked all the way!'

Sidney deposited his hat on the side table. Now that she could see his face, he was the same as ever, the high forehead and kind eyes, although he was full of an unusual energy, as if some of Louis had rubbed off on him. 'It was a very happy detour!' he said. Like everyone else, he was under Louis's spell. She welcomed his gaze as he turned to her. Dear Sidney. She hadn't meant to be unkind in keeping him away.

'I'm glad you have found each other,' she said.

He came forward, his eagerness overcoming his innate reserve. 'My dear,' he said, as he took her hand.

He would be embarrassed if she gave in to emotion in front of the others. She composed herself, dropping her gaze. 'I owe you an apology.'

He leaned to peck her cheek. 'Please, there's no need. I hope you're well.'

Would it have been different, Frances thought afterwards, if she and Sidney had been alone? Would he have taken her in his arms? If so, she would have welcomed his embrace. She had missed it and she had missed him.

The moment passed. Maud was offering lemonade. Louis had gone to the window. 'Where's Bert? He'll be looking for me.'

This meeting felt too important to simply let pass. Frances caught Louis by the sleeve and brought him back beside Sidney, then reached for each of their hands. 'You are already friends,' she said, 'just as I knew you would be.'

Sidney's hand was still. Louis's fingers fluttered against her palm like the wings of a trapped moth. She drew Maud into the group. 'My very dearest friends,' she said, because they had all, in different ways, offered her salvation.

Louis bowed his head. 'I can only hope to be worthy of your friendship.'

'You will be, I have no doubt!' Sidney said.

Louis had made as sudden and indelible an impression on him as he had on Frances. She was pleased. Louis's future as a writer was assured, but from her pleasure she picked out a seed of regret. If only the world could wait a little longer for Louis Stevenson. She would like her fill of him before he disappeared into the places she could not go, the places where reputations were made, where writers jostled for attention and editors watched and listened.

Louis was first to detach himself to go in search of Bertie. Maud disappeared to the kitchen, leaving Frances alone with Sidney.

He clasped her hand. 'I have been no use to you,' he said, his hand on her shoulder. 'Bertie has lost his brother, as for you, I can't begin to imagine ...'

She smiled and touched his cheek, as warm as Louis's but more roughly bristled. 'Don't worry, Sidney. I have been very low but I've survived. I'm sorry I kept you away.' Her eyes strayed to the window. 'Poor Louis,' she said. 'I don't think he had a proper childhood, so he is making up for it.'

Maud returned with more lemonade, laid down her tray and said, 'Well, what do you make of him, Sidney?'

Sidney took a moment then flushed. He clearly hadn't

considered putting Louis Stevenson into words. Then he gave a shake of his shoulders. 'I don't know what to say. He's quite disarming, a mercurial spirit, such a lively mind.' Sidney's face was wistful, as if something had fled his grasp.

'Oh yes,' Maud countered wryly, 'Louis is nothing if not lively.' She looked out towards the garden. Her cousin was the magnet to their thoughts.

Frances caught the sound of Louis's voice through the trees. *A lively mind,* Sidney said. And yet Louis's energy, the nature of his attraction, an attraction no one could deny, was bound up in his physical presence.

'Yes, life, she said. 'New life is what we need.' No one responded. The silence was one of respect. She smiled at them both. 'Vivacity I mean. Someone to liven us up.' Wherever he might be, Louis Stevenson added a rare brightness, a reason for optimism.

Later that afternoon, Frances asked Maud the question that had been nagging at her.

'How old is Louis? He seems very young to have such high ambitions.'

Maud agreed. 'Yes, but let me see,' she frowned as she made the calculation, 'last time he came here was eight years ago, I think he was fifteen. That means he must be almost twenty-three.' This made her pause. 'I sometimes forget he's no longer a child.'

Frances had thought him less than twenty.

Before supper, upstairs at her desk, she turned over the pages written by the man-child. Louis was always spontaneous, always at ease. He was only a few years younger than shy, careful Sidney. How different could two men be?

At supper, Louis was voluble on matters of writing and writers. As they withdrew, Frances walked beside Sidney in the corridor. 'I hope you'll think his writing justifies his confidence.'

She saw the breadth of Sidney's smile in the dusk. 'Don't worry. I think he could succeed by sheer will-power.'

In the drawing room, the dwindling light cast a gentle glow over the faded brocade and made a halo around Louis who sat in front of the window.

'We should have a song,' he said, motioning to the piano. 'We never have a song. Who can play?'

Frances's fingers flexed involuntarily.

'Mrs Sitwell sings and plays beautifully,' Sidney said, 'if she feels able.'

She hadn't touched the piano this summer. Music was an expression of joy she didn't have, emotion she was always holding back.

'We understand if your heart isn't in it, dear,' Maud said.

She'd believed herself incapable, but her emotions were nothing to be ashamed of, her grief had been well-earned. Her friends looked on benignly. They had her happiness at heart.

'I don't know but I'll try,' she said. She stood up and looked through the music. 'Mr Colvin, do come and help. This one, maybe?'

Sidney stood at her elbow, ready to turn the page. She had chosen *Greensleeves*, familiar to everyone. She played a verse as an introduction then invited them to sing. In the second verse she took a breath and sang too, her voice wavering amongst the others. By the third chorus she found her control, she heard her voice strengthen until it was the clearest and most resonant.

Louis, who had flung himself over a formal chair, did not sing. His eyes were closed. 'What sweet sadness!' he said. 'Our Mrs Sitwell has every talent. She's truly divine.'

Sidney touched her shoulder. 'Shall we have something else?'

She picked out Bizet's *Chant d'Amour*. She chose it for Sidney, for his loyalty and his kindness. She let her voice fill the room with the melody and watched her audience, Babington with his hands folded over his stomach, Maud looking out to the garden in some reverie. Sidney was at her side, ready to turn the page. They both knew the piece very well. Glancing up, Frances saw that he was looking not at the music but at Louis, whose head was thrown back as if in a swoon, his slender neck as pale as a girl's.

9.

Sidney would be Louis's teacher, but Frances had been the one to find him and she would not give him up entirely. Next day after breakfast, she led them all to the garden where Sidney took a canvas chair and Louis sat cross-legged on the ground.

'I'll leave you together in the mornings,' she announced, 'and in the afternoon, Louis can be mine.' It was said as a joke but she was staking her claim.

Louis uncrossed his legs and leaned back on his hands. Bertie was calling to him from the house. Here was another call on his good nature.

'What?' the boyish glint was in Louis's eye 'Am I to be divided up like a plum duff at Christmas?'

'The very opposite,' Frances assured him. 'Dividing your time will stop us pulling you limb from limb.'

'You're allowing me no time for recreation,' he said. 'Freedom is necessary to writing, you know.'

Sidney played along, flashing a smile. 'Don't accuse us of being your jailors. We're giving you the help you asked for.'

Louis threw himself back, arms splayed. 'I surrender,' he said. 'I'm your willing slave.' He could have been feigning death, except for the pulse visible near his collar bone.

Sidney's eyes darkened. 'I think it's we who are enslaved to you.'

Frances shooed them away and went to find Bertie. They walked to the village on an errand for Maud, then did a puzzle together. Since Churchill was spending the day in Cambridge, Sidney and Louis had appropriated his study. As she and Bertie came out of the morning room, the men were emerging, still deep in conversation, Sidney's arm on Louis's shoulder. Louis was staring at his shoes with great seriousness, nodding in agreement, as he listened to the advice. They could have been father and son, Frances thought before correcting herself. Sidney's thinning hair, Louis's boyish features, were both deceptive. The difference in age was negligible. They were like brothers who had suffered a long separation and were enjoying their reunion.

Sidney stepped away from Louis and smiled at her. 'Have you had a good morning?'

She said that she had. There was no need to ask the same of the men.

Later, Sidney sought Frances out and told her how, despite his hasty departure from Edinburgh, Louis had brought with him notebooks full of his writing and a horde of books he claimed he could never be without.

Frances deduced this had left no room for clothes. She had never seen Louis in anything but faded breeches, the velvet jacket and a striped cotton shirt. 'What are you teaching him?'

They had decided on constructing an essay. 'He will find a home for it more easily than for a tale,' Sidney said, 'and I know too little of the background to help him with Scottish history.' They were refining something begun on Louis's previous visit to Suffolk, reviewing it line by line. 'He is very attentive. His concentration is complete,' Sidney said.

Frances could imagine it. Louis was hungry for knowledge.

'He's my first real pupil,' Sidney said.

Sidney taught rows of young men at Cambridge–he had taught her–but Louis was the one who mattered now. She saw a spark had been lit between them.

Days fell into a rhythm. She spent the mornings with Bertie and Maud. In the afternoons, the men came looking for her, always in high spirits, like students let out of school. Despite her threat she didn't have the heart to exclude Sidney. They walked together along the fields and hedgerows where Louis picked ears of corn, crumbled and sniffed them, declaring them entirely different from the bearded barley of the north.

They set off one day towards an orchard that lay beyond the church and, as they left the house, she tidied a lock of Louis's hair and brushed a burr from Sidney's jacket, each of them accepting her mothering. It felt natural, especially with Bertie off playing with the village children.

In a clearing, as clouds played hide and seek with the sun, Louis stopped to pick an apple and held it out to her with exaggerated ceremony. 'For Pomona, our lady of the fruits.'

She knew the myth of the deity and her lover who had brought the ripeness of harvest. 'I accept your gift,' she said with a solemn curtsey. 'But I hope you don't want me to eat it. It won't be ripe for another month.'

Louis sighed. 'We won't risk a belly-ache for any myth. But we need something for our professor.'

This was how he usually referred to Sidney, a mark of deference, or was there concealed irony? She couldn't be sure. They were so easy in each other's company.

'You must call him Sidney,' she said, 'Just as I do.' She

called him by his first name only amongst their closest friends.

In response, a question flickered across Louis's face. 'I don't know about that,' he said, 'we men are different. I might use *Colvin* if he'll allow. But we still need a gift for him, a mark of his learning and his fame.'

He scuttled off amongst the trees and returned with an oak twig. 'That Slade fellow,' he was referring to Sidney's professorship, 'isn't his name Felix?' He tapped Sidney's shoulder with the branch. 'This is for our happy professor, our god of learning.'

For a second she thought he would put her hand in Sidney's, blessing the union of his two deities, but Sidney laughed, took the branch from him and poked him in the belly as if it were a rapier. 'Take that, you upstart!'

Louis leapt back. 'No! Unfair! I have no weapon!'

Sidney gave up the sword fight and threw the stick in the air. They watched it fall to the ground, the place where it lay filled with significance.

'Is it pointing to water, do you think?' Louis said.

'Not unless Sidney knows some magic,' Frances replied.

'The magic is in the place,' Louis said, 'or amongst its occupants.'

They left the clearing and walked on. The men scuffed their toes amongst fallen seed-pods just as Bertie would have done.

Later, Frances found the apple in the pocket of her dress and laid it on her windowsill to ripen. It had all been such innocent fun.

If only it could have stayed that way, if only there hadn't been things for Sidney to do, preparations for the autumn term in London and then Cambridge. The pace of everything changed. Autumn was in the air but summer still lay as heavy as a blanket over Cockfield. Louis worked every morning, eager to please his professor. 'Colvin is a hard task-master,' he grumbled, 'but I must take my medicine.'

Frances still walked with him every day. Usually, they were alone and often at least one of them wept. Tears, they agreed, were underrated as a balm for sadness, though Frances made him take off the velvet jacket so as not to dampen the pile.

'I can't keep calling you Mrs Sitwell,' he said one day. 'It reminds me of the hateful vicar. What shall I call you?'

In company she had noticed his awkwardness over a name. *Our good lady* he sometimes said, an ironic avoiding of the issue. When they were alone, she was *My dearie*.

'What would you like to call me?' She was genuinely interested. How did he think of her, a woman ten years his senior who felt as close to him as to anyone.

He frowned as if she wasn't giving the matter the weight it deserved. 'I'll tell you one day. When I know the answer.'

The following week, Maud was organising the annual village picnic and recruited all of them to help. Out on the green, Louis was given the task of slicing bread for sandwiches.

'Excellent!' he said, grabbing the bread-knife with enthusiasm then, before long, letting it slip across the shiny crust to deliver a nasty cut between thumb and forefinger. The baker's wife, horrified, rushed to bind it up. At dinner Louis waved the bandage as if he had taken a blow for the Queen.

Next day Frances walked with him through the shrubbery, along the drive, to the church yard and back. This was their usual route, although points along the way were barely noticed as they gave themselves up to the flow of conversation: the latest letter from his mother, the book he was reading last night.

'Let me see your hand. Is it healing?'

He unwrapped the bandage and she inspected the cut. It's deep,' she said, 'but it looks clean.' The red furrow was exposed and without thinking she touched her finger to its edges and he flinched. 'I'm sorry,' she said.

'No. It's not pain, or if it is, the pleasure is equal.'

Pleasure and pain. She understood. It made her fearful, but Louis was laughing. 'You're like my mother, but not my mother.'

'You did call me your mother confessor.'

'Ah, confession or communion? If taking the wine were like this,' he said, 'I'd be an ardent churchgoer.'

She had no energy to scold him.

One morning she found him in the shrubbery, sitting under a laurel bush with pen and paper. 'It's too hot to be inside,' he said. 'I needed greenery around me.'

She remembered another day, in the spring of another year, finding Sidney in his green shade.

'I'll leave you to your work.'

'No, my brains are too addled. Sit with me, please.'

He laid out his jacket and she complied, resting against the trunk, succumbing to the verdant humidity.

'Do you know Marvell?' he said.

He began to quote the lines but she cut him off. 'No. I know it, I remember.'

'I'm a poor reciter of poetry,' he said. 'But my heart is always in it.'

The contentment she had felt with Sidney had been spoiled by the complications of his kiss. With Louis she was somewhere else entirely. When he reached for her hand, their fingers joined like notes in a silent chord. She closed her eyes and sensed his face close to hers.

'My dearie...'

Somewhere very close, a twig snapped. Louis dropped her hand and they scrambled to their feet as Maud rounded the corner in her stout gardening shoes.

'Oh, you two!' she said. 'What are you doing here?'

Louis rescued them by looking up to the green canopy with great intent. 'Well, we're just listening for the wood finch,' he said, 'Do you think it's the right time of year?'

Maud gave him a narrow look. 'Luncheon soon,' she said and went on her way, the gardening trug swinging from her arm.

When she had gone, they laughed, not at Maud who had the best heart in the world, but at the success of Louis's quick thinking. They were gleeful children who had evaded punishment. He took her two hands and kissed her on the cheek. 'Your existence is a wonder. I wouldn't embarrass you for the world.'

At night it was too hot to sleep. She got up and drew back the curtains, laying her forehead on the glass of the open window, breathing in the darkness. The memory of the morning with Louis had stirred something long forgotten. His boyish vigour, his girlish softness, his lively spirit and lack of inhibition; she bit her lip to quell the rise of her blood.

She bathed her face at the washstand and used the flannel to cool her arms and legs. Her body was awakening from a sleep. She must be careful. Louis wouldn't overstep the mark, but Sidney, whom she had been learning to love, was far away, the memory of his care and constancy blurred and misshapen.

Late in August, she and Louis met as usual for an afternoon walk while Bert was given leave to stay in the barn with the boy who minded the pony. She was carrying her blue and white striped parasol as they set off down the drive.

'I wanted you to be the first to know,' he said, 'I am going home.'

The bright air of morning had congealed to a suffocating heat, like the cream that cook spooned over her fruit tarts. Through the parasol, the sun was dimmed by a haze, the sky, just visible under its edge, a metallic sheen. She stopped in the middle of the path.

Louis stumbled and stopped too. 'Are you all right?'

Home. For Louis this was good news. For her the despair she had shaken off in the last few weeks weighed down on her. Could she bear to be alone again? She affected a brightness she didn't feel. 'You see, didn't I tell you all would be well? What have they said?'

'My mother is ready to have me back, and has persuaded my father to follow suit. I'll be the prodigal son.'

For once his face was closed. She could read neither happiness nor sadness in his eyes.

At the entrance to the lane, he stopped to lean against a hay bale in the corner of the field, picked up a straw and began bending it into meaningless shapes. As she drew him away from the path and into the shade, he threw the straw back amongst its fellows then followed it to the ground where he groaned and stretched out his legs, throwing back his head. 'I need them to have me back. But I need you.'

She sat down beside him, folding the parasol next to his discarded jacket and laid her hand on his forehead. This was the inevitability she had been avoiding. 'We must be strong. We'll be in each other's hearts. Always.' She believed this. The past weeks would lie within her, unchanged, inviolate.

His eyes flickered from her to the trees and to the sky. When she took her hand away, he raised himself on his elbow, bringing his face close to hers. 'You can't go back to Sitwell.'

'I have no choice. At least until we're separated.' I have Sidney, she could have said, but Sidney came and went, an unstable presence.

He grasped her hand, 'I need more than memories of you. I need your smile, your understanding, your open heart.'

'We will find a way,' she said, without conviction. Like him she was at a loss. Some link between them needed to be cemented. She touched his neck above the collar of his shirt, then brushed his pale neck with her lips, a parting gesture. The taste and smell of him (soap, straw, an undertone of salt) was a last indulgence, she told herself, but it could only be a prelude. Before she could withdraw, he caught the back of her head and brought her mouth to his in the deep and endless kiss she had tried so hard not to imagine.

She swam in the luscious darkness, desperately clinging to some semblance of herself. He was a child, but no, he was not. She was his guide, his mentor. He called her Mother. A voice whispered back. *You are not his mother. You do not want a son, not now, not today.* She willed him to pull away, knowing he would not.

The woman she had been would have shaken him off, sent him on his way, a boy who presumed too much. That woman had left and her replacement had different rules for life or maybe none. When Louis's hand, its flimsy dressing still in place, crept to the hollow at the base of her throat, she covered it with hers and guided it lower. The tips of his fingers prised up the ruffled neckline of her dress and strayed beneath. She unbuttoned the bodice of the dress and pushed aside the lace-edged chemise.

His eyes were wide as he cupped her breast in his hand, bowed his head and drank long and deeply. His tongue was caressing the hardening nipple. He was unbuttoning his breeches. The air was singing. She was consumed by desire, her being erased by the imprint of his body on hers. The world flew away and she flew with it.

10.

'No!' At the last moment she pulled away and fell from her dream, a wounded bird plummeting to the straw-covered ground. Louis rolled away from her, cursing, his ecstasy expended on the barren earth.

The long ache of loneliness had taken its toll; Albert's uncouth grasping, Sidney's careful reserve, the anguish of losing Freddie, all of them had left her defenceless. She sat up, fumbling with her fastenings, trembling with the receding wave of desire, aware that such waves did not come singly, a new tide always on the way.

He came to her and raised her to her feet. 'My dearie, what was I thinking? I shouldn't have come at you, not like this. You're still a married woman. Will you forgive me?'

Her body was in a lassitude. It wasn't Louis she needed to forgive but herself. When he took her arm to lead her back to the road, her legs moved automatically. Only when they got to the end of the lane did she feel the ground solid beneath her feet. She was grateful for the emptiness of the scene. She could not have formed a greeting to any passer-by.

By her side, Louis, apparently untroubled, was commenting on the peace of the countryside and wondering if the weather would break. His hand stroked her arm.

'All will be well,' he said, echoing her words to him.

'We are meant to be together. One day we will be. And it came to me just now that I will call you *Claire*. In my mind and in my heart, that's who you are. Claire, it means light you know, and makes me think of air, the country air.'

Names were unimportant. They had lain together. She had so nearly given him her body and her soul. Here they were now, stepping along as one, his lean frame supporting her as she walked. Everything between them had changed because of that onrush of desire.

Louis pointed to a butterfly resting on the meadowsweet, flaunting its peacock colours on trembling wings. 'Look. What a beauty!' The creature took to the air, weaving a trail around them and he laughed. 'It's showing us the way.'

Where she saw a fall from grace, Louis saw beauty. The butterfly flashed its wings and left and she glimpsed the truth, the thing that made sense of what had just passed. Louis had acted in innocence. He would never have set himself against the teacher whom he held in such respect. The knowledge flew at her like a moth against a window. Maud and Churchill only ever spoke of Sidney as a mutual friend; Frances and he were used to practicing discretion. Louis was ignorant of the understanding between them.

She let out a sigh of despair. This was her fault.

'You're exhausted,' Louis said, 'I tired you out.'

She shook her head. 'I just can't see how this will end.'

'Why would it end?'

The rectory with its cordon of trees was in sight. Inside, Maud was tidying Bertie's toys and chivvying him to the tea table. One day soon, Sidney would stride up the drive, a coat over one arm, a bagful of books in the other.

'I'm young,' he went on, 'but I will look after you, you

and Bert. He and I get along like a house on fire.'

Louis not Sidney. She considered this startling proposition. He was offering love and laughter. Albert had offered the same, but although Louis could never be cruel, he might be feckless, an eternally restless spirit. Above all he was too young. She had travelled farther. She was burdened by the knowledge of good and evil.

'I'll write to my mother and say I'm staying longer,' he said.' You and I need more time.'

She neither agreed nor disagreed. She couldn't bear to tell him the truth, that for her it was too late.

A line once crossed could not be easily stepped back over. She couldn't accept his love but she clung on to the memory. In corners of quiet fields and hedgerows they sat leaning together, his head on her bosom. She stroked his hair. He was a child in need of a mother. She did not unbutton her dress and he did not ask to do so.

They must wait, he said, until he was older, until she was free. She turned away. Free from Albert? From Sidney? Louis would have to be told.

On a day of storms, they took refuge in the stable, the parched ground outside turned into a temporary lake. The rain had nowhere to run. Frances sat up, shaking his arm from her shoulder.

'What's wrong?' he said.

She shook her head.

'He leaned forward, his arms on his knees. 'I know what it is. Here we are skulking like thieves, though all we do is love each other. Why is it like this?'

The question was rhetorical. Whatever they did had become clandestine, snatched moments on hot afternoons.

The downpour spattered to nothing. The air was

sharpened by the recent rain. Time for the cruelty of truth. 'I am promised to Sidney. I thought you knew. Everyone knows, we just don't speak of it.' They *had an arrangement*, she explained. One day, God willing, they would marry. 'I'm sorry. I didn't realise you didn't know.' She was going to say that Louis had taken her unawares, but it was she who had surprised herself, yielding so easily to the first kiss.

Louis was silent. She waited for the edge of his anger to dull.

'Colvin, well, well,' he said, his eyes on the ground. 'The happy professor. Or let's hope so, if he's to make you happy.'

'I thought he would have told you, or Maud.'

His eyes narrowed and blinked, cat-like. 'Or even your good self?' he said.

She was a respectable woman being rebuked by a boy, and rightly.

He got up and dusted the straw from his clothes. 'I'm sure you are just the ticket, you and Colvin. I should have seen it for myself.' He smiled to himself. 'I was blinded, of course, by your radiance. Who wouldn't be?'

There was no argument, no pleading for a different outcome.

They never spoke of it directly. In the following days, if she expected Louis to be dismal, the opposite seemed to be the case. He fidgeted with energy, devising new adventures with Bertie, whistling loudly to fill the garden with his presence whenever he was alone.

'Whatever's got into Louis?' Maud asked.

When Frances posed the same question, he said that he was writing, not just the work set by Sidney but something new.

'It's consuming me,' he told her, 'I write half the night. I'm surprised the scratching of my pen doesn't keep the house awake.'

She was relieved. 'I'm glad you've found inspiration.'

His smile broadened. 'I always have inspiration. Sometimes too much. Advice is what I need. And Colvin's gone, just when I need him.' He let this hang in the air, like a ripe pear waiting to be picked.

'You could let me see?'

'If you're sure.'

'Of course.' She could see it was the answer he had wanted. 'Is it an essay?'

'It's a novel. A novel composed of letters.'

'Ah, epistolary. That's a useful discipline.'

When she went up for the night, an envelope had been pushed under her door, bearing the name *Claire*.

With the luminosity of summer on the wane, she took out the page and read it by candle-light. It was a love-letter. A young man, ejected from his family, was writing to his confidante, his saviour, a woman of beauty and understanding. She held it at arm's length, considering the possibility of a *roman à clef*. More likely it was his way of dealing with his feelings, like a valve which regulates gas so that the flame warms the shade without causing it to break.

Next day he was late down to breakfast and Maud had gone off to oversee the laundry. It was unusual for them to be alone together in the house.

'You got my letter?'

'Your letter, yes. I realise it wasn't for me exactly. I can never be Claire.'

She meant it as a warning but he was impatient. 'That's a fine distinction. I wrote it *for* you, if not *to* you.'

She continued with her egg. She had promised Sidney to help with Louis's writing. He was their joint charge after all. 'You'd like me to make a critique?'

'If you would.'

She understood this was a different kind of conversation, a conversation in which no one could be rejected, no one could be hurt. It was fiction, after all.

He wrote his letters; she corrected an expression or questioned some stylistic choice. The words were a veil, a diversion from emotion. Claire stood between them and the feelings which otherwise might take over. But the more he wrote, the stronger the thread was spun. She felt it resonate like the string of a violin, especially at night, picturing him in his room, writing to Claire, writing to her.

The summer was spinning to an end. She and Louis were in the small morning room with Maud and Churchill when Sidney poked his head around the door. They had just taken lunch.

'Hello!'

His dear face was enough to restore normality. The sound of his voice quelled the never-ending jangle of her thoughts and feelings. She jumped up. 'Sidney, how we've missed you!'

The 'we' felt right. Louis, who had been sprawled in a chair, tapping his fingers on the arm, was on his feet too, returning Sidney's smile. The men shook hands and they stood together with Frances in the middle of the room. Louis put a hand on each of their shoulders. 'I see we are a three-sided object, a triangle, or a tripod. Perfectly stable but only when all three legs are in place.'

Frances could hear no irony. Louis was an open book.

Maud laughed over his sudden devotion to the discipline he had abandoned. 'You're an engineer after all!'

Churchill insisted on disputing the geometry. With Louis a head taller than both Sidney and Frances, the figure was wrong. Nonetheless, Frances was quietly pleased. With Sidney here, surely all really would be well.

The next morning, she was in the garden, helping Bertie into the boat and laughing with him as it rocked. 'Be careful!'

'Mama this is only a puddle and I'm in my old clothes.'

Louis had taught him how to row in his very first week at Cockfield. Despite the summer sun, his hair was growing darker. He was growing up fast, and would soon be able to look after himself.

Sidney appeared at her side. 'Not quite autumn,' he said. The willows around the pond, untouched by the summer drought, wept soft and green. If she and Louis had left some trace of passion in the air, Sidney did not sense it. She drew her wrap around her, shy of his proximity. 'Where's your student?' she asked.

'I decided to take some air. I've set him some work.' They watched as Bertie dug an oar into the gravel and propelled himself away from the bank. 'Has he told you about his novel?'

'A little.'

'You know it's a tale of family feud,' Sidney said. 'The hero, an only son, is sent away in disgrace. Sounds familiar?'

'I've seen a little of it.' She was pondering exactly how much of the writing Sidney had seen, how much she might not have. 'I noticed the parallels with his situation.'

'That's not necessarily a fault. It's very often the way with first novels I suppose, though I'm not sure in this case it will reach a conclusion.'

'The feud or the novel?'

Sidney laughed. 'At least the feud is settled,' he said.

He meant Louis's dispute with his father. Fiction and reality were so easily blurred.

'I think he finds his novel a welcome relief from your essays,' she said.

A shrug. 'I dare say. Nothing that keeps him writing is a bad thing.'

Without Louis's company, Bertie had tired of the pond. Sidney went to help him back onto the pebbled margin and he ran off to the house, calling over his shoulder. 'I'm hungry, I'm going to find Cook.'

They followed behind, Sidney worrying at the novel. 'I asked Louis if his hero will be accepted back by his family in the end. Apparently, it all depends on the advice of a lady. She will intercede on his behalf. The way he describes her, I'm not sure if she is a guardian angel or a mistress.'

Sidney was looking towards the house where the French windows were illuminated. The words were carried off on the breeze that was chasing shadows across the water.

'In fiction anything is possible,' she said. 'Life is very different.'

'Of course!' He kissed the top of her head. 'It only struck me that Louis's heroine must be modelled on you.'

'Me?'

'And why not? You're an angel to all of us.'

A fallen angel, she could have said.

Sidney went on, 'I've reminded him that a novel is well and good but he must finish off his essay before anything else.'

The piece they were concocting was *Roads*, an appreciation of Suffolk. *Claire* was not only fictional but would be given up before too long.

Frances took Sidney's arm, steady and warm. She must grow used to it again. Upstairs in her room, another letter from Louis to Claire lay on her desk, pleading for attention. She would look over it quickly and return it. With luck it would be his last.

11.

At their final dinner together, Sidney made his announcement. Before heading north, Louis would spend a few days in London.

'I have lodgings in Hampstead,' Sidney said. 'A few days to ourselves and we'll have *Roads* ready for publication.'

Louis was exultant. 'That North Sea haar gets on my chest. It does me no good, nor does my parents' constant fussing. London—imagine! We'll see the sights and have some high jinks.'

Maud's expression was doubtful.

'Don't worry!' Louis rushed to assure her. 'The good professor is sure to keep me in check.'

Sidney said, 'I can only spare a few days. I still have my autumn lectures to polish up.'

Louis made a bow of thanks. 'I will treasure every moment of such erudite company.'

Frances was startled.

Louis should be leaving for Scotland. Louis must leave for Scotland; she was relying on his departure. Disbelief fought with a pang of jealousy at Sidney, for stealing Louis from her. 'I had no idea you were planning such a thing.'

Sidney, registering her annoyance, was also puzzled. 'Louis and I have had so little time together,' he said. 'But if he'd like longer, couldn't he stay with you? Chepstow Place is very convenient.'

For a second she thought this was a trick, that Sidney suspected something and wanted to force a confession. She dared not let her gaze settle on Louis.

'With me? With us?'

'Sitwell won't object, will he? Louis is practically his cousin after all.'

In her mind she placed them together: Louis and Albert, herself and Louis; this the greatest jeopardy, but how could she object?

'A very good idea,' she offered and this time could not avoid Louis looking at her from under his eyebrows, concealing merriment. Sidney was playing into his hands. 'Although I'm not sure we have room...'

Maud was oblivious to the undercurrents. 'Albert's usually elsewhere, isn't he? And a box room will suffice for Lou. He's slept in ships' cabins, remember.'

Louis sprang to life. 'Yes, Sitwell is Maud's relative and that makes him mine. I have so many I forget the odd one. And it's high time I took a look at the Vicar of Roost!'

This was one of his many names for her husband. He jabbed the air with his fork, as if Albert could be popped like an overripe melon.

'Well...' Frances had run out of excuses. Louis Stevenson, looking at her across the table, watching for her reaction, could not be shrugged off as easily as she had hoped. She reminded herself it was Sidney's idea, as if she could not have refused to have Louis if she had wanted to.

A week later, she ushered Louis into the narrow hallway with its faded runner and polished wood stair rail. Sidney hovered behind. Her observation about space had been a real one. They had only three real bedrooms, one was Albert's, one was Bertie's, and since the start of the separation she had taken the eyrie on the top floor. She had arranged for Bertie to come home from school that weekend and was putting Louis, as Maud had suggested, in the small room next to the downstairs closet. He would not complain, and however respectful he might be, she couldn't bear the close company of those long fingers, the light in his eyes.

Louis removed his disreputable straw hat and dusted himself off. 'Here we are!' he said. Then, lowering his voice to a stage whisper. 'Is he here? The Vicar?' He could have been a school-boy on the lookout for a farmer whose apples he was stealing. Frances shook her head. Albert would be in later, she had made sure of it, it was the only time she had wished it so.

If a stay with Sidney was meant to steady Louis's purpose, she doubted it had worked. His smile was entirely mischievous, and Sidney, relaxed and at ease, looked to be on holiday. When she asked how they had been entertaining themselves, they came up with some story about Louis pretending to be a tramp.

'It was a serious matter,' Louis said. 'I'm convinced the law is weighted against the poor.'

'Since his disguise failed utterly,' Sidney said with a laugh, 'We shall never know.'

He stepped back, preparing to leave. Even if Albert came back to find them together, Sidney had a perfect right to be in her house. She could ask him to stay to tea, but that was only to delay the inevitable. She was tongue-tied.

Sidney, always alive to the unspoken word, said, 'Sadly, I need to get on. Take care of Louis. Send him home in good spirits.' He raised his felt bowler as he left.

Next morning, she and Louis walked in the park. Once

or twice his hand brushed hers, inadvertently she was sure, and the air crackled with an electrical energy which ebbed to leave behind a shimmer of suppressed longing. The memory of the last few weeks was imprinted in every footstep, every casual remark.

They got back to a silent house, silent but no longer empty. She thought of Bertie, soon to return, so fond of Louis, and how poor Freddie would certainly have felt the same. Except, if not for Freddie's death... She pushed the thought away.

'No one at home?' Louis said, glancing up the stairwell. His hand encircled her waist and his head dropped to her shoulder. 'Don't push me away, please.'

She covered his hand with hers, holding it against her side as if to staunch a wound.

'Don't be sad,' she said. 'We will always be close, just not like this.'

He took out a handkerchief, turned away and blew his nose noisily, a judgement on her coldness. If only he knew the heat that was stealing through her veins.

The following day, Saturday, they chose the Embankment where he watched the bustle of small boats, a freshening breeze blowing the river odours to the opposite bank.

'Isn't this just as good as Suffolk?' he said, and she knew he was expressing what she felt but couldn't say; the heady feeling of being by his side, the ache in her throat, the knowledge he would soon be gone.

He was scanning the river, up and down stream. 'Where are the ships, the steamers?' he said.

She explained they left downstream from Tilbury.

'Is it far?' he strained his eyes as if he needed to see the embarkation point.

'Oh yes,' she laughed. 'Several miles. Too far to walk.'

From their conversations she had pictured him plying a boat down a river or tramping over heather-clad hills. He had visited Europe more than once. Gulls were wheeling low over the grey river. All of the time she spent with him was a preparation for his leaving.

'What will I do without you?' he said, a rhetorical question, surely.

'You have plans, friends, your studies to finish. I'm the one who'll miss you. I'm often alone.'

'You have your professor.'

'He's very busy. Writing is my main comfort.' It was Churchill Babington who had reminded her. It had been good advice.

'I sometimes forget you are a writer. Both Claire herself and Claire's critic.'

He turned back to the river where a rowing boat with a single occupant was struggling against the current, then reached for her hand.

'Although I don't write like you,' she said.

Sidney had schooled her to be rational rather than lyrical. She thought of Louis's easy flamboyance and the heartfelt pleas of *Claire*. 'I like to form sentences, muster arguments. Anything else would feel like letting go,' she said.

On the far bank, clouds gathered over the jagged line of rooftops. 'I am all for letting go, as you well know.'

'I suppose both are required. The trick is to know when and how. With Sidney's help you'll have a great future.'

Would Sidney constrain him, curb Louis's natural talent? Make him something other than his natural self?

'Why don't you write to me? Not to Claire,' she said quickly. 'Not love letters.'

He was silent, searching for her meaning. 'You'll listen to me, and guide me?'

She could not bear him to be sad, not on her account. She squeezed his arm. 'Isn't that what I've always done?'

'I can comfort you too,' he said, 'when you're troubled and alone.'

'I would like that very much.'

At last the old playfulness was back. 'What my lady asks for, my lady will be granted.' He kissed her hand.

With letters from Louis, London would be bearable again. Without his turbulent presence, London would be safe.

PART THREE

Consolation

... all that you have told me, all that you feel for me, Consuelo – is so much better than I feel myself to be that I begin to loathe myself as an imposture.

Robert Louis Stevenson to Frances Sitwell,

14th February 1874[*]

* Booth, B.A. & Mehew, E. (eds.) (1994-5). *The Letters of Robert Louis Stevenson.* New Haven/London: Yale University Press. Vol.1, p.482

12.

The day after Louis left, a letter arrived, another the following day. Words, words, words. His thoughts on his journey home, on his parents, on their time together. *The best time of his life.* She had thought letters would constrain him, but words were his be-all and end-all. His pen flew in time to his thoughts, a rippling melody careering up and down a keyboard. She was overjoyed by his fluency, but unnerved by the unguarded fervour piling up on her doormat, like sea-foam after a high tide.

The housekeeper eyed another two envelopes as she set them on the hall stand. 'Something else from Edinburgh?'

'My friend's cousin, you remember him? I'm helping him with his writing. He's expected to send me something every day.'

Mrs O'Leary shrugged her indifference. Frances was sure she would pass this on to Albert who would accept her assurances of 'that young man with nothing better to do.'

A week later, she had four long letters. She was replying as best she could, using the address he gave her at his university club just in case his parents should misconstrue the missives from a woman in London they had never met.

Her letters were halting and dull compared to his lucid

and colourful prose, but she encouraged him as best she could. He wouldn't write like this for Sidney.

A few weeks later, Sidney came down from Cambridge and they met in a tea-shop on the Strand. It was a relief to be in his presence. She was spending too many hours in the company of Louis Stevenson. His letters astonished her but also made her anxious. His words were as enticing as his light-fingered touch.

Over tea, Sidney reminded her what a wonderful summer it had been, bringing as it had the gift of Louis Stevenson, a new talent and a new friend.

She couldn't disagree. 'I suggested he write to me. Look at this.'

Across the white tablecloth, she handed Sidney one of Louis's longer screeds. These letters, she sensed, must not be secret, although she had selected this one for its scarcity of endearments.

'You want me to read it?'

'I think you should know how much he is writing and how often. Is it healthy, do you think?'

Would Sidney see there was more than composition at stake? She watched his eyes skim over the opening lines then slow down to absorb the detail of Louis's family travails, the loving descriptions of his native city and its surrounding hills. 'So vibrant,' Sidney murmured, 'and very charming.'

'Yes, to be encouraged?'

'Absolutely. It's as if in writing to you, something's unlocked. These are invaluable. There are passages here that could be worked up into…'

Sidney saw only an essayist in the making, a writer who had found a muse and a mentor. He saw no danger but then why should he? He had no reason to doubt her or Louis. He'd been absent for too much of the long hot summer.

He grinned in friendly collusion. 'I have letters too, of course. Nothing quite like this! I don't always have time to reply. You on the other hand, you must do all you can.'

Their letters had Sidney's blessing: this was what she had wanted and what she had feared. The more Louis wrote, the more she was laid open to his words. Perhaps she should have brought a more tender letter, one where he called her, despite her warnings, by the name Claire. But that would mean baring her soul, and for what? An unconsummated union she had put behind her.

She closed her eyes for a moment. When she opened them, Sidney was leaning forward. 'You look a little wan my dear, are you all right?'

Reading and rereading Louis letters, composing her replies, was tiring. She could have used rouge but had none. It simply wasn't her habit. 'I'm only as worried over Louis as you are.'

He reached over the table to squeeze her hand and his touch was a surprise, his hand steady where Louis's caress was quick and insubstantial.

'We need to get him down here,' Sidney said. 'I hear he weighs no more than a feather.' His frown dissolved into warmth. 'But these letters, you're keeping them, I hope?'

The question was unexpected, the answer obvious. Of course she was keeping them. She treasured them for their reminders of shared laughter and his fleeting touch. She would never give them away.

'Their quality is striking,' Sidney went on. 'He might want to revisit them. They'll have some future value, I'm sure.'

Louis's legacy. She hadn't considered it and tossed the thought aside until the very next week when another letter arrived.

'Please keep this letter, Louis wrote, it's my only record of those thoughts about Montaigne.'

She had assumed his letters were for her alone, or for himself, to ease his mind or allow his imagination to run free. This passing comment, along with Sidney's question, gave her pause for thought.

Chepstow Place,
Monday Sept 21st, 1873
Dear Louis,
I'm sorry my letters can't match yours for grace and wit, but I'm happy they spur you on to writing more. I will keep everything safe just as you asked and have found the ideal resting place, a rosewood box brought back from our time in India. When I open it I can still smell spices and sandalwood. I've emptied it of its dusty souvenirs and I place each letter there, thinking, as they multiply, that they will keep each other warm like chicks in a nest. Will they ever fly from here? Perhaps in the far future. For now they are mine as that tender loving part of you is mine.

I do fear for you, though, on the volcano of family ructions that threatens to explode any time. Your health will suffer. I can tell from your letters it's suffering already. If only I could be there to stroke your head and hold your hand.

I can't deny I'm very tired. London and the febrile presence of Albert do not help my nerves. Loneliness is bad for me. I gather my energy for writing to you, it calms me as nothing else can.

She reread it before sealing the envelope. *Stroke your head and hold your hand*. This was more than she had meant to say. His ardour was infectious. She could contain herself no more than he could.

In his next letter he thanked her for her care of him, telling her how he carried her letters with him in his jacket, keeping her next to his heart. She was reading at the breakfast table. She smiled at the metaphor, then the smile contracted. The coffee on her lips was cold and bitter, the taste of toast and honey sickly sweet.

She had sent every letter to the usual poste restante. What was the point if he simply carried them around? Close to his heart perhaps, but easily taken out to reread and lay down anywhere in a careless moment.

Mrs O'Leary came to clear away and Frances waved away the unfinished breakfast. She must write to Louis and she must write now. She couldn't risk any misunderstanding. Never mind his parents, she had Sidney to think of, and the odious bishop's proctors who were examining her separation from Albert. Nothing must stop that.

His reply was immediate, he agreed, reluctantly, to destroy each of her letters as soon as he had replied. Her headache disappeared. Relief coursed through her like water. She could be true to Louis; she had ensured her safety.

13.

As the letters fell like autumn leaves through her door, Sidney hatched a plan to have Louis apply to the English rather than the Scottish bar. He made his escape from home by feigning a trip to Carlisle and went straight to London and Chepstow Place, where he arrived in a state of near collapse. Her joy at setting eyes on him was eclipsed by worry. She helped him upstairs to Bertie's room where he lay coughing, no longer the pleading lover but simply a sick man.

'There's a doctor in Mayfair who'll know what's best,' Sidney announced. 'I imagine a spell abroad would be in order.'

To Sidney the continent was a cure for everything. When the doctor agreed and recommended a stay on the Riviera, Louis's parents came flying down to London to reclaim him, taking him to their hotel, then going straight to Harley Street to ask Dr Clarke to give an account of himself. Afterwards, Frances and Sidney were summoned.

In the hotel room, with Louis wrapped in blankets and looking on from a chaise, Thomas Stevenson appeared very much as Sidney had described him, 'A gruff northerner, not as stern as he would like us to think. He means well for his son.'

'Thank you for helping Louis,' he said to Frances, bending into a slight bow, his eyes solemn in his ruddy

101

face. Next to him, Margaret Stevenson was surprisingly young, demure and guarded. She smiled her thanks. 'We are in your debt, I think, yours and Mr Colvin's.' She was simply dressed but in the latest fashion, and Frances caught the flash of diamonds in her droplet earrings.

'Not at all,' Frances replied, 'he is such...' she would have said 'a dear boy' but in front of his mother, to whom he was the very dearest boy, she thought better of it. 'A dear friend,' she concluded, 'and very talented.'

Margaret Stevenson's chin tilted imperceptibly, as if she would be the judge of that.

'The doctor has persuaded us,' said Louis's father. 'Although we were against it, his mother was against it, Louis must winter abroad.'

'Yes,' Margaret was emphatic, 'we know Menton well. We're happy to let him go.' She and her husband had done everything in their power to keep Louis in Edinburgh. She was turning defeat into victory.

From behind his mother's back, Louis raised his arms in celebration before letting them fall back, his smile spreading from ear to ear. Now he could escape the Scotch weather, his persistent sickness, his overly-solicitous parents.

'Will you take tea?' Margaret asked and Frances welcomed the chance to sit down. She arranged her skirt, maintaining the upright posture her mother had taught her. She would be the respectable matron, just like Margaret Stevenson.

Louis's father smiled in gratification, believing everyone satisfied.

Whether this outcome was defeat or victory, Frances couldn't tell. She would miss Louis but had enjoyed two unexpected weeks of his company. She had no argument against his journey south. A greater distance might be helpful to her, to both of them.

As soon as Louis had left, letters arrived from Paris, Sens and Orange. She flew with him to the scent of lemon trees and the blue-grey mist of olive groves.

Chepstow Place,
November 18th, 1873
Dear Louis,
I take pleasure from your safe arrival, your fine view of the sea, the gardens and views you describe so exquisitely. I am truly grateful for these things and the way you convey them to me. If you wish me to be honest, my spirits are locked in winter gloom. I could scream with loneliness.

Sidney has been busy in Cambridge and has barely written me a line. On Friday, at my wits' end, I went to Norwood to call on Mrs Colvin. We have little in common apart from our care for her son, but we keep each other company from time to time. I arrived feeling chilled and in the sitting room (I should have worn my winter boots) a draught around my ankles turned my feet to stone.

My hostess was no more cheerful. 'The cold is in my bones,' she said. I agree winter in England is hard to bear. 'Yes, I'm so pleased' she added, 'that my son will soon be off to the Riviera with this Stevenson fellow.'

You can imagine my feeling of abandonment. Never mind that Sidney hadn't shared this with me, I had to hear it from his mother. My anger is directed at him, running off to the sun, leaving me here with my dreadful husband and my frailty, but you, my dear, will bear the brunt of my low spirits as you are the one to whom I tell these truths. You must forgive me my selfishness as I forgive you yours.

The debilitations of winter have been lightened by your poem. 'The river of my life' is chequered indeed and I bear 'both flowers and thorns'. What can I say? I hope that one day the blooms will outnumber those hateful briars.

Yes, your letters are still safely stored. Albert still threatens me with his presence but has no interest in my possessions. I hope you also keep your promise.

The violet you picked for me was a poor shrivelled thing after its journey, but I applaud the love with which it was sent.

I'm worried about your state of mind. Are you becoming dependent on opium? It brings only temporary relief, my dear, do not rely on it.

I say this as your faithful friend,
FJS

Chepstow Place,
November 20th, 1873
Dear Louis,
I don't think you can imagine how this house imprisons me. In the daylight hours I think I see my dear departed Freddie peeking out from behind chairs and curtains. Without Bertie's voice echoing up and down the stairs, I have nightmares that he has followed his brother to his grave. My head aches constantly and yesterday everything I ate was expelled soon after.

If I could I would come south, but a married

woman does not have such freedoms nor the means to exercise them. I miss my two dear friends but I do not deny you your obvious pleasure in each other, if only I could be there to share it.

Your letters are a real comfort. S.C. writes to me of your adventures in Monaco and those picnics on the rocks; but only you have taken me to that very spot with its drift of sea-pinks, the pungent aroma of herbs, the startling glow of the early sunset. I will reply to him after I have replied to you. My pen moves almost as much as your own.

As for Claire, it was time for her to go. She served us well in the heat of last summer but you must not cling to her or the feelings she embodied. I have read Sand and I see Consuelo with her musical soul as a worthy successor. If I cannot have her freedom, I shall try to borrow her wisdom to help calm your troubled mind. But you must believe, my dear, that you are perfectly sane, if sometimes too given to emotion. The trick will be to moderate the inner turmoil without losing the vigour and originality that imbues every word you write.

It is my sanity that has been at issue these last weeks but knowing you are well will keep me steady.

Take care of yourself. Allow Sidney to take care of you.

I sign myself your friend and your dear,
Consuelo

The two men sent her the same news in such different ways, Sidney formally affectionate, Louis's letters inveigling her in their infectious spontaneity. They were addictive, as he was addictive. Her loyalty to Sidney was being sorely tested. If she could have gone to Menton, what would have happened? She had cleaved to Sidney for safety's sake. Why should she hold out against the attractions of someone who gave what Sidney could or would not, someone to smother her with love.

Rue Monçeau, Paris,
December 16th, 1873
Dear Louis,
You will have heard I was so wracked with fever that Albert sent for my sister who had the sense to take me back with her to Paris, and so here I am, a little closer, my dear, to the loving glance and wistful smiles I miss so desperately.

As for the incident at the Casino, I am as surprised as you that S.C. took himself off there. I never had him down as a gambler! But how dreadful that he was there to witness the horrific suicide of another player. I cannot imagine the effect such a violent and bloody scene would have on him, on anyone. May God deliver us from such extremes of human despair!

What a blessing you, dear Louis, did not go with him and were safe in your rooms, ready to help when he was so distraught, although it's strange to think of your holding him and singing him a lullaby as he shivered. I applaud your brotherly affection and solicitous nursing.

S.C. has told me none of this, no doubt wishing to erase it from his mind. I thank you for your care of the man who cares for me and for relating the things he prefers not to share.

Now you are back in Menton and Roads is published! You are right to be planning a party. Here is the beginning of future glory, Robert Louis Stevenson, a writer to be remembered through the ages.

I hope the new hotel in Menton is to your liking while secretly hoping it will be so unsatisfactory you will give up the Riviera and come to Paris.

Forgive my teasing. My health is still out of sorts, but Suka and I will raise a glass in celebration of your achievement.

Your dear
Consuelo

14.

In Paris, her sister was watching her seal a letter and start on another. They were in Frances's room, where she was using the dressing-table as an escritoire. 'Can't you write to them both at once?' Suka said.

Running her hand through her hair, Frances considered writing one letter instead of two, addressing Louis and Sidney together. She looked up and spoke through the dressing-table mirror. 'No. That wouldn't work at all.'

Then there were no more letters. For Sidney this was not unusual. His travels were always combined with business so he had many other letters to write. For Louis it was unheard of. Without the sound of his voice, her days were empty.

'What is wrong with you, Frannie?' Suka asked. 'You can't sit still. Anyone would think there were fleas in here and I can assure you there are not.'

'I might go to the post.'

'That's a terrible idea. Henri went first thing this morning and with that cough you should be staying in.'

Suka was right, but Frances could write no more without a letter to respond to. Writing was Louis's lifeblood. He must be ill. But surely in that case Sidney would have written to tell her.

She scanned the strip of sky visible above the boulevard. A pigeon would be a good omen, she told herself, a starling would signify illness, a raven death. She cursed her superstition and tried to find other distractions, but there was nothing that didn't add to her anxiety.

Later that morning, two collared doves perched on the balcony of the building opposite. This was a sign. Louis had taken her at her word and had boarded a train for Paris. The picture was vivid in her mind. The men would leave Menton together. In Paris he and Sidney would say goodbye, Sidney travelling on, Louis stopping in Paris to visit bookshops and to call on Mrs Sitwell, 'just to see that she is recovering'. He would find lodgings.

He and Frances could spend their days together; he would tell her about the people of Menton and their entertainments, how he enjoyed them but was ready to leave them behind. She needn't burden him any more with her illness and depression: they could talk about his future. Her future was a blank page. Her separation from Albert would soon be finalised. It was what she had longed for, but the prospect brought both excitement and dread. She had never lived alone.

At lunch she confessed to Suka that she thought Louis might be going to visit. This was the only explanation for the dearth of letters. 'He is obviously in better health and has just been waiting for the right time.'

'And Sidney?'

She frowned. 'He won't have time. He'll go back to Cambridge. The spring term starts soon.'

On a shelf by Henri's desk there was a railway timetable. The edges of its well-thumbed pages slid treacherously under her fingers. Yes, a train had left Menton early yesterday. With the right connections, passengers would reach Paris late that night.

The hours were devoured as she tidied her books and

her writing desk, reread chapters of *Consuelo*, marked passages she and Louis could talk about.

At bedtime, she berated herself for putting faith in the random habits of birds. Louis, with his blithe rejection of the church, was turning her into a pagan. She could not find it in herself to say her prayers but she slept peacefully, knowing her loneliness was at an end.

She was right and she was wrong. The bell clanged next morning as Frances had known it would. She was dressed and her hair carefully arranged. She had borrowed Suka's pot of rouge. She heard voices at the door of the apartment and went into the narrow hall where a figure was standing with his back to the light, shorter and more solid than Louis, flashing an anxious smile.

'My dear, how are you? I've been so worried.'

She accepted Sidney's unexpected embrace, puzzling at the texture of his winter coat when she had been waiting for the softness of velveteen.

In her sister's curtained salon, Sidney's face was livelier and more mobile than she had remembered. His eyes were innocently clear.

'It's good of you to come,' she said.

He looked puzzled. 'I knew you were unwell. Didn't you want me to?'

'Yes,' of course she had, just not as much as she had wanted Louis.

He had brought some southern air with him and she felt the blood run quicker in her veins. The rooms where she had been happy to hide felt stuffy and confining.

'We should go out,' she said to Sidney.

'Are you well enough to walk?'

'Yes, I think I am.'

Outside the streets were damp underfoot and as they turned towards the river they were met by a chill breeze. 'Is this too far?' Sidney asked.

'No, the air will do me good.'

'You will be missing the sun,' she told him, 'and Louis.'

'I needed to know you were well. Besides, Louis has given me some errands. I can be useful to you both.'

So Sidney would go back, but she no longer begrudged him his time in Menton. For her, the Parisian boulevards and the walks by the river would be enough of a respite from London.

The following day, he called early with a cab which took them to the Bois de Boulogne, Paris's new pleasure ground, laced with lakes and grottoes. 'If it freezes there will be skating,' she told Sidney. 'Louis loves skating.'

Sidney frowned, disconcerted by the arrival of Louis into the conversation. She rushed to justify it. 'Is he writing much?'

Sidney grimaced. 'Not as much as he would have us think. But he is full of ideas.'

Ideas she could help engender. Lulled by the warmth of the coach, she closed her eyes in a moment of unexpected contentment.

Sidney nudged her gently 'Are you asleep?' She roused herself and shook her head. 'I have some news,' he said. 'A college is being set up in Queens' Square, for working men and women, to improve their prospects. They need a superintendent. I've taken the liberty of mentioning your name. What do you think?'

She knew of the college and approved of its aims. She had never thought of taking employment but how much better that would be than living in the hope of making a living from writing, waiting for an editor to look favourably on her work.

Sidney read her mind. 'The work is mainly in the afternoon or evening. You'll still have some time to see friends and pursue your other interests.'

Sidney's idea would grant her not just an income but also independence. She was no longer dozing in a carriage but planning her life after Albert, scurrying in her mind from Paris to London. Queens' Square was on the edge of Bloomsbury. 'Where shall I live?'

He squeezed her knee in a small gesture of triumph. 'I made enquiries. Burne-Jones knows of a small house on Brunswick Row. It will be free by the summer.'

He had thought of everything, a place for her and for Bertie too in the holidays, somewhere close to Sidney's London haunts.

When they got down from the carriage, the day was subsiding into sleety darkness. Paris, she realised, brought other kinds of freedom, and at the door to the apartments she threw her arms around him without inhibition. 'Sidney Colvin, you are a good man.'

He stood with his chin resting on her head, giving a small sigh. 'Only for you, my dear, only for you.'

She straightened his hat for him and squeezed both of his arms. The omens had failed her. She had wanted Louis but God knew better. She needed Sidney.

15.

Brunswick Square,
23rd June, 1874
Dear Louis,
You are back in your hometown. From your letters I know its cobbled streets as if I had walked them myself. Even in summer I see you skating on your loch, weaving figures on its frosty carpet. Yes, I am quite cross you passed through London and didn't stop to call on me. I would have loved to set eyes on your dear face and shown you my darling house. It hides in a narrow alley but the glories of The British Museum are only a few streets away and my place of work is on my doorstep.

Best of all, my life is free of Albert's hateful presence. An empty future beckons and I shall fill it as I like, with people and things which are dear to me.

I hope your mother and father have given you the welcome you deserve. I hope they won't keep you too long. You must stretch your writer's wings. Sidney tells me London is waiting for you. Don't forget your Consuelo's heart beats at its centre.

Your dearest,
FJS

In early July, Louis returned to London. From their lodgings in Hampstead, Sidney sent a note saying his visitor was, 'in a state of high excitement'. He gave no further explanation.

Next day, returning home from a morning in college, she put her key in the lock and, sensing a movement behind her, turned to see Louis on the pavement, rumpled, pale, his face lit with joy.

'At last,' he said, 'It has taken me forever to find you.'

Unable to contain her pleasure she went to him, then held back from an embrace. Glancing down the deserted street, she took him by the arm, 'Come inside!'

'Now I'm here,' he said as he followed her, 'I like it. More than I thought I would.'

The maid, Maddie, had heard voices but Frances waved her away to the scullery. In her sitting room she stood back to look at him.

'I like it too.'

'We could be happy here. I feel it in my bones.'

The 'we' was an oddity but then Louis was full of oddities. Her house was a haven, a sanctuary, and with Sidney's help she was gradually making it her own. He had purloined a tiny desk for her from Morris, beautifully carved, and Suka had sent a cheerful rug whose colours gave life to the room.

Louis's hair was longer, his moustache had come into its own. He held a ridiculously large hat in his hand and his eyes darted to every corner of the room, as if something or someone might be lying in wait.

'I've been with Colvin,' he said. 'He kept me all morning at his blessed Savile or I would have been here sooner.'

She couldn't bring herself to defuse his ebullience. She tried to hold herself apart from it. 'You would have missed me. I was at college, preparing some accounts.'

This evoked a frown. Something annoyed him about her college role. 'It's not right for you to be a clerk.'

'Superintendent.'

He shrugged, as if the distinction was meaningless.

'Won't you sit down?'

He shook his head. 'No.'

His mood was sliding from excitement to undisguised resentment that she should work for a living, as if she had a choice.

He frowned again. 'Is Bert here?'

'No, he's at school for another week.'

Louis was restless and ill at ease, full of pent-up emotion, like a kettle full of steam that pushed against the lid.

'What's wrong?' she asked

'You should have told me.'

'I tell you everything.'

He shook his head and stepped towards her. 'Colvin. The first comer. I deferred to him. I thought he was marrying you.'

She should have allowed the embrace on the doorstep. Now his feelings were overflowing and mingling with her own. This was what she had feared. He caught her to him and smothered her with a kiss. The old sensations lapped around her feet, catching her in the undertow. Then he pulled back, leaving her stranded. She groped for the back of a chair, befuddled by the sensation of his lips on hers, the onslaught of desire and its sudden withdrawal.

'I don't understand,' she said.

'You led me on.'

She shook her head. Had she encouraged him? She had failed to push him away. She had offered loving friendship. Now she was being punished, but for what?

'Colvin can't marry you. Not while the vicar's alive!'

'But you knew that.'

'I did not! You told me you were promised, engaged, on the point of marrying.'

'It's true.' Amid the shifting sands of her feelings for Louis Stevenson, the ground was firm beneath her feet. 'I will marry Sidney, one day. It's only a question of time.'

He threw back his head and barked a laugh. 'Look, I would push Sitwell in the stinking Thames if I could, but failing that, the man might live forever!'

He reached for her hand and squeezed it with the urgency he used on that first afternoon when her fingers smarted. So much had happened since, she couldn't fathom what point they had reached. 'What matters is I am free of Albert. I can live as I please.'

He took two steps across the carpet square. His arms were around her waist, his cheek against hers. 'Consuelo, Claire, my dearest dearie.'

She had chosen Sidney for his loving constancy, the steady arm under hers. All that slid away under the touch of Louis's hand on her cheek. He fell on her neck, clasping her against him. He smelled of clean laundry and London smoke.

He was too strong or maybe she was too weak. She was the lightning conductor, the sap-filled tree that would burn like driest tinder. He kissed her again. His hand moved towards her bosom and through the silk and calico her nipple sensed his touch before it arrived. Using all of her will-power she pushed the hand away but he lowered himself to his knees, laughing as his forehead found the curve of her belly, his face pressed against her secret warmth. She sank to the floor next to him, drowning and falling. Her blood sang the old song. He raised his head and his tongue grazed her ear-lobe, a gunpowder spark of desire. He breathed in her ear, 'If you are free of Sitwell, you can be free of Colvin too.'

A line had been crossed. 'No!' She wrenched herself away and pushed herself up off the floor, hoping Maddie hadn't heard her cry. She reached again for the chair, wishing it were a less flimsy thing. She needed the strength of an oak.

He was standing too, his face coloured by unquenched desire. 'What do you mean, no? There will be no more nos!'

She retreated behind the chair, sat astride it, clenching the sides like a knight on horseback. 'No.'

It seemed she had only one word to offer and he deserved more. She reached into her heart, searching for the truth. 'I don't want to be free of Sidney.'

The simple fact shocked her. It was a thing of wonder, diamond hard. It lay between them and Louis was startled into silence, shaking his head, turning away from the hard gleam of truth.

He muttered his objections to the wall. 'What can he give you? He has no means. He told me so himself. You will be penniless. You might as well live in happy poverty with me as with him and his dull mediocrity.'

She felt anger rising. Sidney was not mediocre. Louis knew that too. 'Please sit down. You're not yourself.'

He shook his head like a dog who has dived in a pond and needs to rid itself of the wet. 'It's you who must be yourself, the one I saw last summer. You desired me, you still do.' His eyes narrowed. 'Your heart beats for me, remember?'

Did she say that? The words she'd put so thoughtlessly to paper were coming back to haunt her, a literary flourish taken by Louis as a promise. It was a disaster, a punishment for her weakness, and lack of foresight.

'You're twisting my words.'

'You mean your heart beats for him?'

She couldn't answer. She felt a great deal for Sidney but not passion. The heart wasn't everything, was it? If Louis didn't know that, she couldn't tell him.

In the wake of the storm, they were mute, like sailors shipwrecked on the beach, trying to regain their strength. He gave two trembling breaths and hung his head, his hand clenched to his chest in a theatrical gesture of love and pain.

'I came all this way. I kept you *here*, I sent you my *every waking thought*.'

She touched a hand to his face, remembering the weeks that had been enlivened by his letters; her black despair, his rhapsodies of lemon trees and Riviera sun. 'And they were all dear to me. They always will be.'

'But you'll stick with him? A fine man but he won't love you as I do. Don't ask me how I know, but I do.'

She wouldn't be drawn into an argument over Sidney. It was enough that she and Louis were in disarray. 'I won't change my mind.'

He was petulant now. 'I can't just go away. I won't, when we could live and love *as we please*. You were meant for better things, better places than this.'

'Where exactly could you take me?'

'Anywhere! Paris! Menton!'

She had been in Paris, but it was Sidney who had come to help. She clung to that moment and the decision she knew to be right.

But Louis was unstoppable. 'You would love it. I could show you Scotland. There are worlds for us to conquer!

And Bert. You know what good chums we are.'

She gave him a long look. He would see the sticking point.

'Look,' he reached again for her hand and she let him take it. '*Ordered South* is to be in *Cornhill*. It pays well. Soon I'll have means of my own.'

She shook her head. 'I can't give up what I've taken so long to gain.'

His was a soul beyond price and she was calculating his worth. She was shocked at her practicality.

He was scathing, 'It's not about the coin. It never was. We belong together.' He took her hand and kissed her fingers. 'You could have no one more faithful than me. I'm your loving son, your heart's desire. You're my priestess, my mother confessor...'

How much she wanted to save something from this disaster. She would take the blame if only he would agree there was blame to be laid.

'I can love you too, as a mother loves a son. Anything more has been a weakness. My weakness.'

He narrowed his eyes. 'Only weakness then, only lust? I found beauty, or thought I did.'

'A beautiful weakness, if that will do.'

'One you indulged at your convenience, then, when no one could see or hear?' He was accusing her of treating him as a lover, a paramour. But he had come to her at Cockfield in that exact guise.

His voice was unnaturally calm. 'Or do you want that still? Secret trysts, passion indulged when time and circumstances allow?'

He was testing her. These things happened all the time, fleeting unions when the opportunity arose, occasional planned deceptions, consolations for the drabness of life as it must be lived. It was wrong, or was it necessary?

Louis narrowed his eyes as if he read her mind. 'Love is wasted when it hides in corners. I know that well enough. Wasted and defiled. We could have a full and perfect union…love, friendship, nourishment.'

He wanted everything, he wanted too much.

They were both exhausted. 'I think you should go,' she said. 'Maybe we can talk again. Differently.'

His voice was edged with bitterness. 'You'd leave me with nothing?'

As he had left her, all winter, alone and unwell. He suddenly crossed his arms around his stomach and grimaced in pain.

She took his arm. 'You're very pale. Let me call you a carriage.'

He shook her off. She rang the bell and asked Maddie to run to the main road. The girl shuffled in the doorway. 'Where shall I say?'

'To Hampstead,' Louis said, 'To Colvin, damn his eyes.'

As he left the room he swayed and clutched the door-jamb. She could give him no more. She let him right himself and leave.

Hearing Maddie come back from outside she called to her again and scribbled a note to be sent to Sidney. It said simply, *take care of him.*

Afterwards she sat with her head in her hands. She was worn out. She wished Sidney were here, a reminder of her real life, surely her true self. But Sidney couldn't answer the song that Louis sang within her.

16.

A day and a night passed. Another man was in her sitting room. Where Louis had been willowy, Sidney was angular. Where Louis had been pale, Sidney was pink with perplexity, fidgeting with the hat he had taken off and was crumpling in his hands. There could only be one topic of conversation.

'How was he, last night?' she asked.

He looked away to the window and the empty lane outside. 'Simply dreadful. I was seriously worried.'

'And today?'

Sidney's gaze returned to the room and settled on her with a quick smile. 'A speedy recovery. Remarkable almost.'

'So you dispensed the right treatment?'

Sidney took her literally. 'We resorted to chloral but he is none the worse. A case of desperate measures. Though you know he's not averse to remedies of that kind.'

No more details of Louis's collapse were to be forthcoming. There was something in Sidney's short replies that felt accusatory, Louis was improving *no thanks to her*.

Had Sidney taken chloral too? She pictured the men, easing Louis's pain or simply seeking pleasure? She brushed the picture aside.

He was surveying the room which he hadn't seen since she had first moved in. 'This is all right, isn't it?'

'It's perfect,' she reassured him. 'Or it will be.'

'I'll keep my eye open for some more prints. Japanese or European, what do you think?' He went to the mantlepiece and picked up the framed photograph of Bertie and Freddie, the boys stiff in their best clothes in the photographer's studio. It was already a year since Freddie's death. It troubled her that the photograph was more familiar than the memory of his face.

'Do you think you can be happy here?' Sidney asked.

Louis had said they could be happy, meaning he could. She stood next to Sidney who was running his hand around the frame. She needed to bridge the awkward gap between them. 'Of course I can be, I will be. Bertie likes it too.'

He put back the photograph and she kissed his cheek, determined to drive the ghosts from the room, the dear son, the importunate friend. She must look to the future. Sidney smiled at her vaguely and drifted to the window.

'Sidney, please sit down, you're putting me on edge.'

He sat down with some reluctance. 'I can't describe the state he was in last night.'

She had thought the matter closed, but Sidney was working it over in his mind.

'Yes. I'm sorry I was the cause.'

'I assume he... proposed himself to you?'

Proposed himself, she had to smile. She reached across from her chair and touched Sidney's knee. 'If you mean he threw himself on me, yes. I'm sure you can imagine.' She would say no more. She could be laconic too.

'He told me in Monaco that he loved you but wouldn't press his case.' He let a moment pass. 'You knew of this, I assume.'

Frances nodded. 'I knew he was...enamoured.'

'I know you wouldn't have encouraged him.' Frances

acknowledges this. 'But he thought we were to marry very soon. I had to put him right. I could see he was agitated.'

Her hands were folded in her lap. 'Yes, that was the nub of it.'

'Although it's only a matter of time, until we do marry.'

It was a relief to have him confirm it.

'You did make clear he can't expect anything from you?'

Sidney's formality was a help. She nodded. 'Of course. Where is he now?'

'I left him at the Savile. He'll be looked after there.' He met her eyes. 'He says he won't give you up.'

Is she a noxious drug, a draft of chloral? 'Well, he must.'

She had replied too quickly. Sidney's suspicions were aroused. 'Frances, is there something that has given him hope of… intimacy with you? A future even?'

She studied her right hand and the ring with the amethyst, set in silver. It had belonged to her mother. Her wedding ring was jettisoned long ago but it had left a pale circle on the ring finger of her other hand, the ghost of Albert Sitwell, except Albert still lived, casting a troublesome shadow. She smoothed an invisible crease from her skirt. 'I have been quite clear with him,' she said.

'And yet he had to be corrected?'

She sighed. Her ultimate loyalty was to Sidney. He shouldn't need reassuring. 'You know how impetuous he is.'

She was rescued by Maddie who put her head around the door to ask about meals for the day. Frances excused herself and went to the scullery with the maid.

When she returned, she sat down again. Sidney deserved some explanation. 'You remember, last summer, Louis was writing about a woman called Claire?'

'Ah, yes, the novel?'

'It was a novel of letters, which he sent to me. I had offered to comment and correct. Those letters were very... uninhibited. I'm not sure he could escape his own conceit. It was clear I was taking the place of his heroine. Occasionally his letters to me, the real me, have strayed in a similar direction.'

Sidney was looking at her intently, more intently than she would have liked. He leaned forward, more intrigued than angry. 'He writes you love letters?'

'Not any more. But sometimes there's an undercurrent. His pen goes farther than his intentions.' She leaned forward again, appealing for understanding 'You know how fragile he can be,' she said. 'And how he relies on us. I try not to upset him.'

Sidney's awkward angles seemed to soften. 'I sometimes think he has us dancing to his tune.'

They exchanged a rueful smile. 'Anyway, Claire is gone,' Frances said. 'I try to encourage his writing, not his feelings for me. If I failed for a while. I'm sorry.'

There was no need to mention Consuelo, who could also be dispensed with.

Sidney sat back. 'Very well. I can see how it might happen. He gets so quickly...inflamed.' He spoke of it like a disease only Louis suffered. Sidney didn't think she could have caught the same infection, but then he had never lit that same fire. 'I've had a word with him,' Sidney said. 'I have promised to help him in his career. But he must stop bothering you.'

A year ago, they had stood in the drawing room at Cockfield, laughing together, an uneven triangle that would stand the test of time. Now she was a bargaining chip in some tussle between Louis and Sidney.

'He doesn't *bother* me. Surely we're all friends.'

Sidney was impatient but stayed in his chair. 'Friendship is fine. He must give up other claims. You must make sure he sticks to his side of the bargain.' A bargain Louis hadn't agreed to, not in so many words. 'Otherwise, he may persist. And we can't help him if he is always...at you.'

She flinched at the expression. 'Listen to us,' she said, 'As if he were a wayward child or an unschooled puppy.'

Sidney surprised her with a laugh. 'A puppy! I can see that!'

She stood up to bring the awkward and necessary meeting to a close. She and Sidney embraced as they always did.

'Can you make some kind of peace with him?' Sidney said. 'Perhaps a letter, a very clear letter?'

Letters held dangers of their own. 'I can't make peace from a distance.' She frowned in concentration. 'I have to see him.' She needed to secure Sidney's trust. 'You could be there too. A joint agreement.'

She was surprised that Sidney balked, blustering. 'Oh I don't think so.' He got up to leave, kissing her cheek. 'You will make things right, I'm sure.'

Sidney trusted her, but the triangle of friendship would never be the same. Some force of nature had thrown it in the air to land warped and twisted out of shape.

Since Sidney, a confirmed unbeliever, would feel no jealousy, she invited Louis to go to church with her. When he knocked at her door on Sunday morning, under the wide-brimmed hat the old light was in his eyes. He gave her a formal bow.

'Madame, I am here to escort you to your place of worship,' following this gallantry with, 'I can compare the English form of nonsense to the Presbyterian.'

She sighed and resisted the instinct to take his arm, nor did he offer her his. They were acting out parts written by Sidney.

'It's good to see you looking so well,' she said.

'We have Professor Colvin to thank for my recovery.' He frowned into the sky where a few house martins were circling. 'Luckily he had some very good remedies to hand.'

'Chloral, yes, he told me.'

'Not to mention the balm of his affectionate nature.'

Sidney as a *balm* was a novel concept. Louis had such a way with words. 'I'm pleased you two are such good friends.'

'More than friends. He's promised himself to me, to my career as a writer.'

Sidney had said the same but it sounded different coming from Louis. Sidney had promised himself. Hadn't she done the same?

This was her first church visit since moving to Bloomsbury. She remembered the lightness she had felt in having him by her side all those months ago in Bayswater. They were always walking a tightrope between love and friendship. It might be a strong and stable walkway if only the danger didn't always lurk on either side; the rising pleasure she took from his company, the heightening of her senses in being close.

St. George's had a pleasing elegance. 'Good Heavens!' Louis said as they turned the corner. 'London does its churches well.'

'No better than Edinburgh, surely?'

He was doubtful. 'For the most part, the Kirk is unassuming. We would rather contemplate the perils of damnation than the joy of Heaven.'

As they entered, he offered his arm and she took it for

the short distance to the strangers' pew. A few heads turned, but had no reason to question what the matron and pale-skinned boy might be to one another.

The church was bright with sunshine. Louis stood for the first hymns but did not sing, so that her voice rang too loudly in her ears. Otherwise, the only thing he refused to do was to kneel in prayer, his bony frame towering over her and the other worshippers. If she turned her head, she could see his fingers spread on his knees.

As they left the church he said, 'I asked to talk to you and all we've done is sung a few dull hymns.'

'I can't think what there is to say, except I hope we can be at peace with one another.'

'If I didn't know better, I would think that Colvin has put you up to this.'

She looked straight ahead. Sidney wanted this peace but so did she.

'He has your best interests at heart. We both do.'

'I expect to be in London more from now on and I intend to see you. There will be things we can do together,' he went on, 'when I'm free from my infernal studying.'

She hadn't thought of this, that she might see him more than previously. His presence so far had been intermittent, short intense encounters, the gaps cushioned by letters. He might begin his imprecations all over again. She began to see how his absences were easier to bear.

'I've promised Sidney I won't let you overstep the mark.'

A yelp of laughter. 'The mark? Our professor should look to his own behaviour I think!' He smiled to himself, 'Though I shouldn't complain. He has saved my life more than once.'

He was talking to himself. Frances couldn't follow but understood the men had put their rivalry aside.

He tucked his arm through hers again and she didn't draw away. His tone was conspiratorial. 'Never you mind what jinks we men get up to. He will be sound for you, I have no doubt.'

If Sidney was to be sound then so must she. He had given her a task to complete. 'You must give up all idea of being with me, as a husband, or a lover.'

His face was concealed by the hat. He lengthened his stride, driven by irritation. She had done too much pleading. He said something over his shoulder which was blown away on the wind. At the corner of the street, she caught his arm. 'You're going too fast for me.'

They ended up in the central garden of a square. In the hour before lunch, it was empty and they had the choice of any of the benches set under the trees. 'Sidney and I will be married one day.'

He folded his arms and stretched out his legs, looking down their long length then looking up at her with a piercing look.

'I value his support and his friendship,' he said, 'I can hardly keep pestering the lady who apparently belongs to him.' He took a breath, looking down again, studying the pale fingernails. 'I still don't believe he loves you as I do.'

'I think there are many kinds of love.'

He turned to look at her. 'That's very profound for a Sunday morning.' He turned the hat around in his hands by its brim. 'So, I am permitted to love you in my way while he loves you in his?'

This wouldn't work. There would be no end to it. *Make him promise*, Sidney had said.

'I don't suppose I can stop how you feel. Can you promise not to say it? Not even to think it? Then you will give your energy to where it should be.'

A glimmer of amusement. 'Do you speak to Bertie like this?'

'Yes, sometimes I do.'

'And this will make me good in your eyes?'

'Yes. And in Sidney's.'

He took her gloved hand and kissed it. 'I suppose you have been merciful.'

She closed her eyes to avoid the sight of his head bent over her hand then brushed his cheek with her fingers. 'Dear Louis.'

'May I write to you still?'

He would not hold back in his letters. They would make a nonsense of anything he agreed.

'I'll have to think about it.'

'And in the meantime?'

'Write temperately.'

His narrow eyes watched her. 'So I must be good. And for Colvin I must work. I hope I don't become a dull boy.'

A dull boy. That would be the very worst outcome.

She asked Sidney about Louis's writing to her. If he forbade it, so would she.

Sidney was vociferous. 'No, don't stop him! Think how much of him we might lose.'

Later she would see this was her second mistake, to let him go on. There was no way he could be stopped.

He wrote to her as his *Madonna,* his holy mother, but she wasn't deceived. Images of faith were useful allegories for his covert desire. He would be good, he said, he was being good. Frances was under no illusion: the words were only words.

From time to time, he came to London and there was an increasing distance between the voice of the letters and

the man who stood outside her house, twisting his hat in
his hands.

> *Brunswick Row,*
> *December 13th, 1874*
> *Dear Louis,*
> *I saw you in the dusk but thought my eyes deceived
> me. If you had told me your train was delayed we
> could have spent more time together. Your company
> is always a joy, but don't forget the vow you made
> to form elegant words and elegant thoughts, the true
> end of every writer.*
> *Yesterday I was reminded of Donne;*
> *"Sir, more than kisses, letters mingle souls;*
> *For, thus friends absent speak."*
> *Take this from me, a letter for a kiss. Be strong
> in your intentions. Live well.*
> *Your dearest friend,*
> *FJS*

He replied with what he called a Christmas kiss, long and
lingering. She should have been more careful in her choice
of words. It was as if her pen had chosen for her.
Trammeled in the net of their correspondence, she was
almost glad when, a year later, Louis passed his exams
for the Scottish bar, threw off any pretence of practising
law and took to travelling, principally to France with his
artist cousin, Bob. His letters became shorter and less
frequent. For Frances it was a kind of freedom, but without
the line connecting her to Louis, part of her withered and
she felt herself grow old.

Then, a year later, Louis was in love. The news trickled
down to Sidney and was soon all over town. That young

Scot, darling of the Savile, was skulking in Paris with a woman he'd met in the artists' colony at Grez. Rumour had her as American, outlandish, married, with several children. Her name, strangely enough, was Frances, but she was always known as Fanny.

PART FOUR

Friendship

But we are all travellers... and the best that we find in our travels is an honest friend. He is a fortunate voyager who finds many... They are the end and the reward of life.

Robert Louis Stevenson, *Travels with a Donkey in the Cevennes*, 1879

17.

Paris, 1877

Fanny Van De Grift Osbourne (Dutch stock, American upbringing, unwise marriage) woke to the sounds of early morning Paris, the clatter of wheels, the screeching of birds, and the all too familiar feeling of hunger. The aroma of freshly baked croissants drifting up from the shop downstairs was an unbearable temptation, but she and Louis had no money for luxuries. She burrowed back under the bed-clothes, reaching for Louis, but he was wide awake and wouldn't be distracted by seduction.

He sat up. 'We have to go to London.'

Long before she met Louis Stevenson, Fanny was a traveller, although more from necessity than preference. When her husband, Sam, took off for Nevada to work a silver mine and asked her to join him, she and their four-year-old daughter Belle went the long way around, from Indianapolis to New York and to Panama, by trains and boats and sometimes on foot.

It was a gruelling journey, but she got there, and she was born practical. She did her best to fit into the miners' rough settlement and make a half-decent home out of next-to-nothing. But Sam announced they must move on, and that was just the beginning. Time after time, they decamped from one lawless city to another until she worked out that this was his way of getting out of trouble— trouble usually meaning debt.

She grew tired of it all and for a while they lived apart, but after they settled in Oakland, it looked like things had changed. Sam found a proper job and she began to make friends of her own. Hervey was born a year after their first son, Lloyd. They felt like a real family.

Then she heard rumours that Sam was seeing another woman. And Fanny wouldn't be made a fool of. It was her turn to move on, somewhere Sam wouldn't follow. Those new friends encouraged her interest in art and with their help she decamped to Europe, where she and Belle, seventeen by then, could study painting.

Later, Fanny would remember the hopeful start in Antwerp, with its fine buildings and cosy lodgings, but the optimism was ill-founded. Hervey, barely five, fell ill and doctors recommended a move to Paris. It turned out nothing could be done, and for the rest of her life she was haunted by his last desperate days as he lay coughing and in pain, making pitiful moans as he bled to death in her arms. She would never recover from the horror, the grief and the overwhelming loss. A lock of his soft blond hair went with her always, next to her heart.

If nothing else, that darkest of times propelled her, grief-stricken and exhausted, into the depths of the French countryside where she found friendship and consolation at an inn at Grez-sur-Loing, summer home to a group of artists. There, she and Belle, with the younger Lloyd, were a curiosity at first, but they were accepted, and it was peaceful. She was no longer on the run, but she had come to realise that nowhere was permanent. There would always be a time for moving on. Travelling was in her soul.

It was at Grez that she met Louis Sevenson, skinny and

febrile, travelling with his artist cousin. It was a myth that Louis jumped in through a window and into her arms but straight away something about him got under her skin. Louis had depths she wanted to explore, possibilities she couldn't put her finger on.

He and the cousin came and went, but each time he and Fanny met they would take up the conversation as if he'd never been away. He was a writer and he was a talker, the most dazzling she had ever known. They barely stopped talking to make love, and that was more energetic and satisfying than she would ever have believed.

She and Louis had plenty in common; they were both on the run, she from her marriage, he from his overprotective parents. Both of them were emotional wrecks, Fanny of course still grieving for poor Hervey. And Louis? He was always too excitable, laughing or crying to the point of hysteria. More than once, she had to slap him back to his senses. They knew they belonged to each other and returned together to Paris, living in the Latin Quarter. She encouraged him to write fewer essays and more stories. They might make money and they were much more fun.

She wanted no one else. He said that falling in love was like entering a darkened room. She had been there all along, waiting for him.

Except now they must go to London. On top of his chronic lung condition, he had an eye infection. 'I can't go on like this,' he said that morning as she gave up on her idea of love-making and crawled out from under the bedclothes.

Another journey was only to be expected, but what about the practicalities, she wanted to know, in particular the money?

'Belle and Lloyd can stay here,' he announced.

It wasn't impossible. There were friends to look after them, or to look after Lloyd, as Belle was forever proclaiming herself independent.

'What about a hotel? Will your father pay?'

He was leaning back, hands behind his head. 'He's sent me thirty. I don't want to ask for more. Maybe Colvin will help.'

Fanny's mouth, already dry from sleep, grew sour. Colvin was Louis's editor, an arrangement that seemed to suit them both, although Fanny sometimes questioned Colvin's judgement. Woe betide Louis if he put a comma in the wrong place, or ventured beyond the editor's narrow view of literature. 'Too British,' Fanny said of him. Louis corrected her. Sidney Colvin was English: the Scots were a different race.

'I know he's strict but he's good for me and he knows people. He's the one who got me published.'

'How can he help? I thought he lived in Cambridge?'

Louis made a mou. 'You're right. He has no London house. I can find a cheap hotel.'

But what about Fanny? They would need two rooms. Sam might be thousands of miles away but she was a married woman; it would do her no good if he knew she was with another man, then there was the disapproval of Louis's London friends. To them she was an interloper, a foreigner they had never met.

Another frown and a sigh from Louis. 'I suppose there's always Mrs Sitwell.'

By now, Louis had told her his whole life story, at length and in considerable detail. Why had she never heard of Mrs Sitwell?

Louis got up and began to dress. Fanny filled a pan with water to make coffee. 'And who might she be?'

Louis explained that she was 'attached' to Colvin.

'Attached? How exactly?'

He told her about the brutish ex-husband who still had some sway over her.

It never failed to surprise Fanny that when marriage was meant to be the key to a good life, people spent so much time and energy trying to extricate themselves. Herself included.

'Mrs Sitwell has been a great help to me,' Louis said. 'She took up my cause. We used to write to each other. Very often.'

If Louis needed a supporter, Fanny assumed Colvin took that role. What part did Mrs Sitwell play? In any case the writing had come to an end. There was no Mrs Sitwell on any of the letters Fanny took to the post or carried back to their lodgings.

Still, her antennae twitched. 'A great help? How exactly?'

Louis gazed somewhere into the middle-distance, which in their cramped rooms gave only a view of the dingy bedroom wall with a dark stain occupying one corner. It had a particular shape, like a man with a hooked nose. She should point this out to Louis, it had the makings of a story. He rolled to look at her, his head propped on his elbow, the red eyes giving him a distinctly demonic look. 'She is a writer too, but it's more that she just understands me. She always has.'

She hooked her arm around his skinny waist and twined her legs around his. 'Like I understand you?'

He put his head on her shoulder, laughing softly. 'Mrs Sitwell's understanding is of a different kind.'

Fanny was only partly appeased. When it came to the bedroom, she and Louis were such a great match, but she didn't like to think she was simply a replacement.

Louis was still pondering. 'Mrs Sitwell has been like a mother to me.' The smile was one of absolute satisfaction, as if he had finally solved a riddle. 'Yes, she has given me a mother's love.'

Fanny huffed. How many mothers did a man need?

But beggars (in this case literally) couldn't be choosers. Louis wrote to Colvin, who would ask the mysterious and motherly Mrs Sitwell to accommodate Fanny for a few days while his eyes were attended to.

On the whole of the journey, the train from Gare du Nord, the hateful sea-crossing and on to London, Louis coached her on the likes, dislikes and expectations of Colvin and his circle, including this Sitwell woman. It made her twitchy. It was as if his future depended on these people. Fanny would like to have told him otherwise, that between them they could have the world at their feet. But right now, they had nothing. It irked her that she would need to be liked, and she was nervous of letting Louis down.

18.

It was October. Fanny had injured her foot and was in no state for a first trip to England but treatment for Louis's eyes was urgent. In London, gusty winds blew up on every grey corner, snatching at their clothes and throwing Fanny off balance. When Colvin met them off the train, he and Louis greeted each other like long-lost brothers while she stood by in terrible pain. By the end of that first day, she could barely walk. What a pitiful picture they must have made, Louis with his crusted eyes, she with the agonised limp, and Colvin somehow manoeuvring them into a coach. Along the way, they crossed the river and Colvin pointed out the dome and portico of the British Museum, then they came to a halt in a narrow alley, surely one of the gloomiest corners in all of London.

'A bit of a back-street,' Fanny muttered to Louis.

Colvin turned towards her, a good profile spoiled by dry skin and meagre hair. He smiled thinly, 'Bloomsbury is a good address, and very convenient.'

Fanny was ready to believe him. She needed a place to sit down. Colvin rang the bell and Fanny waited for a maid to answer, but the woman who stood smiling at the door was no housekeeper. Her eyes were deep and soft, her dark brown hair gleamed even on this grey day. She wore a day-dress of dark green silk, not the latest fashion but well-cut, its high neckline offset by a deep V of tassels ending at her tiny waist, all enhanced by expert corsetry. Fanny tried not to look as awe-struck as she felt.

'Do come in,' said their hostess, who also had the smile of an angel.

When extolling Mrs Sitwell for her motherly virtues, Louis had somehow failed to mention how incredibly beautiful she was. Not only that but she exuded some inner calm, a stillness that would be hard to ruffle.

Fanny envied her this, as much as the beguiling looks. She herself was a good seamstress and could pretty herself up in a decent dress, but her character was obvious and open to everyone. She wore her heart on her sleeve. Although she guessed their ages to be similar, she would never be able to cultivate Mrs Sitwell's poise, her air of quiet mystery.

Here, on a narrow doorstep in Bloomsbury, was real beauty, nor could Fanny see in Mrs Sitwell the hauteur such comeliness often bestowed. Fanny suspected she went through life ignorant of the effect she had on others. Modesty, you could call it, but perhaps also a kind of blindness. Frances Sitwell should be seated in a grand drawing room, besieged by admirers, yet here she was in a London backstreet, accepting the obeisance of a stuffy academic, a penniless writer and his lame travelling companion.

Louis removed his battered hat and waved it in front of their hostess. 'My dear Mrs Sitwell!' Luckily, he didn't attempt the bow which would have toppled both of them over. 'Here we are, orphans of the storm, seeking only shelter.'

Fanny was in too much discomfort to notice if anything in particular passed between him and the lady on the doorstep.

'Louis!' said their hostess, the smile never wavering. 'It's wonderful to see you. And, Mrs Osbourne, we're so pleased to meet you at last, despite the painful circumstances.'

Their hostess certainly had all the social graces. If she had reservations about Louis's renegade American, she gave not the slightest sign.

'Fanny here is in a bad way,' Louis said, as if he himself were the picture of health. 'They've looked at her foot, but it needs time to heal.'

'Please come in,' Mrs Sitwell said. 'Let me find you a seat.'

Inside the tiny house, Colvin took charge, fussing over Louis while Louis fussed over her. *She must sit down, have you a stool? Are you alright dear?*

Fanny was eventually settled in a corner with Louis next to her and a cup of tea in her hand. When the flapping and fluttering subsided, she addressed Colvin and his paramour. 'I'd be obliged for you not to call me Mrs Osbourne. I'm trying to rid myself of that name. Fanny will be fine.' She could only take so much British formality.

'Yes, of course!' Louis said, and so that matter was settled, though in the ensuing pause no one suggested Mrs Sitwell should be called by her first name, later discovered to be Frances.

With the pleasantries concluded, Fanny laid down her cup, folded her hands in her lap and closed her eyes, wishing only for the throbbing in her foot to subside.

Removing herself from proceedings was an art she perfected over the next few weeks. A day-bed was manufactured for her in the rear of the sitting room, away from the window. Each morning, Colvin and Louis arrived together from the hotel where they were staying and, along with Mrs Sitwell, and immediately embarked on some dry discussion about writing or writers. If Fanny broke in with an opinion, Louis was ready to include her, but Colvin invariably shut her down. It was easier to retreat into silence, closing her eyes to give the impression of a light sleep, although her wits remained very much about her.

She could hear how Frances Sitwell's musical tones smoothed over disagreements with light-hearted affection, although her ear failed to pick up any special understanding between Louis and his former correspondent. On the other hand, there was something between the three of them, Louis, Colvin and Frances, a bedrock of understanding, born of a long-established friendship, Fanny supposed. But had they spent much time together? They had met years ago at the home of Louis's aunt, 'a special time, a special place', Louis called it. Fanny made a mental note to ask him what had made it so special. The obvious answer was Mrs Sitwell, with all her gracious charm. But maybe Colvin was part of it too. With him, Louis was surprisingly precocious, venturing ideas which were wild even by his standards, then accepting Colvin's criticism with good grace. Colvin, too, was more mellow, more boyish than he had at first appeared. Fanny could tell that amongst the three of them, much was unspoken: opinions, memories and private jokes were taken as read. Frances Sitwell presided with quiet indulgence, lending her presence to the alchemy, exuding some secret knowledge Fanny would never have.

Before lunch, the men left for their blessed club, and the two women were left alone. Mrs Sitwell was lovely but she was not idle. She worked two mornings and most evenings at a charitable foundation set up to educate working men and women. Fanny admired her for her independence. She had no official tie to Colvin. She bore with cheerfulness what she called a dull secretarial job. This position and a few published book reviews – she hoped to progress to essays – allowed her to live here and make a home for her son in the school holidays. 'Professor Colvin' (occasionally 'Sidney' slipped out), was attentive and encouraging.

'Where does your professor live?' Fanny asked after a few days. Surely the hotel with Louis was only temporary.

'He has rooms in Cambridge, or he stays at his mother's house in Norwood.'

Colvin was the director of the Fitzwilliam as well as the Slade Professor in Cambridge. None of this sounded particularly convenient for a London life. Fanny could hardly ask if Colvin ever shared a bed with his almost-betrothed, but she felt no male presence here, and there was no passion in the air.

Fanny watched them dance around each other, as if touching would be an embarrassment. When the men left, Fanny gave herself up to a hug from Louis while Colvin planted a chaste kiss on Frances's hair and stood by the door, waiting for Louis to join him.

If they weren't lovers, they were certainly good friends, and presumably Frances valued Colvin, as Louis did, for his literary and artistic connections: one afternoon she took herself off to tea with Georgiana Burne-Jones, no less, and her jewel of a writing desk was a gift from William Morris.

Was this proximity to art and culture enough to sustain her? Mrs Sitwell seemed happy with her lot. But Fanny didn't envy her the ascetic, argumentative Colvin. What did the woman do for pleasure? Where did she go for love?

When Frances had offered Louis her lifelong friendship, she had not anticipated it being put to the test in quite this way. She was pleased, of course, that he had found a new love. She had urged him for so long to think of her only as a friend. This mistress (they were lovers, surely) would be a more suitable object of his desire. No woman enjoys being superseded in a man's affection, but she wished him well, Frances reminded herself, she wished both of them well.

While Louis and his lady were at a distance, all of this was academic. It was a different matter to have them on her doorstep. Louis, so much his old effusive self, still made her heart stop in its tracks. On a first impression, the small dark woman on his arm looked to be his opposite in every way. She stood stolidly beside him, dark-skinned with unruly hair and a hint of pugnacity in her expression. Louis wore an extravagant Tyrolean hat with the cloak Frances had chosen in Paris wrapped around him. Mrs Osbourne was hatless and the dress she wore under her cape was embellished with a collar and a cravat. Next to Louis, the effect was almost manly.

Installed indoors, Mrs Osbourne (it was a struggle to call her Fanny) accepted Louis's conspicuous devotion but was otherwise mostly silent. When she did speak, her observations, perhaps sharpened by the pain of her foot, were as disconcerting as her brooding presence in the corner of Frances's sitting room.

However much Frances wanted to like Fanny Osbourne and put her at her ease, in the days that followed, it proved remarkably difficult to keep the woman entertained. When provided with a pile of novels, Fanny left them untouched on the table next to her day-bed.

'You don't care for Eliot?' Frances said, picking out *Silas Marner*, her particular favourite.

Fanny dismissed the greatest writer of the age with a flap of her hand. 'These people take too many words over everything.'

Fanny still couldn't walk any distance. One afternoon, Frances went to the kitchen to speak to her maid, and found her guest sitting at a pantry shelf with a pile of thin white papers and a heap of tobacco. Next to these raw materials was a growing pile of cigarettes. Fanny looked up, unabashed at being caught out. 'I'm making myself useful. I know Louis is running short.' She was taking a pinch from the pile of tobacco, her hands neat and skilful.

'You smoke yourself?'

'Don't worry, I wouldn't do so in your fine house any more than Louis would.'

Frances nodded, acknowledging the courtesy. 'If only I had a garden,' she said, 'It's the one thing I miss about my old home.'

'I'm used to making do with what I have.'

Frances approved Fanny's philosophy, and sympathised. This woman had few comforts. 'You could go by the front door. There are very few passers-by.'

Fanny raised her eyes from her task. 'I'm much obliged.'

That evening Frances asked if she had enjoyed her

cigarette and received the reply, 'I expect you think me a heathen,' she said.

'It's not for me to judge.'

Fanny's face lit up in a rare and mischievous smile. 'I'm sure there are plenty who will.'

Frances returned the smile. Sidney had said as much, that Fanny with the dark skin and fiery eyes was too exotic, whatever that meant, but Frances saw her as just a woman doing the best she could.

'You must be missing your children.'

'Children! My daughter is a grown woman and much too keen to remind me of the fact. If she'd had her way I would have gone after Louis's cousin, Bob.'

'His cousin?' This was the easiest rejoinder. Frances knew little of Bob Stevenson but imagined Fanny Osbourne mounting a horse and scattering the eligible young men of Grez in her path.

'Belle has always been too much like me,' Fanny went on. 'Handsome and strong-willed. She has the artist Frank O'Meara in tow. Who knows what will come of that? Lloyd, now, is a sweet boy, just nine years old and already good company.' Her voice dropped. 'Hervey was the most beautiful. They say God takes those he loves.'

'Oh!' Frances was shocked. No one had mentioned a third child. 'You lost a son?'

'Not so long ago, I can't tell you the horror of it. To see him suffer. To hold him in my arms as he died.' She bit her lip and her head dropped. Perhaps she regretted her directness.

Frances went to the mantle-shelf where she took down the photograph of Freddie and Bertie. 'My older son Freddie died. He was eleven.' *He was alone,* she could have added. If only she could have stroked his forehead as Fanny had done for her boy. She often wondered if holding Freddie in her arms would have saved him. They had told her that Freddie suffered no pain. Frances was grateful for that if nothing else.

Fanny Osbourne studied the picture. She gave a bleak smile and handed it back. 'Eleven? Six more years than I had of Hervey.' She fumbled in the pocket of her dress and held out a photograph. The face was cherubic, the hair, left long, was angelically blond.

Frances took the picture. 'What a beautiful child,' she said.

They stood together, contemplating the pictured boy. A gesture was needed to acknowledge their shared sorrow, but they weren't ready to embrace. Instead, Frances touched Fanny on the arm and said, 'I may have a spare picture-frame you could have. It will stop this from fading.'

Fanny held her gaze. 'I'd be very much obliged, thank you.' Then a change of tone. 'Where's your other boy, then?' as if Frances had mislaid him.

'His school is in Marlborough.'

'You only see him in the holidays? I'm surprised you don't want him with you.'

So much of Fanny's conversation sounded like reproof.

As the days passed, they became more attuned to each other. Knowing about her artistic ambitions, Frances offered to get Fanny paints and an easel.

'Thank you, but the standing would be too much. These days I think writing is more my métier. I can be more useful to Louis that way.'

Frances had heard none of this. 'You'll collaborate?'

'We each have an interest in crawlers, you know, the gothic tradition.'

Frances couldn't think of a reply. Would Louis change tack in his writing? Was Fanny Osbourne any good?

'I know, I know,' she went on. 'Colvin and his like want every word to gleam with polish. I think, just get the story down, ramshackle if need be, see if it's worth telling. See if it will sell.'

When Frances shared this with Sidney, they were alone. At last Fanny was well enough to go out and Louis was taking her on a short carriage drive.

Sidney, sitting opposite Frances, crossed his legs and frowned. 'She fancies herself a writer?'

'She may have talent.'

He rolled his eyes. 'Or sees the chance to share an income, come the day.'

'You're very cynical about your friend's true love.'

He gave her a wry smile. 'Can you blame me? We know nothing about her.'

This wasn't quite true, not by then, but Sidney, she suspected, couldn't come to terms with Fanny's hold over Louis.

A week later, it was decided they could travel back to Paris. On the doorstep, Fanny, with Louis next to her, thanked Frances profusely. 'I'm a difficult guest at the best of times, never mind when I'm laid up. You have the patience of a saint.'

Frances shook her head. 'I'm glad I could help.'

Louis stepped forward to clasp Frances's hand, his touch a shock of remembered sensations. 'What would I do without you?' he said, seemingly oblivious to her reaction. 'You must write to me more. I miss your letters. Colvin's talk is all business.'

Frances missed his letters too, but she was not deceived. Too much had changed for them to write as they had before, effortlessly and at will. And Fanny Osbourne had other ideas.

'Louis,' she said. 'You have letters from the whole world, and I know hardly a soul here in Europe. When things settle down, I shall write to Mrs Sitwell, if I may.' She nodded to Frances. 'I hope she will return the compliment.'

The dark, determined eyes held nothing but the offer of friendship. Frances was gratified. She and Fanny Osbourne had more in common than she had imagined. Her letters would be diverting, and they would deliver news of Louis without creating turmoil in her heart.

After Louis and Fanny returned to France, Sidney disappeared to Cambridge. Autumn was drawing to a close when he and Frances walked together in Hyde Park on a Sunday afternoon. There were drifts of leaves by the side of the path and Sidney was studying the sky where geese were forming a straggling V before flying south.

Frances followed his line of vision. 'When will we see them again, do you think?'

Sidney seemed surprised, as if his thoughts had been elsewhere. 'Will we see her again? The husband may claim her back.'

'I don't think so. She's devoted to Louis. I can picture them married, can't you?' This succeeded in catching his attention.

'You really think so? She is so...outlandish.'

Yes, Fanny Osbourne's looks and manners were unconventional. Sidney's tastes were more decorous. 'Not the easiest companion,' Frances admitted, 'a little strange, but we began to get along. You don't find her attractive?'

He shook his head vehemently. 'Not, not at all. Not...'

She could have prompted him to finish the sentence;

not like you was surely what he meant. She went on. 'They are so affectionate. She rolls his cigarettes. Imagine!'

Sidney was shifting beside her, his eyes straying to the lake and beyond. 'Last night, Louis spoke of you. He hoped I was *finding comfort* with Mrs Sitwell.'

The exact meaning of *comfort* floated somewhere between the water and the sky. She had to stifle a sigh of exasperation. Louis's meddling was outrageous, but he was right. She thought of Sidney's cautious courtship, her turning aside from anything more than a kiss. She reached for his hand.

'There have always been practicalities.'

Sidney was suddenly assertive. 'Practicalities can be overcome. I'm planning another trip to Brittany. Walter and his wife would like to join me.' Sidney had been to France a year ago with friends and described it on his return: the rugged coastline, the gentle hinterland with its neat cottages and scudding clouds. 'It's bracing, but rarely cold. Do you think you would like it?'

She liked the sound of *bracing*. 'Where would we stay?'

'I imagine we would rent a house. Something fairly spacious.'

She liked the sound of *spacious*. They would take long walks and come back healthily tired. After a glass of port, they would retire for the night and there would be no question of her and Sidney sleeping apart. The door would close behind them, she would hold his dear head in her hands and they would give each other what, after all this time, they both most decidedly needed and deserved.

20.

Fanny Osbourne did write, as she had promised, from Paris, but after a few months the letters ceased. Frances knew Fanny had gone back to America and her future with Louis was uncertain, until, to Sidney's horror, ('he'll never stand the journey') Louis crossed the Atlantic to claim Fanny as his own.

Grosvenor Hotel, London,
18th September, 1880
My Dear,
I must apologise for not having written in so long. When Louis arrived in California, he was close to death and I was in such vexation, struggling to get him well. Then I had to free myself from Sam Osbourne. At last, we divorced, and in May, Louis and I became man and wife. I wonder now how I ever doubted this was the right thing to do. We had a mad honeymoon, on an old silver mine, with only a few planks between us and the sky. I sometimes think these were the best of days, clean air, simple food and solitude with just Lloyd, my boy, Louis's playmate, to keep us company. But family allegiances couldn't be ignored. Louis's parents paid for our return and so began another long trek and ocean voyage. I admit it was a

comfort to find Colvin on the quayside to bid us welcome.

To my surprise, Louis's parents have taken me to their hearts. His mother advises me on what to wear and the gruff father turns out to be an absolute dear. I have him purring like a kitten!

In this whole year of trials and triumphs I have looked forward so much to seeing you and still it is not to be, because Louis's health is my first concern. If only those doctors didn't seem hell-bent on testing my resolve. He must have a cold apparently, but not the cold of Edinburgh. Davos! The thought of it makes me shiver.

I really did expect that on our way to Switzerland we could call on you (how I miss your dear house!) but first you were away and now this hotel is keeping me prisoner. Every evening a gang of Louis's friends turn up to make a fuss of him and keep him up too late. He loves the company and says they want to help. I call them hangers on, waiting for Louis to do something extraordinary then reap the benefits of friendship. Henley especially glowers at me. I know that behind my back they call me Louis's jailor.

If only we had time for our real friends, you, my dear, and your stalwart professor. Your joint love for Louis is plain as day and I am so grateful you have accepted me into that association of hearts and minds.

They say Davos is very pretty and there are men of letters there so maybe it won't be so bad. I hear you have been very busy with your translation. An entire book on the buildings of Venice! I admire your industry, but please think about coming to visit when it's done. It would cheer me more than anything to see your dear face.

*   Fanny V de G Stevenson*

Hotel Belvedere, Davos,
12th December, 1880
My Dear Frances,
Another cri de coeur! This town is pretty enough with the alpine light but the daily procession of sickly men walking up and down is depressingly English. They even call it the promenade!

*   Colvin is here but where are you, my pretty friend? Just as in London, the men love Louis to bits and I am, as ever, shut out. He is very taken up with Addington Symonds and his old friend Edmund Gosse. They fawn over him, their latest pet, while Symonds's staid wife views me with suspicion. Wherever in the world we rest our heads, I am doomed to be alone with my anxieties.*

*   I have no real company other than my two boys – Louis and Lloyd are always in cahoots over something – and the cold disagrees with me. I eat too much and Louis calls me his butterball. He is eating just as much but gains not an ounce. The world is an unjust place.*

*   Colvin's arrival is a double-edged sword. I love him dearly but he has thrown himself into the company, encouraging Louis to talk and argue endlessly with the English contingent. Worse, in the daytime, he and Louis throw themselves down the mountain on toboggans and hurl snow at each other, yelping like schoolboys. Louis becomes feverish and overexcited, and your professor grins in triumph over*

Louis or perhaps over me. It's my fate to be his
keeper and the enemy of his friends, except you, my
dear.

S. C. tells us your translation is a triumph! May
more work flow from it if you so desire. I understand
you must be in London with Bert (almost grown-up!)
and this is a bad time to travel, but I do miss your
lovely face and charming company.

Think of me in this mountain fastness. L. sends
his best regards but is intent with Lloyd on printing
a magazine with a toy printing press and cannot stop
to write. You see how I am marooned!
Fanny V de G Stevenson

21.

It was as Frances had predicted. Louis and Fanny were married. And as she had also foreseen, Louis never stayed in one place for long. His *Inland Voyage* and *Travels with a Donkey* were testament to his love of travel. But while Sidney raved about the crisp winter light of Davos, Frances found herself content to be in London.

The previous year, on the recommendation of Edward Burne-Jones, she had won a commission for the translation from French of a book about Venice. The work was exacting but satisfying, and now that it was completed, the fee was a useful supplement to her income.

At Christmas, Bertie was home from school and they visited her sister, Louisa, recently settled in Surrey. For once she had family around her. When she returned to Brunswick Row, she was delighted to find Fanny's letter awaiting her, but let Louis and Fanny, Sidney even, wander where they might, she was increasingly fond of her home.

She gave the letter to Bertie to read. The boy who had played pirates with Louis would shortly leave school, but still loved to hear from his childhood friend. He took out a handkerchief, coughed into it and blew his nose. She thought he was tearful. 'Don't be sad! I know you miss Louis but he is well and happy.'

He shook his head. 'I'm not crying. I think I picked up a cold in Surrey.'

Frances sighed. Louisa's house had been draughty. She sent Bertie to bed and asked Maddie to make beef tea. She told herself not to worry. He had always been a strong boy. With some cosseting, he would soon recover.

That same night, she woke in the early hours to hear Bertie coughing and was filled with dread. By the time she reached his room, he had fallen asleep, but from the door she heard how his breath rasped in his throat. This was no common cold.

In the morning, she took him breakfast on a tray and tried to make light of it. 'We'll soon have you up and about.'

He was shivering and turned away. 'I'm not hungry. Maybe later.'

In the next few days, no matter how much healthy broth she gave him, how often she stoked his fire or how gently, on a warmer afternoon, she coaxed him into the garden for the benefit of fresh air, the truth was unavoidable. He was seriously ill.

Sidney, returned from Switzerland, visited as often as he could. He stroked her hand as she gazed into the fire and wished away the horror that was to come. The doctor had diagnosed consumption, an extreme and virulent kind. *Dear God, let my boy survive.*

'You should take him to Davos,' Sidney said. 'It's his best chance.'

She was sceptical. The journey would exhaust him but her friends and her sister agreed.

Bertie, too, sat up in bed, cheeks flushed. 'Uncle Louis is there. His doctor will help me. When I'm well, we can go tobogganing.'

She had no faith in Davos or its doctors, and for once in her life had no real desire to see Louis Stevenson. Who was he except a ghost from her past? But, to keep up the appearance of hope, she boarded the boat-train, holding Bertie by the arm as he stumbled at her side. Her heart failed her. There would be no coming back, her only comfort would be to nurse him as he died.

Sidney went with them to Paris, from there Frances journeyed alone with Bertie propped up beside her, talking with feverish excitement of their arrival in Switzerland, then slumped in exhaustion, his cough more chesty, more persistent. As she helped him down from the carriage in Davos, she glimpsed faces at the hotel windows looking down on them and hastily withdrawing. They had made their assessment, and knew from grim experience the unlikelihood of recovery.

At the reception desk, the concierge gave her a message. It was from Louis, in the distinctive hand that grew ever more spidery and difficult to read.

I have got Bert a toboggan for when he is recovered. Ask the hotel to fetch it when he is able. We shall have him out in the snow before long.
   L.

Louis and Bertie were of the same mind, but she didn't show the message to her son who was clinging to the hotel desk. It would have been an act of cruelty. She wrote a short reply, regretting they would not make use of Louis's gift. It should be left for other hotel guests to enjoy.

She gave her note to the concierge. 'Is Mrs Stevenson in the hotel?'

A regretful shake of the head. Mrs Stevenson had left for Paris on account of her health. Frances felt the loss, the one person to whom she could have unburdened herself.

Not for Frances the delights of afternoon walks or dinner table conversation. What she saw of Davos she saw from the window of her room, the daily procession of men wrapped in greatcoats as described by Fanny, brown faces belying their frailty.

She saw Louis only from a distance or heard his voice as she passed the dining room, the Scotch accent undimmed by so many journeys across Europe and America. She heard his old confidence and a new-found maturity. He didn't approach her and she didn't want him to. He couldn't help. No one could.

Two weeks later, Sidney arrived. As she watched over Bertie, he sat writing at the small desk by the wall, the scrape of his pen grating on her jangled nerves. Downstairs, there was singing. She travelled from bed to window and back again, unable to settle.

'Come down to dinner,' he said. 'Bert will be all right for an hour and it will do you good.'

Sidney deserved her company and so she tidied her hair and took her seat with him at a corner table in the busy salon. Across the room the guests sparkled in the brightest lamp-light, as noisy as a flock of birds. The invalid life was something they embraced. Louis sat with a group of six, taking part in some heated discussion that broke into unrestrained laughter. Seeing her, he turned away from his companions, brought his laughter under control and raised his hand in a formal wave, a gesture of sympathy. She caught sadness in his eyes before she looked away.

Sidney began to enumerate the men who sat around

them, this eminent professor, this acknowledged wit. She laid her hand on his. 'This is no place for me, not tonight. I'm going back to Bertie.'

'I'll sit with you,' he said.

She shook her head. 'You should join Louis.' Propriety demanded they have separate rooms. She had no idea how late he stayed up or what merriment occurred.

A few days later there was a knock at her door. When Frances answered, Fanny Stevenson threw her arms around her. 'My dear, my poor dear.'

Frances would have lingered in her muscular embrace, so strange and yet so needed, but Fanny went straight to Bertie, stroked his forehead, put her plump hand over his wrist and spoke quietly. 'You don't know me, Bertie, but I've heard so much about you. I'm going to send my Louis to see you as soon as I can drag him away from my son. Lloyd idolises him, you know, just as you do.'

Maybe it was the tone of her voice or the mention of Louis, but Bertie's breathing seemed to quieten and he fell from restlessness into sleep. This was what Frances needed, a friend who didn't need her to explain how she felt since she had no words to do so.

Fanny held her arm. 'You'll be no good to him if you don't get out of here. I'll find somebody to watch him. Put your coat on and meet me in the foyer.'

Frances had no strength to argue.

The light outside, as bright and hard as a diamond, made Frances's face ache, a pain she welcomed. She had been numbed by the stuffy hotel rooms. She thanked Fanny. 'You were right. I need some air.'

'It does me good to get away from *my* invalid for an hour,' she said.

Frances absorbed the knowledge that Fanny Stevenson's invalid was more likely to recover than hers.

'How is he?'

'Disobedient.' Louis was dismissed in a word.

'You haven't been well.'

Fanny laughed. 'We're a pair, aren't we? He's not to smoke and I'm not to eat. We spy on each other. If I find him with a cigarette, I get to eat bread and butter. You can see I grow no thinner.'

It was true she was stout, as if she and Louis would always match each other in bodily extremes. When Frances's boot skidded on an icy patch of snow, Fanny caught her just before she fell. It was a matter of surprise to both of them. 'I am steadier than you,' Fanny said. 'Not like in London.'

Fanny pointed out people around them. 'Symonds and his wife, poor woman. I've told Louis to be careful.' A knowing look, the voice lowered. 'He goes to Venice, you know, to photograph gondoliers.'

Did Fanny really fear for Louis? With his long hair and foppish gestures, Louis could play the part of an aesthete to perfection, but surely his devotion to Fanny was obvious.

Frances asked about Fanny's daughter, in America and expecting a baby. 'I'm sorry we didn't see you when you were last in London.'

She sighed. 'In London they all want Louis for themselves. It's the same here. They forget he belongs to me now.'

It was her right to be possessive. Louis had made his choice.

'I just wished they wouldn't keep him up so late. I can say nothing to shift them. If I try, they think I'm a cowgirl with a lasso.'

Fanny might be forty or more but the picture was apt. 'I'll remind Sidney you're anything but.'

'Colvin isn't the worst of them by any means. And Louis wouldn't be without him for the world.'

Frances remembered the stories of snowball fights and envied the men their carefree fun.

In their time at Davos, Louis did not call to see Bertie even once. In her mind, Frances tried to excuse him: he didn't wish to flaunt his new family in her face, Bertie's frailty reminded him of his own. But with Sidney disappearing back to Cambridge for the spring term, she felt abandoned. Only Fanny saw the need to bear her up. By then, death was the only end in view.

'I should tell you,' she told Frances one day, 'that Louis is writing you a poem, you or Bert, or both of you, a memorial you might call it. It's the best he can do, he says. I felt like saying *go and see the woman, sit with the boy and talk to him*. But men are hopeless around death.'

Albert had thrown himself into the practicalities of Freddie's passing, Sidney had simply stayed away. On this too, Fanny was almost certainly right.

They buried Bertie at Davos in April. Frances thanked Louis for giving her son a breath of immortality in his poem *In Memoriam, FAS*. Francis Albert was Bertie's full name. The title she supposed was to preserve her privacy although she wished Louis had been more personal, more familiar for the boy who had loved him like a brother. 'For Bert' would have given her more solace. She puzzled over some of its lines, trying to find a message in them. Bertie had lived *all the singing season*. She was the one who had sung all her life. At Cockfield, Louis, tall and young beside her, turning the pages, or sometimes kneeling next to the piano at her feet. She folded the poem and put it away. It was a formality, like the polite wave across the dining room.

She returned to London alone, as she had known she would: one boy, so nearly a man, was left in Switzerland, the other lay in an English graveyard under the grey skies of Kent. She opened the door to the home she had made for herself and Bertie and was overwhelmed by the silence she had once enjoyed. In the sitting room, she picked up the photograph of her boys and turned it to the wall. She had never felt so alone.

Louis's story filtered through to her in his letters to Sidney and Fanny's letters to her. He continued to make a name for himself with his travel writing and he was assembling a collection of essays for publication. *For Girls and Boys*, he was calling it, as playful as ever, as if they were all children, living in an age of innocence.

22.

Braemar Village,
28th August, 1881
Dear Frances,
I write to let you know that Colvin is here, arriving on yet another dismal afternoon of rain which makes me long for the frost of Davos and its honest cold, even if it was of no use to you and your dear boy. I do think of you in your sadness and hope any letter is a brief distraction, even if I have only my fears to share.

Summer it may be and Louis's parents are so delighted to have us here, but I fear the place (Pitlochry was even worse) will be the end of him. He haemorrhages continually and I worry his next breath could be his last. He spends most of the day in bed with a respirator which uses pine oil. The stink of it is all over the house. Amid such mayhem he has strangely found a new seam of writing joy. In the evenings he entertains us all with a tale called The Sea Cook, *an adventure story for boys. It's a marvel to see him so wrapped up in a story and enjoying the attention of an audience. His father especially listens avidly and suggests improvements!*

Otherwise, Louis is forbidden from talking for large parts of the day and as usual I defend his door like Cerberus at the gates of hell. The family at least understands my savagery.

Gosse, the poet, is here too, and since he swore obedience to my rules he is permitted to play silent chess with Louis. I know he will be true to his word. He and Louis met as boys and have always been close. According to Louis, he is on his way to an assignment in Inverness. Louis disapproves. A mistress? I didn't ask. His wife is an accomplished painter. If he's a troubled man he gives no sign of it and he clearly adores Louis.

When S.C. arrived, Louis was particularly bad and I had to keep everyone downstairs. Next morning, I found him at the back door getting into a spare pair of wellington boots. If he couldn't see Louis, he said, he might as well get some fresh air. Poor man. I said he would get his turn and that afternoon I took him upstairs with my usual warnings. Louis, who had been dozing, opened his eyes when he saw Colvin and raised an arm, smiling widely. 'Colvin! She let you in!' I gave him such a frown he said no more. Colvin sat down on the chair beside the bed and grasped Louis's hand and so I left them to their reunion.

Afterwards he thanked me for looking after Louis. 'No one can ever have enough of him,' I said, 'I have to portion him out.' Colvin laughed and told me some story about Louis saying just the same thing years ago, likening himself to a Christmas pudding, telling me to ask you for the whole story, because you were certainly there. Your professor is quite the conundrum, adoring Louis just as he adores you, but then Louis has this effect on everyone, men and women.

I had forgotten that Gosse and Colvin are friends too and spend much time together when Louis's door is closed. On our single fine day, I saw them on deckchairs on the lawn, their heads together, no doubt on some literary topic too abstruse for the likes of me. You and I must be grateful we have each other for when our men retreat to their private world.

I just wanted to let you know, dear, that you are in our thoughts and that while we would love to have you, I know it is too soon for you to travel and anyway this vile weather would do your spirits no good.

I fear we will be back to Davos for the winter. Who knows when you and I will meet again, but I look forward to that day above anything.

Look after yourself and send me any London news I need to know.

Your dearest

Fanny

23.

Bournemouth 1886

Davos, Hyeres, a welter of trips in between, always hoping to find the perfect climate, the perfect spot for Louis to be well. He would say he was happiest at Hyeres, where he and Fanny found blissful solitude in a tiny house too small for visitors, but that happiness was fleeting. Louis continued to spit blood. Frances knew that Fanny was constantly anxious about outbreaks of cholera in the region.

Sidney was appointed Keeper of Prints and Drawings at the British Museum. No longer tied to Cambridge, he could take his rightful place at the centre of literary London. The post came with a house, one of several attached to that grand institution. Following the success of her Venice translation, and helped by Sidney's new position, Frances began to contribute to art journals. He persuaded her to find a new house too, a modern building in Marylebone, with all the latest conveniences. At first she missed her Bloomsbury hideaway, but she enjoyed the larger space and the light from her new bay windows. Suka, whose husband, Eugene, had died while working abroad, came back from Paris to live in London and declared Frances's new home terribly grand.

Then a letter arrived from Fanny Stevenson. Their sojourn in the South of France, which for a while had been such a success, had come to an end. They were driven back to another English promenade, this time at Bournemouth. A house had been found and bought for them by Louis's father. Fanny had her doubts about the move to England, she wrote that she feared the climate would prove unsuitable, that Louis would be plagued by the attentions of too many friends who were already celebrating his 'homecoming.'

Be assured, she added, *that all other visitors will be kept at arms' length if you and S.C. as much as hint you are on your way. What heaven it will be, to live on the same island as my pretty friend, to look forward to many meetings and conversations.*

Fanny had proved a good friend and her letters were entertaining. They also revealed a life strung between love and eternal anxiety. As for Louis, he had written to her asking for her advice on his *Child's Garden* and thanked her for her response. His letters were formally polite. They hadn't met since Davos, and that had been a miserable affair.

Louis took to visiting Sidney in London. *Louis is enthralled by his new home. Such history, such culture!* Fanny wrote. *I shall think of him as The Monument.*

Suka was very taken by 'The Monument'. 'How perfect for Sidney!' she said.

Frances stayed away during Louis's visits, feeling oddly unprepared for a reunion.

Winter and a series of chills prevented travelling for a while, but in the middle of the following summer a new railway station opened in Bournemouth. Sidney pointed out they could get down and back in a day, and Fanny would hear no more excuses.

Sidney, by now a regular visitor to Louis's home, declared they would make a weekend of it and booked his usual sea-front hotel, and so the following morning, with the sea winking on their left, he and Frances stepped along the promenade where many others were already taking the air.

With a breeze on her face, Frances tasted salt on her lips, wondering why she had put off this trip. 'Louis always loved the sea,' she said.

The house was at the head of a green valley leading away from the sea-front. The name Skerryvore, paying tribute to the lighthouse built by Louis's grandfather, was carved above a lamp next to the door. Louis was putting down roots.

Fanny came to the door straight away, stouter than before, with shadows under her eyes, and threw her arms around Frances. 'At last!'

Her embrace spoke of warmth and of settlement. She and Louis were no longer wanderers. This was their home.

A small dog yapped at Fanny's ankles. 'Come and see the invalid', she said and shooing the terrier away, led them through to a drawing room. Through the window Frances glimpsed a long and sloping garden but saved her attention for the man facing away from the door on a sofa. He was wrapped in a blanket, his slippered feet stretched in front of him.

'Here they are!' Fanny announced.

Louis half turned to greet them. 'Come in, come in', he said, with an airy wave of his hand. His voice was unchanged. It could have been nine days rather than nine years since he had arrived with Fanny in Bloomsbury.

A chair was placed at the foot of the sofa for the use of visitors and Frances availed herself, sitting at his feet. Once upon a time he had paid court to her. Now she was the supplicant.

'Doesn't she get more beautiful all the time?' Fanny said from across the room. 'There should be a law against it!'

Louis replied to Fanny but looked at Frances. 'I admit no woman ever looked so good in a bustle.'

His eyes were full of the old playfulness but the corners were crinkled and the forehead creased. His hands were laid on the cover but he didn't reach for hers.

'I'm sorry I couldn't come before,' she said.

He didn't ask for a reason. 'You're here now. Fanny has been desperate to see you.'

Fanny was fussing with the maid and asking what they would like for lunch. Sidney was saying Fanny must show Frances the garden.

Frances and Louis sat in silence. He closed his eyes. 'Listen to the birds out there.'

Frances absorbed the birdsong and the sunny room, created by man and wife. Fanny and Louis in newly acquired domesticity. It suited them and she quelled a pang of envy.

Fanny insisted on showing her round. Louis's slew of books, the travel memoirs, *Treasure Island* and the *Child's Garden* had brought him solid acclaim and the house reflected his success. Good furniture was softened by Fanny's more exotic choice of rugs and wall-hangings. There were photographs and paintings, tasteful and amusing knickknacks given by friends. The garden was huge.

'I didn't know you liked gardening,' Frances said.

'Nor did I until I had one. It's my favourite place.'

She showed Frances her new dahlias and red-flowered runner beans on the beginnings of a vegetable plot. In this corner of England, Fanny could still be a pioneer.

After lunch, it was warm enough for Louis to go outdoors and they walked down the chine as far as the sea, the men together, the women arm in arm behind. On the way back, Louis stopped, sat on a low wall and took a lungful of air.

'I could love this place.'

'If only it loved you,' Fanny said.

He barked a rueful laugh.

Sidney chimed in. 'The people love you, both of you.'

Sir Percy Shelley, the poet's son, and his wife Jane were frequent callers and Henry James had a chair set aside for his personal use.

Fanny grunted. 'Too well, I think. They bring their illnesses with them. Then there's the damp. Any one of these could kill him.'

Louis was unperturbed. 'No one lives forever. It's not perfect but it will do for now.'

Frances saw Sidney open his mouth to speak and then think better of it. If this was *for now*, where else could they possibly go?

For the short walk back Sidney and Fanny went ahead and Louis offered Frances his arm.

'I'm glad you and Fanny are friends. It means we can be too.'

'Yes. We've all found happiness after all.'

'Your professor always has the air of a string stretched to breaking point, but he's happier than I have ever known him.'

'We're very lucky, I know.'

'You're more of a married couple than my wife and I will ever be. We are always at each other's throats.' Frances said she saw no sign of discord. 'That's because we're on our best behaviour. You two make us civilised.'

24.

Back at Skerryvore, Fanny persuaded them to stay to supper. 'You're not like the others,' she said, 'We can tell you when to go.' She took Sidney by the arm. 'Come along, Mr Monument. I want to show you a painting we bought recently. I'm not sure it's in the right place and you have the very best eye.'

Did Fanny really want Sidney to herself? The two of them were never quite at ease. In any case, Sidney beamed his acceptance and they left with the dog yapping at their heels.

Louis settled back onto his sofa with a sigh. 'Being by the sea is very fine, but I am confined here like a weevil in a biscuit.'

Frances laughed. 'A weevil? I don't think so!' And yet there was something worm-like about Louis in his blanket, and confinement was certainly not in his nature. *For now* floated back into her mind. He and Fanny clearly weren't as settled as she had thought. 'You won't stay here?'

He smiled narrowly. 'We'll stay for a while. After that, who knows? I leave such decisions to my sturdy Van de Grifter. She is the mistress of my destiny!'

He lay back, head tilted, that long neck curved in submission. Why shouldn't he leave the practical things to Fanny? She had energy for both of them.

'Can I get you anything?' she said. 'Another cushion?'

'No. Your presence is enough. I'm enjoying having you here. Although you always did reduce me to wordlessness.'

'That's not true. We used to talk for hours.' She had no intention of raising the past, but now that they were alone, it was unavoidable. 'And we had our letters.'

He lay still, his eyes on the view from the window. 'I was just thinking of those the other day. Did you keep all of mine?'

'Of course I did. I have every one. I'm surprised you had to ask,' she said.

Her rosewood box had accompanied her from Chepstow Place to Brunswick Row. It sat in sequestered silence, behind the curtain in her hall, under the pile of winter clothes which were mothballed and folded on top, just as in summer the warm things were laid away. She welcomed the gleam of polished wood and the feel of it under her hand as one season slipped into another. She couldn't imagine being without it.

Louis shifted under his blanket. 'Things can easily go astray. And you see the state of me. I have to think of what will be left of me when I'm gone.'

He was being melodramatic. Louis Stevenson would never be reduced to a box of letters. Still, if he had to talk of death she had a question for him. She touched the back of his hand to be sure of his attention. 'And did you keep your promise to me, my one request?'

He smiled. 'I often thought I would not. Some weeks my jacket pocket bulged with all those sheets filled with your tenderness. But dinna fash, my dear. I am a man of my word.'

She took the use of Scots as a sign of sincerity. She pumped his pillows and they sat in silence until the others returned.

She tried not to think of the likelihood of Louis's death. Her letters had been destroyed and, whatever should befall him, that was for the best. But as for his letters to her, she was too wrapped up in the moment to ask what he meant her to do with those treasured words, the troubling mementoes of things that might have been.

After supper, Louis talked about Hyeres, enjoying Fanny's irritation since it was she who had dragged him away. If this was them 'at each other's throats' it was a skirmish in a playful war.

At eight, Sidney stood up to go.

'Not yet, please!' Louis said. 'I was hoping our nightingale might sing for us.' After all these years he rarely addressed Frances by her name. A glance to Fanny, 'If my keeper will allow it.'

Frances had not sung in years. After Bertie's death, she had told herself she would sing no more, but here she was, amongst her dearest friends, and what was life without music? As they settled in the drawing room, she sorted through the sheets on top of the piano and called to Sidney to turn the pages.

'Goodness,' Fanny said to Louis, after the first piece. 'You never told me she could sing!'

'Everybody knows she can sing!' Louis answered. 'It's her particular gift.'

Fanny was still in awe. 'You could be on the stage with that voice!' she said.

Frances was becoming accustomed to Fanny's adulation and she liked how it allowed Sidney to preen himself. 'Now, what else shall we have?' she said. Amongst the music she found the *Chant d'Amour*, something else that spoke of the past. As she sang, Sidney's eyes were on the music. Louis hummed softly, moving his fingers on the blanket as if picking out the notes on an unseen clarinet.

The following year, Louis's father Tom Stevenson died and *for now* had come to an end. Not long after, Louis announced he and Fanny would sail for America at which Sidney took terrible offence, suspecting Fanny's influence. Frances understood his pain at Louis venturing beyond the known confines of Europe. She also knew it was pointless to argue or complain. Louis had never been well in Bournemouth and he had a huge following in America. Fanny was probably blameless.

Somehow a reconciliation was engineered and Frances went with Sidney and a group of Louis's friends to wave Louis off at Tilbury. He had finally got to see where the steamers drew in and cast off.

On the dockside, there was almost a party atmosphere as Louis, his wife, and his mother leaned over the rail, waving to the crowd. Sidney, the only dissenter from gaiety, insisted on going on board to see Louis and the family settled.

Frances standing next to Edmund Gosse, one of Sidney's closest friends,

let out a sigh. 'Do you think Sidney will sail off with them?'

'Yes, poor Colvin,' Edmund said. 'Louis is practically his raison d'etre.' He hurried to correct himself. 'After you, of course, Mrs Sitwell.'

Frances wasn't offended. Sidney's involvement in Louis's work was tantamount to an obsession. And Gosse… What had Fanny said about him at Braemar? How he adored Louis and competed for his affection. And something about Edmund having a lover. That couldn't be true. Gosse and his wife were as devoted as Louis and Fanny. They held famous Sunday teas to which invitations were like gold dust.

As the ship moved off, they could see Sidney scrambling from the departing boat into the tender which would bring him back ashore. That much was a relief. 'What am I to do with him?' She asked Gosse.

'If anyone can save him, 'Edmund said, 'it will be you.'

Sidney came hurrying along the quay to join them and, as the ship drew away and the figures on deck grew smaller, he joined in the waving. 'He'll be back,' he said to Frances. 'Before winter, I'm sure of it.'

She was unconvinced. Louis had his wife and his mother with him and Fanny's son. Her daughter, Belle, was married with a child in San Francisco. If things went well, what was there here to bring him back?

The company trooped back from Tilbury to the hotel where Louis had stayed the previous night. With their hero having set sail, proceedings took on a doleful air. Frances watched Edmund chatting to a lugubrious American she recognised as Henry James. Gosse smiled at her over James's head and nodded towards her, no doubt explaining her presence to the American to whom she had never been introduced. She in turn tried to signal with her eyes that she wanted to talk to Edmund. An idea was forming, and it was Gosse's opinion she required. At last he extricated himself, leaving James to amble towards the drinks table. 'Is something wrong?'

'You must introduce me to Henry James,' she said. 'But first I have something to ask you.'

Edmund had a round face, given to smiling. 'Then ask away!'

'If Sidney were to hold soirees at the museum,' she said, 'do you think people would come? People like these?'

Edmund surveyed the room as he considered her question. 'I think they would. Especially with a hostess alongside him.'

She was known as Sidney's friend and companion. To be his hostess was another step.

'Someone as becoming and insightful as you,' Gosse added, with a noticeable twinkle. 'Just to soften Colvin's… rigour, shall we say?'

Gosse was right. Sidney liked company but in discussions, he could be stubborn as well as rigorous. She could give in more gracefully, or agree to differ if the need arose, but her reviews were appreciated for their directness. Her presence would be more than decorative.

'I can be rigorous too,' she said with mock severity.

Edmund inclined his head. 'I stand corrected. But I assure you, Mrs Sitwell, your rigour, if it should be required, will be very much easier to bear.'

Frances was satisfied. And as Henry James bore down on them, ready for Gosse's introduction, she glimpsed a new arrangement between her and Sidney, one where she could be, if not his wife, then more of a real partner. With Louis gone, it would be good for both of them.

PART FIVE

Exile

So far, so foreign, your divided friends
Wander, estranged in body, not in mind.
Robert Louis Stevenson,

'To S.C.'

25.

London, January 1894, six years later
Frances ran her hand over her new upright piano, grateful
for its sturdy presence, grateful for all of the circumstances
that had made such a thing possible: a good address, a
pleasant room and now an instrument with a warm tone
and a mellow sheen. Sidney too was as content as she had
ever known him. His salons were the highlight of each
month: writers, artists and editors flocked to them. Frances
enjoyed her place at his side, his companion, hostess and
fellow authority on art.

With one last part of the piano, she put aside the
counting of blessings to dress for the outdoors. It was a
fine day for January but the museum was an omnibus
ride away and Sidney was expecting her at two.

In Great Russell Street, she plotted a course through
the lines of visitors crowding the museum steps and looked
up towards the window of the Keeper's House. Yes, Sidney
was watching for her.

Once she was inside, he took her hands to chafe them,
even though his dry fingers were colder than her own.
'My favourite dress,' he said and kissed her cheek.

She gave him a reproving smile. 'You said that last time,
when I wore the green.'

He held up his hands. 'Can't I have more than one
favourite?'

She put her cheek to his and smoothed her skirt. He never failed to make her feel appreciated.

Sidney's man, John Humphries, had brought the straight-backed chairs from the dining room and arranged them in a semicircle. Frances nodded her approval and went across the corridor to where the table was laid for afternoon tea. Having completed her inspection, she came back and retreated to the window seat where she looked out to the museum forecourt.

'Whom are we expecting?'

'Most of the usual crowd. Henry James is out of town. Gosse is bringing someone new.'

Yes, she could see Edmund now, on the museum steps, shaking hands with a younger man whose unfashionable frock coat was made more conspicuous by a red and purple woollen scarf. A man of modest circumstances, Frances assumed, doing his best to fit in. When the men came in, Gosse introduced the newcomer as Matthew Swift. They took seats together and Frances imagined Swift asking discretely about the unexpected lady in the room. Amongst friends, she and Sidney's 'arrangement' was common knowledge. With strangers it did no harm to cultivate an air of mystery.

The afternoon took its usual course. After some literary discussion, tea was served and Sidney introduced her to Matthew Swift, slim and almost blonde, his manner poised between eagerness and diffidence.

When it came to aspiring writers, Sidney deferred to her, allowing her to separate the wheat from the chaff, the poet or essayist worth pulling from the sea of hopeful wordsmiths from those left to drown in the morass. She was good at drawing people out and she enjoyed it. She gleaned that Swift wrote poetry when he had the time.

His wife was expecting a child. As the guest left, Swift thrust a bundle of paper into her hands, for which she thanked him. Most likely the work would be dull, derivative or both, but something had brought him to Edmund's attention. Maybe a new talent was lying in wait.

Afterwards, they had their routine. Sidney took the chairs back to the dining room because after hours of conversation he enjoyed the simple physical activity. Frances picked up the books and pamphlets left lying around the room and replaced them in Sidney's study. It was as large as the drawing room and hedged around by bookshelves from floor to ceiling. Only a framed poem by Rossetti and two separate photographs, one of Louis, one of herself, were allowed a section of wall-space.

When Sidney came to find her, she was standing by the globe next to his desk, spanning the spaces with her fingers, tracing the trade routes which carried letters and parcels from Samoa—Louis and Fanny's home for the last two years.

Sidney stood beside her. 'It looks such a small distance.'

She frowned. Surely it was a world away, but Sidney had survived Louis's departure, perhaps he was even more at ease with his friend confined to the pages of monthly letters, compared to his brilliant but enervating presence.

Sidney hated the omnibus and so rather than take a carriage, they settled for a walk back to Marylebone. With darkness a fine drizzle had arrived. On the pavement outside, he shook his umbrella open so that its black dome reached over both of them.

As she leaned in towards him, he reviewed the afternoon just past. 'Another successful soiree! How was Mr Swift? Amiable, I thought.'

She remembered Sidney glancing over to where she was interviewing Swift, his eyes resting on the young man, making some private assessment.

'He gave me some of his sonnets.'

'Ah,' Sidney was sympathetic. 'Let's hope they're worth reading.'

In her drawing room, Maddie had brought the fire to life. Frances plumped into her favourite chair, surrendering to its enveloping softness. In a moment of liberation, she kicked off her shoes.

'Goodness, have I tired you out?'

She shrugged. 'Not you especially. It's good to come home.'

The curtains were open and the room was illuminated by the glow of the street-lamps outside. Sidney flashed a smile as he sat down and stretched out his legs, his arms flopped over the arms of the chair, at ease with himself and with the world. . Frances was grateful again for everything that Heaven had bestowed on her.

It was a quarter to eight. 'We could go to bed,' she said, surprising herself. 'Or Maddie will have left supper, if you want it.'

He got up and stood beside her, stroking her hair. 'I'm sure supper can wait.'

Sidney was a considerate lover who had learned how to arouse her. Under his touch she cried out in the moment of release. Somewhere beyond her pleasure, she was aware of Sidney's long exhalation as he withdrew and expended himself into a handkerchief laid ready on the bedside chest. In Brittany, when they had become true lovers, a child was out of the question, and they had taught each other acts of intimacy that fell short of full congress. Now her womb was unlikely to quicken, but this, she supposed, was the legacy.

Sidney rolled back towards her, nuzzling her shoulder. For some reason she was irritated. Was this remnant of the past just a habit, or did he need the moment of separation, the private communion with the square of white cotton?

His voice broke the silence. 'What are you thinking?'

'I'm thinking how lucky we are.' Absolute truth was not always necessary. 'Shall I get Matthew Swift's sonnets?' she asked. 'We could read them together.'

This was a ruse to keep him next to her where she might rouse him again. She suddenly wanted to test him, to have him not hold back.

He sat up. 'No, you'll only get cold. And I should go. It's my duty night.'

The Keepers took it in turns to act as museum caretaker. She sighed. 'You should have said.'

'I didn't want to spoil the evening.' He dipped his head to kiss her cheek, his stubble abrasive on her skin, then dressed quickly. 'Let me know what you think about the poetry.'

When he had gone, she got up, reached for her shawl and slid her feet into her slippers, curling her toes in the silk lining. Her peak of satisfaction was slinking off to hide in the dark corner beside the bed along with the soiled linen.

From the window she watched Sidney pause on her doorstep. The drizzle had let up to reveal a yellow-blue haze of lamplight and a few stars scattering the sky. She knew that he regretted leaving the warmth of her bed, but also that he was happy to be walking back to Bloomsbury. The museum was his home, just as this was hers.

She wasn't ready to sleep and so, before climbing back into bed, she fetched Swift's sonnets and leafed through them. She had turned off the gas and lit an old oil lamp. The poems, in Swift's even hand, were surprisingly lyrical, much better than she had expected. She would tell Sidney that both style and choice of subject were reminiscent of Keats, but far from a slavish imitation. She lay back against the pillows and drew her shawl around her shoulders. Tonight these poems were all the company she needed.

26.

The next day, Frances was eager to share her thoughts on Matthew Swift with Sidney. It was late afternoon and she was about to leave home for the museum when the letter arrived in an envelope bearing the stamp of Lambeth Palace. She opened it quickly, assuming it was from Albert, who was still honorary chaplain to the Archbishop of Canterbury and had a habit of using palace notepaper to raise occasional money matters. Then she stopped in her tracks. The note was from the Archbishop himself. Albert Sitwell had died.

Whatever the circumstances, however unloved the soul, death can never be entirely disregarded. Albert was the prevailing wind of a great part of her life. She allowed herself a moment to give her husband, the father of her sons, some respect. In the drawing room, the letter still in her hand, she paused in front of the mantlepiece where she still kept the old photograph of Freddie and Bertie in their school uniforms. Her poor boys. Freddie, a short bright line of laughter in the weave of her life. Then Bertie, whose death still weighed so heavily around her heart. She had left him in the bleak landscape of Davos. She should never have taken him there. She wished she could have brought him home.

She left the letter next to the photograph. A line from Tennyson came to mind. *Tho' much is taken, much abides*. Life without Albert, absolute freedom from the situation that bound her to him, it was almost too much to take in. Hadn't she been congratulating herself on her contentment? Now she was dizzy at the prospect of more. She held herself back from the edge of mounting excitement. She must tell Sidney the news.

In Bloomsbury, she found him in the small lounge he favoured in the afternoons, looking over the tree-lined margins of the museum grounds. It was a place to shrug off cares, but something, she could tell, had unsettled him. He greeted her hurriedly, wringing his hands as he did so. Surely news of Albert's death hadn't arrived before her?

'Sidney, what's wrong?'

He rubbed a hand over his face. 'I had a letter from Louis. You had better come and see.'

Word from Samoa usually made Sidney jumpy with excitement, sometimes joyful, never downcast, but then letters to and from the Vailima estate took many weeks. Replies become detached from questions, comments divorced from what gave rise to them. Whole letters could be lost, leaving misunderstandings which needed months to be ironed out. As they went through to his study, she put aside thoughts of Albert.

On the desk a letter was uppermost, the paper of such poor quality as to be almost transparent, the hand unmistakable. Sidney shook his head and pushed it away. 'I was too outspoken in my last. He is very tart in his reply. Rightly I suppose.'

A reprimand from Louis was out of character. Sidney had a tendency to self-flagellation. 'Why don't you let me see?'

He handed over the last page of the letter. For Louis it was very direct. Sidney could raise no interest in Samoan politics. Louis urged him to exercise his imagination and find some sympathy for the Samoans, Louis's fellow islanders.

Frances sighed. 'Sidney, they are his people, some of them part of his household. You must do as he says, put yourself in his shoes.'

Sidney's appreciation of art and literature wasn't matched by an ability to empathise. As Frances sat down on the extra chair, he raised his hands in helplessness. 'It's simply unimaginable.'

'But he tells you everything. You have all his descriptions and maps and accounts of his expeditions.'

'So can *you* imagine what it's like there?'

Frances didn't see everything Louis sent to Sidney, but from Fanny's letters she had a clear picture of how her days were spent taming a tropical jungle while Louis applied himself to writing. Then there were evenings of music and song, and parties with the crews of passing ships. Frances took pleasure in visualising these scenes and the places in which they took place, but Sidney seemed incapable of the imaginative leap.

Samoa was distant but not unreachable, and Louis had visitors all the time. 'Maybe you should go there, then you would understand.'

Sidney shook his head. 'No. It's too far. I go green just crossing the Channel.'

She went to him and stroked his head. 'Never mind. You'll write back. All will be mended.'

He leaned against her, staring at his blotter, as if trying to make sense of the inky smudges. 'You must tell me what to say.'

Sidney must do his own making up. She remembered the reason for her visit. 'I have some other news. I heard this morning. Albert has died.'

'I'm sorry, what did you say?'

There was nothing wrong with Sidney's hearing. She had hoped to distract him, but asking him to deal with more than one thing at a time was a mistake. She held out the letter from the Archbishop and he sat down with it.

'Well, we knew he was ill, so it's not unexpected.'

She reminded herself she'd had time to take in the news. Sidney was some way behind, not to mention distraught over Louis. All the same, she could have shaken him. The news had thrown her more than she had expected. She needed Sidney to give her a lead, to reassure her all would be well, not just well but better.

He drummed his fingers lightly on the desk. 'Did you want to talk about the sonnets? I saw Matthew Swift earlier, walking in the park. We should put together some suggestions for him.'

Swift's work was the least of her worries. Sidney should have been thinking of their joint future. If only he had put his arms around her and said 'how wonderful' and 'now we can marry' then she would have been comforted. She would have felt loved.

Oxford and Cambridge Mansions,
18th February, 1894
My Dear Fanny,
So good to hear from you again. I hope you managed the Christmas celebrations you were planning and that the household are all in good health.

I expect Sidney will have divulged this news but he has been very distracted of late and works much too hard. So, in case he hasn't, my husband of old, Albert Sitwell, has finally gone to meet his Maker

(although what fate the Maker will dispense can only be guessed at.)

Of course, you never met my cruel Vicar but I know Louis will want to hear. Since the death of my poor boys I had little to do with him, but his absence is still significant, perhaps in ways I still have to discover.

I found the news quite disconcerting but I am becoming accustomed. I must decide how best to embrace my new freedom.

Warmest wishes to you all.

As ever,

Frances

It would be months before there was any reply. Frances felt herself to be in a limbo, broken only by a visit from Maud Babbington. Since her husband, Churchill, had died, Maud had returned to family in Portsmouth, but Frances's new apartment made it easy for her to come and stay, often for a weekend, occasionally for a month at a time.

Maud at least appreciated the silent upheaval caused by Albert's death. 'Has the funeral taken place?' she asked.

Frances shook her head. She hadn't enquired. 'I've mourned his sons. To weep over his grave would be hypocritical.'

'And Sidney?'

Frances had no answer ready.

'Let me guess. Sidney would rather not contemplate a change in your circumstances?'

Frances was forced to agree.

'Don't worry,' Maud said. 'He will get there in the end. And in the meantime,' there was a decided twinkle in her eye, 'you and I will raise a glass to Albert's demise. We have all wished him gone often enough.'

Maud was right. Frances thought of Louis's threats to run Albert through or drown him in the Thames. It was time to celebrate.

It was more than two months until the next batch of letters arrived from Samoa, parcelled up and sent to Sidney for distribution around London. In his study a large packet lay open on the desk and he was sorting through the contents with enjoyable energy. Frances felt his enthusiasm, the tiff with Louis forgotten.

'Anything for me?' she asked, thinking Fanny would have replied.

He picked up an envelope and handed it to her without looking up from his task. 'Just this.'

The envelope was not in Fanny's hand and marked simply *Madame*. It was from Louis. It was rare for him to write to her directly, and for a moment she saw him standing before her, his head inclined in a mock bow, a flicker of laughter in his eyes. The flap was folded, not sealed, and when she opened it, a photograph fell to the floor which she picked up and studied. Sidney stood up and looked over her shoulder.

Tusitala was written in pencil on the back, Louis's island name, and this was his island self, still thin in face and body but less wasted, cheek-bones prominent, hair cut short, signalling his transformation for life in the South Seas. No longer the sick man, he was the Teller of Tales.

'Ah,' Sidney said, 'How changed he is, but still the same.'

She felt his breath on the back of her neck. She stepped away and tucked the letter into her purse.

That evening she had a class to teach and so it was late when she read Louis's letter at home, in the warm haze of firelight. Louis seemed to revel in this new life, as familiar to him, she supposed, as any of those he had tried in California, in France or in Bournemouth.

Frances threw back the curtains to let in the last of the evening light. The sky was streaked with the purple of sunset after rain. It stretched across the whole world, even to the distant mountains of Samoa. She would like to have embraced everything that Louis was embracing. Was a new day dawning on his Vailima estate, or had this day, just lived, yet to arrive? She would ask someone about the complexities of geography and time.

Reading on, she frowned. Fanny, he explained, was busy in the garden but joined him in sending good wishes and reminders of her love. Surely he had written because of Albert's death, and yet he barely mentioned it.

She held the creased pages in her hand, the familiar scrawl, the unexpected welter of longing combined with the frisson of danger. Her fingers itched to take up her pen. They were old friends. What could she do except reply?

Oxford and Cambridge Mansions,
26th May, 1894
Dear Louis,
What a joy to have your letter and the photograph. I picture you on your pony on that rough path and sense your new grasp on life. My first duty, though, is to berate you for such maudlin thoughts and this strange desire for death.

If such a thing were possible I would shake you by your shoulders. You are well and successful and you are barely forty. You have everything to live for. I hope you will take this advice from your Consuelo and your Madonna. Do not spend too much time looking inward. Many more books are in your heart, waiting to be written. Make sure they find the light of day.

I'm surprised you have so little to say about Albert. My heart has been strangely confounded by his death. It is indeed a pity he lived so long, and yet what good would it do to expend more words on the man? I dare say you are right to leave it there.

Your dearest friend,

FJS

Across the hallway, snug in its corner, she had the box containing all his other letters, from Scotland, Menton, Paris. She could put this last there too, but this was a different time, a different Louis. She laid it in the bureau and propped the photo on the mantelpiece against her cloisonne vase, a reminder, not of times gone by, but of the future they each deserved.

27.

In June, Sidney announced that he would spend the summer in Wiesbaden to stabilise his health. College was closed for the summer. In a week or two, Frances would go with Suka to a favourite boarding house on the coast.

On the day when all this was decided, Frances sensed another lull approaching, a lack of momentum she didn't appreciate. Arriving home, she saw Louis's photograph winking at her from its place above the hearth and Matthew Swift, almost as lanky, almost as interesting, sprang unbidden to her mind. After all, Sidney thought he was to be encouraged, and in his absence Swift could benefit from her advice. A little tea-party would be ideal. At least four were required for a company and so she invited Swift, Suka and Stephen Phillips, a poet who favoured epic verse and was a regular at Sidney's salons, for the Saturday after Sidney was due to leave.

Suka came early. Swift and Phillips, the latter rotund and amiable if a little too ingratiating, arrived together. Suka began by recounting stories from her time in Paris which she managed to describe as much more gay than Frances remembered. At least this put the men, Swift especially, at their ease. He lost the nervous flutter but remained formally polite, although she liked the way he flicked his floppy hair from his forehead as he spoke. Frances wanted to recreate the connection which had occurred on their first meeting. She would certainly rather read his sonnets than Phillips's strained pentameters.

'Have you brought anything new for us?' she asked.

He shook his head. 'I'm afraid not. I was waiting to…'

Phillips cut in. 'What about your villanelles?'

The younger man flushed, 'They're not ready. *Not yet.*' The emphasis was for Phillips who must have read the first drafts. She liked the idea of villanelles, a challenging form for someone with little time on his hands. Her interest quickened. Maybe Swift, with a group of other poets, could put together a collection, something modern but rooted in tradition. Could this be the project she was looking for?

She leaned forward and patted Swift's leg in encouragement. 'I'm very much in need of entertainment so do send your poems when they are finished. Or if you're passing, just put them through my door.'

Her touch, an instinctive gesture, startled Matthew Swift whose eyes widened before he smiled. 'Thank you, I will.'

She wanted to keep the smile in place. 'Make sure you do.'

Phillips told them he was attending an evening of poetry and music at the Savoy Hotel the following weekend. 'Perhaps you and Mr Colvin will come?'

The Savoy was garish and the music would be mediocre by Sidney's standards. She was relieved to be able to decline. 'I'm so sorry, but Sidney has gone abroad for a while.'

Phillips inclined his head. 'Then perhaps I could accompany you myself?'

Frances was dumbfounded. Phillips was no more than an acquaintance.

Suka, after a muffled cough of surprise, was first to recover. 'We should all go – all four of us!'

This was equally preposterous, as if they were young people with no responsibilities or attachments. Suka knew Swift was married and was simply being mischievous.

Matthew Swift saved the day. 'I'm so sorry,' he said, with the slightest gleam of amusement in his eye. 'I'm needed at home at the moment.' He had read the situation and Frances tried to convey with her eyes the gratitude she felt. 'In fact, I really ought to be getting back now.'

This was a cue for the men to leave. Phillips made a great show of bowing and kissing her hand before repeating the performance with Suka.

Frances turned to Swift. 'Don't forget those villanelles. In fact, wait here a moment.'

She hurried across the hall and in her bedroom searched along the spines in the bookcase until she came to what she was looking for. When she came back to the hallway, Phillips was calling a goodbye and Matthew Swift was alone. She held up the book. It was the standard collection of villanelles. 'Do you have this?'

His face brightened. 'I've been looking for a copy!'

She offered it to him. 'You must take it.'

He held it on his open palms. 'I can't possibly.'

'It's just a loan and you must pay me interest. In poetry of course, at least two poems for every month of ownership.'

'Thank you,' he bowed his head, 'I'll return it as promptly as I can.'

He held her eyes. He was not so shy as she thought and she liked him better for it. 'I would rather earn substantial interest than have it back *too* soon.'

He nodded again, stepped back and, bowing over her hand, barely brushed her fingers with his lips in a gesture that was very different to Phillips's obsequious chivalry.

'Off you go,' she said quickly. 'I'll see you soon, I hope.'

In the sitting room, Suka was laughing over Phillips. 'The cheek of the man! You had better marry Sidney or all of London will be courting you. And I know what you're thinking…but Matthew Swift has none of Louis's originality.'

Frances opened her mouth to argue. Despite the pleasure of seeing Matthew Swift respond to her, he could never take Louis's place. She didn't want or need him to. As for marriage, Frances thought, perhaps it was a mirage. Whether it arrived or not, she needed a life of her own.

The trip to Devon was not a success. The weather was poor, and Suka constantly incited her to a merriment she didn't feel, insisting on outings to concerts and variety shows. Frances would have preferred to stay in and play a hand of cards, except Suka constantly confused suits and never remembered what had been dealt.

Returning to Marylebone at the end of their fortnight away, she was flooded with relief to sit down and enjoy what she'd been longing for, a room devoid of company. But this respite would be short-lived. The next few weeks were the busiest of the college year when she helped with the new term's administration alongside her few hours of teaching. On her first evening back, she pushed open the heavy door with its opaque glass pane and crossed the foyer to the registration desk at the foot of the stairs. Here, the new Superintendent, waiting to leave, tipped up the wooden counter-top to let Frances come behind and greeted her before departing. Frances dropped her wrap in the office behind the desk, and told Irene, the other helper, to leave too. She had a family, and supper to prepare.

'Thank you,' Irene said and blew her a kiss. 'You're an angel.'

Glancing through the ledger, Frances was gratified by the night's attendance. She took special interest in the women who attended college. When she had the opportunity, she engaged them in conversation, eliciting their circumstances. If any were truly indigent, she put them in touch with charitable foundations who might offer help. Frances had never been poor, but she knew that a warm coat or extra bowl of soup could make all the difference between a student continuing or disappearing from the record.

With the early evening flurry past, she glanced down at the attendance book, recognising many names from previous terms, until she came to the page where the ink was fresh. These were the newcomers, four gentlemen and six ladies, the second of whom was Lucinda Swift, entering classes for Arithmetic and English Literature.

Surely it was a coincidence. There must be several families of that name in London. She ran her eyes over the other details. The address in Lambeth was inconclusive as she had no idea where Swift resided. The date of birth put Lucinda in her mid-twenties. Frances's eyes flicked to the start of the line and the space for *Title*. Lucinda was indeed married.

She glanced at the clock. Classes ended at nine when students returned to the desk to sign out. The book was left on the counter for this small procedure; they needed to do no more than place a tick on the page and most barely stopped as they hurried home. Frances, in the process of closing up for the night, locked the office and lingered by the desk, feeling a little surreptitious, although she couldn't think why. It was her job to make sure everyone ticked the book.

As soon as the bell rang, voices echoed above the stairs, followed by a flurry of skirts and boots. First down were the old-timers, chatting as they crossed the hall, calling their goodbyes to each other. Behind the rush, a few others came down more hesitantly, newcomers struggling to remember names, to absorb the lesson just given, glancing around to remind themselves of how it would be next time. She called them over. 'Sorry, just one last thing to do, thank you.'

The last of them was Lucinda Swift, tall, as tall as her husband (if indeed it were he) in a decent cotton dress, tying a plain bonnet over pale brown hair.

'Mrs Swift, I hope you enjoyed your first class.'

The woman looked at her without speaking, perhaps she didn't catch the question. She had clear grey eyes and a steady gaze. Her face was wan but her clothes were more than respectable. The foyer had emptied except for the two women. In the silence Frances felt she must speak again. 'Forgive me, but might I have met your husband? A poet?'

Lucinda's face was disfigured by a frown. 'Possibly, I suppose. When would this have been?'

'Earlier this year, at a literary gathering, and again more recently.' Frances would rather not have pursued it but the silence needed to be filled. 'He may have mentioned I lent him a book.' She smiled and held out her hand. The counter was not designed for such a gesture and her hand hovered awkwardly, awaiting a response. 'I am Mrs Sitwell, by the way.'

'How do you do?' The hand barely touched hers and, with a smile of polite incomprehension, Lucinda Swift turned to go.

On Frances's walk to the Metropolitan Line, the

pavement vibrated with the passage of a train. Settled into her seat, she saw there was no reason why Lucinda Swift should have known her. With the college porter jingling his keys so ostentatiously, she could hardly have kept the girl chatting. It was foolish to take Lucinda's sullenness as a rebuff, although if Matthew was to be her protégé, it would be better if his wife could offer some support.

28.

The final part of her journey home from Queens Square was a short walk along Edgware Road where the wind quickened. Frances fastened her small cape around her neck, and wondered how long it would take Lucinda to get to Lambeth and what kind of house she and Matthew Swift kept there. Would he be busy over his idylls, or be standing by to take her coat, a cup of tea at the ready?

The idea of tea led her to her kitchen where Maddie had left the range lit. Listening to the kettle grumble then sing, she reminded herself it was a good thing that Lucinda Swift, like so many young women, wished to find employment. As regards the workings of the Swifts' marriage, Frances had been single for too long to judge what passed between a husband and a wife.

The kettle had done its work. The water swilled into the teapot and after a few minutes she poured it into a cup. Yes, the girl was well enough to come to college, if a little pale, and she could be sure that Matthew Swift was no Albert. A sudden memory made her slop some tea into the saucer. When she'd first met Matthew Swift, his wife had been expecting a child. That was months ago. Why was a new mother joining an evening class?

The kitchen was not overly warm, but boiling the kettle made a noticeable difference. Then Frances was suddenly not so much warm as ridiculously hot with a burning face and damp forehead, as if she were in the tropics. She closed her eyes. It wasn't the first time this had happened. Only last week, Suka had teased her about fanning herself just after she'd been complaining of cold.

She went to the door for some air, took her lace-edged handkerchief from her sleeve and dabbed her face. All this about the Swifts was strangely troubling. She thought back to the odd tea-party, Phillips over-confident and overbearing, Matthew Swift graciously deferential, signalling a readiness for friendship. Presumably there was no child. She hoped her efforts to draw him out had not been misinterpreted. She had no intention of coming between a man and wife.

On a Friday in September, in the late afternoon, Sidney arrived unannounced. Maddie showed him into the sitting room and he came towards Frances smiling, arms outstretched. Frances rose in pleasure to meet him, although somehow their steps were out of time and they bumped awkwardly against each other. She laughed as she rubbed her nose and gave him a more sedate, if less spontaneous, hug before holding him at arm's length. His face was unmarked by the usual worry lines and his skin had the glow of good health and good humour.

She smiled. 'How well you look!'

'Yes,' he kept hold of her arms. 'I feel so much better for having been away.'

'So, you had a nice time?'

'Very pleasant. Very restorative. And you are well? And Susan?' Sidney refused to call Suka by her pet name.

'Susan was as she always is. I survived.'

She invited him to sit down. There was something different in his demeanour, something other than returning from a good holiday, not his usual anxiety, more a kind of anticipation.

'Sidney, what is it? You are all on edge.'

He leaned forward, gripping the arms of the chair as if he might otherwise float above it. 'No, not on edge exactly. You see I've been thinking.'

'Thinking? Goodness. I thought Wiesbaden was more for walking and talking.'

Sidney frowned, as if Germany had slipped below the horizon. 'Ah yes, but I suppose what you said stuck in my mind while I was away. Then I spoke to Gosse.'

She had no idea what had perked him up so much but was pleased he was no longer fretting over Louis. She pictured him and Edmund lunching together at the Savile, exchanging news amongst its leather chairs, white linen and deferential staff, or so she imagined, since as a woman she had never been inside.

'And what does Edmund have to say?'

'He was telling me Louis may be in Australia next year, on a lecture tour.' Sidney's eyes were especially bright, his smile quite startled her. 'Gosse suggested we could go out to meet him.'

She wasn't sure what to say. 'Australia is a very long way.'

Sidney looked at his hands, pausing before some big announcement. 'Exactly. It made me realise that I shouldn't wait any longer. I should visit Louis now.'

'You mean go to Samoa?' She was astonished.

He leaned towards her so that his eyes were on a level with hers. He might resist new ideas, but once his mind was made up, nothing would stop him. 'Australia may never happen and Louis won't come back here. It's as you said. I should make the effort.' He smiled sheepishly. 'It will be quite the adventure.'

She had sowed the seeds of this before his summer trip, issuing the challenge without ever thinking he would take it up. She felt unsteady, as if the earth was spinning too fast on its axis. 'What about the Edinburgh edition?' Sidney had been consumed by the preparation of a new collection of Louis's work, something to produce a steady income for Louis with a percentage due to Sidney.

'It's at the printers. Baxter is going out next month to take him the first bound copies.' Charles Baxter, Louis's lawyer friend from Edinburgh, took charge of the finances.

'You'll go with him?'

Sidney shook his head. 'Afterwards, I think. I'd rather have Louis to myself.' He stopped to correct himself. 'I mean…'

She smiled at Sidney. 'You'll have a lot to talk about. Fanny and the family will understand. You'll find some quiet moments.'

He reached for her hand. 'Thank you.'

She understood his gratitude. She had given him the idea. There was no suggestion she should accompany him. Perhaps if they had been married… She preferred not to let her thoughts wander down that route. Let Sidney go, let her conversations with Louis be confined to pen on paper, or take place through Fanny. That arrangement had worked very well for many years. Even that last letter to Louis had been a mistake, stirring up half-forgotten emotions.

'So, when will you go?'

'Maybe in the early spring.'

Frances dropped his hand and got up, patting his shoulder. 'Let's hope the seas are calm at that time of year.'

She imagined him returning with photographs and

souvenirs. The idea was unsettling, like Louis arriving back in their midst.

Maddie brought a tea tray and they sat together at the occasional table. Sidney was about to speak but she put her hand on his to stop him. She had forgotten she had a question to ask.

'When did you last see Matthew Swift?'

Sidney blinked at the change of tack. 'I can't quite think...'

'While you were away, he and Stephen Phillips came to tea with Suka. Soon after, I spotted Matthew's wife in college. I thought she was expecting a child'

Sidney had caught up with her train of thought. 'Ah, yes. A sad loss.'

'The baby didn't survive?'

He shook his head.

'How dreadful for them.'

It was odd that Sidney knew this and she didn't, but if he and Matthew still walked in the park, something she'd forgotten until now, they might share more personal matters. She felt sorry for the Swifts, but there was no reason for Matthew to have mentioned it to her and Lucinda was clearly making the best of a sad situation.

She directed her attention to Sidney and his plans. 'I'm sorry Maddie did no baking,' she said. 'I wasn't expecting you.'

'I'm not hungry. I had lunch at the club.' He smiled at her indulgently. 'Cakes or no cakes, we should do this more often. We should spend more time, I mean. Just us. At leisure. Would you like it?'

'To see more of you? Of course. But you are always so busy.'

'Exactly, as are you. And so, I've been thinking...'

She laughed out loud. 'Goodness, two thoughts in one day? Germany has made you very profound!'

He clicked his tongue in exasperation. Her laughter was apparently out of place.

'I'm sorry,' she said. 'Go on.'

Sidney was grave. 'I was thinking of this before Germany,' as if he didn't want that country implicated, 'and then today when I saw Gosse ...' He broke off, shook his head and started again. 'It's been several months since Sitwell's death. You and I are free agents. I *will* go to Samoa,' (this with noticeable emphasis) 'but when I get back, I think we should marry. Frances, dearest, you will be my wife, won't you?'

<h1 style="text-align:center">29.</h1>

When Sidney left, Frances was truly bemused. Should she be more excited? Suka would be giddy with joy but that was not Frances's way, and if Sidney's proposal felt like something of an anti-climax, she had only herself to blame, distracting him with pointless questions about the Swifts when he was champing at the bit to claim her hand. Sitting on her divan, she inspected her hands, noting that she needed to attend to her manicure. A rough nail was not in keeping with how she wanted to be seen, especially now that she was to be Mrs Colvin, although they had agreed not to spread the word just yet. Sidney would talk to his mother and no doubt include the news in his next letter to Louis so that Fanny (Frances wanted so much to tell her) would know soon enough.

Dear Sidney. She congratulated herself on not having pressed her case straight after Albert's death. They'd both needed to come to terms with that event. *All in good time* had always been his motto. Sidney's other tenet was *Louis first* and for years she conspired in that principle. Now, though, she might like to have taken first place, to have been offered marriage, if not before his trip, at least before it was discussed. But the logic was against it and Sidney liked his logic.

From the mantlepiece Louis's photograph regarded her with amusement. She got up and turned it at an angle so as not to be under his gaze. Marriage was what she wanted. Soon she and Sidney would be man and wife, under one roof, like Edmund and Nellie Gosse. It was Gosse who'd persuaded him about Samoa. Did he also suggest marriage? His famously successful union might well have provided the nudge Sidney needed. Frances was happy with the comparison. Seeing how Nellie thrived in a happy marriage while pursuing her career as an artist, Frances needn't worry about giving up her freedoms.

Moving would be a mixed blessing, but she could accustom herself to the museum house. While Sidney was planning his trip, she would make enquiries about who had overall charge of the premises. They were gracious but too formal, weighed down by dark furniture and heavy paint and the curtains in the drawing-room were faded. She would argue it was time to redecorate.

When a note arrived from Sidney's mother inviting her to visit, Frances set off with more than her usual enthusiasm. She had no love for the Sydenham cottage where Mary Colvin had been forced to move some years ago, but she would embrace her official welcome into the family.

As she walked from the station, a wind got up. The sky was a shabby autumn pewter and the road between the avenue of trees was strewn with leaves of rusty red and gold. She increased her speed to fend off the chill, knowing there would be no fire.

At the house, Frances was let in by a maid and led to the dark sitting room. Mary Colvin would not see seventy again but she was far from decrepit. There was resolve in her shoulders, the face more hawklike than feminine. She was known to exert her will with a tap of her hand on the arm of her chair, even if there was only a single maid and a paid companion rather than a line of servants to do her bidding. The walking stick by the side of her chair was a new acquisition and looked more like a weapon than a means of support.

The companion was away visiting family in Sussex. As Frances sat down, Mary tutted at the maid for being too slow in organising tea. Mary inclined the stick towards Frances. 'So, my dear, are you pleased you have what you have always wanted?' There was a gleam of humour in Mary's eye. They had accommodated themselves to their respective roles, the mother who would always have the upper hand, the woman who had claimed her son's affection. For the first time, Frances wondered how this had been for Sidney, with two women to appease. 'I know you want to see Sidney happy,' she said.

Mary laughed. 'Sidney, happy? I will settle for married!'

Frances bridled. As if anyone would do!

Her hostess shrugged an apology. 'He was a solitary child. I thought he'd stay a bachelor. Then he chose a woman he couldn't marry. Perverse as well as solitary!'

Frances was irritated. Sidney wouldn't be the first man to want what he couldn't have, but in his case the obstacles were real and his love beyond question. 'He is very happy at our plans for marriage. It was his suggestion, not mine.'

Mary sat back, relenting. 'I dare say if anyone can make him happy, it will be you. He has stuck with you long enough. And you with him. He's not the easiest man.'

'He is kindness itself!'

His mother rearranged herself in front of the unlit fire and considered its empty blackness. 'Too late for children, of course.'

For a moment, Frances heard this as a reproof, but Mary's voice was edged with regret. Frances had been expecting to discuss wedding plans. This turn in the conversation left her at a loss.

Mary's eyes were half-closed. 'I had daughters, you know, three of them. Buried on our old estate.'

Frances knew only of Sidney's brothers, one deceased. He had never spoken of sisters. 'I'm sorry, I didn't know.'

'Sidney has been son and daughter to me. Maybe that was too much to ask of him. A daughter would have been more of a friend.'

If Sidney had been here with them, his mother would have been the same as always, perfectly polite, a little domineering. Without him she was an old lady living just too far from London, estranged from her old friends and her old life. Still, Frances didn't like to think of her as lonely. 'He is very attentive to you.'

'I know he's busy. Stevenson may be gone but he's still a thorn in his flesh.'

A less thorny creature than Louis was hard to imagine. Or did Mrs Colvin have a point? Sidney's friendship with Louis entailed the occasional hurt as well as a mountain of work.

'His being in the Pacific doesn't help,' she agreed. 'If only he hadn't gone quite so far. Still, Sidney will be overjoyed to see Louis again.'

Mary raised her eyebrows. 'He's gracing us with a visit?'

Frances responded without thinking. 'Louis' health couldn't stand it. But Sidney is looking exceptionally well, so I don't think the journey will be a problem.'

The hooded eyes snap open. 'What journey is this?'

Frances could have bitten her tongue. Apparently Sidney had told his mother of their marriage but not the voyage that was to precede it. She rushed to assure Mary that nothing had been booked, that Sidney probably wanted to have everything finalised before divulging his plans.

Mary was not persuaded. 'It will take months and cost a fortune. Can't you talk him out of it?'

It had been Frances's idea, at least in the first place, but in Mary Colvin's drawing room, the enterprise suddenly lost its glamour and became a foolhardy venture. She needed to remind herself it was necessary. 'It's important for him. You know how close they've always been.'

Mary's mouth pursed in distaste. 'I don't like Sidney depending on him. Spending money on a visit will hardly help.'

The cost had crossed Frances's mind but she wouldn't begrudge Sidney a visit to his dearest friend.

Mary narrowed her eyes. 'If I were you, I wouldn't rush into matrimony until his debts are paid, particularly those to Stevenson.'

If Sidney owed money to Louis, Frances was in the dark, but she wouldn't show her ignorance to Mary Colvin. Instead, she turned the conversation to the future and promised that when she and Sidney were married, Mary would be looked after. The old lady was mollified. She had offered no congratulations and avoided any mention of wedding plans, but perhaps Mary Colvin had got what she wanted.

***

Frances went straight from Waterloo to the museum.

'I gather from your mother you're in debt to Louis.'

Sidney's face caught the setting sun, reflecting and enhancing his embarrassment.

'It goes back a long time.'

'The engravings?'

When Sidney was director of the Fitzwilliam, he'd managed to lose a valuable set of prints by leaving them unattended in a carriage. They were never recovered, leaving him responsible for the considerable cost. Louis, along with other friends, had to bail him out and it remained Sidney's greatest embarrassment. So out of character, Frances thought at the time. And yet, every now and then there was some kind of accident—a lost manuscript, money unaccounted for. Each was a shock, to his colleagues and to himself. Famously punctilious in his work, Sidney had a careless streak and it pained him to be reminded.

He shook his head in impatience. 'The engravings are paid for. I asked Louis to help with life insurance, for Mother.' He flushed, seeing the trap just as he walked into it.

'Sidney, you know Albert has left me with next to nothing.'

Because of Sidney's lack of funds, she had been forced to work. She had been lucky to find employment that suited her, the college, translation, some well-regarded writing on English art and artists. None of this had irked her, but what might she have achieved without the need to earn a steady income? How much more time would she have had to write for herself, to enjoy the company of their London friends?

Sidney was vexed. 'I'm paying him back. I'll soon be able to foot the insurance bill myself.'

International success had left Louis comfortably off, although with Fanny's family to think of, he was never free of financial worries. Still, Louis would understand that Frances was Sidney's priority. 'Have you told him we're to be married?'

'I was leaving it until I saw him.'

'And why didn't you tell your mother about the trip?'

His discomfort was obvious. 'I will do. She's easily upset.'

'As she is by our marriage, apparently. Her comments were hardly enthusiastic.'

She watched him flounder. He could hardly say the wedding was more important when the trip to Samoa came first. 'I'm sorry. I didn't intend for you...'

'To bear the brunt of your mother's anger? If you had been open with her, I might not have done. No one likes an argument, Sidney, but I didn't have you down as a coward.'

She had been going to suggest they attend a concert. Mendelssohn's Hebridean was his absolute favourite, recalling, he always said, not just Scotland but his beloved Brittany. The evening was spoiled. She asked John Humphries to call for a carriage to take her home, and hang the expense.

30.

On her doorstep, Frances faced the uncomfortable fact she and Sidney had had their first disagreement. And so soon after agreeing to marry. It was hardly a good omen and it made her uneasy. Everything she had taken for granted, her feelings for Sidney, the care she had lavished on him, their entire future together, was thrown into doubt. In the darkness, she fumbled with the key which was worn and refused to turn as it should. There was no one to call on as Maddie had the evening off.

Once inside, she steadied herself. If she'd learned anything, it was to look to practicalities. It would be foolish to go into marriage without any recourse to funds. If, God forbid, the worst should happen to Sidney en route to Samoa, she would be left no better off than now. All this might be an over-reaction but it felt like a lesson, the same lesson she learned from her time with Albert, never to rely entirely on anyone else for a home, for an income, for peace of mind.

She paused in front of the hall mirror, assessing how people saw her–unmarried but rarely alone, a respected literary hostess, a woman who, beyond fifty had kept her looks. As time went on, as her skin dulled and slackened, would they see just a lonely old maid?

On her hall table was a thick envelope bearing her name. It was a sheaf of poems from Matthew Swift.

Grateful for an occupation, she took them to her room where she read, as she still often did, by candlelight, allowing the words and shadows to play together on the page, lulled by the captivating rhythm of Swift's poetry.

Next day, it was easier to dwell on the poems than to return to the unresolved situation with Sidney. The villanelles made pleasant night-time reading but would an editor consider them sentimental? She began to doubt her judgement. She was wary of asking Sidney, and anyway Matthew Swift was *her* find. He still had her book and his company would be welcome. It was easy to find his address from the college roster. She sent a note asking for the villanelle collection to be returned.

No reply arrived, and December had blown in when she came home one evening to find Swift, complete with the red and purple scarf, hovering on the steps. It was Sunday and dusk was spiralling into darkness, but there was no soiree. Sidney was busy planning his trip and she was disinclined to play hostess.

'Mr Swift, how nice to see you.' She had come up behind him and made him jump.

'I brought your book. I'm sorry it's late.'

The book or the hour? Both she supposed. It had been six months since the tea-party, almost a year since they had first met.

He stepped aside to allow her to cross the threshold and their arms brushed in passing. The outer hall was dim with the light behind him. She caught the gleam of a smile.

'You did ask for payment,' he said, 'You've had my writing?'

She inclined her head. 'I have indeed. It has been my night-time companion these last few weeks.'

Did 'night-time' sound over-familiar? Surely not and anyway it was true. 'Come in and we can talk about it.'

Inside, she removed her heavy wrap and hung it on the peg. As she raised her arms to unpin her hat, she was aware of revealing the contours of her body and hastily brought her arms down, smoothing her skirt to restore a more decorous silhouette.

In the sitting room, she invited Swift to sit and he chose the armchair by the fire which Maddie had encouraged to a welcoming glow in expectation of Frances's return. With the curtains drawn, the room felt smaller and more intimate. She heard Maddie calling to ask if anything else was required, and Frances went to tell her no, she could leave if she wished.

Frances closed the sitting room door behind her. 'There, that's better.' She meant simply to reduce draughts, or did it make the room too private? It was only just after five but the early darkness felt more like late evening, the hours before bed. 'I hope the book was useful.'

'Very. I've invested in a copy for myself.'

She went to her writing desk where the villanelles lay. If she had known he was coming, she would have made some formal notes. Her thoughts on his poems lacked focus.

The top four sheets contain a single poem called *Doves*. She flicked through the rest and carried the stack to the small sofa opposite Swift. The man was on the very edge of his seat, but it was natural to be apprehensive when your work was the subject of discussion.

She strove for objectivity in what she might say to him. 'I'm not surprised the villanelle has become popular,' she began. 'It sits with our Pre-Raphaelite school, don't you think? The desire for the formality of a bygone age. I must say I rather like it.'

He was silent. He must know something of art, surely, to write with such intensity about lovers released from separate cages, free to circle the earth but searching only for each other.

Over the incoherent hubbub of wheels and voices drifting down from Marylebone Road, the clock ticked. She must dismiss him or admit to what she knew at first reading, that the poem with all its romantic sensuality was about herself and him, lovers freed from unhappy unions. She knew it but chose to ignore it. After all, she and Sidney were not unhappy – goodness knows where Swift had got that idea – they were just temporarily at odds. Still, she enjoyed the poetry, the adulation, the sweep of sentiment, the thought that she could move a young man to words of love. Now she must deal with the consequences, the words made flesh, the writer sitting close to her, expecting his love to be returned.

The silence between them was too long. She must speak, or something in the room would snap with the force of a violin string stretched too tight, ricocheting who knows where. On the chair next to Matthew was the knitted scarf, the mark of a family man.

'I was so sorry to hear of your wife's sad loss.'

His eyes flicked up. 'Mr Colvin told you?'

'Eventually, although I met your wife and deduced...' he registered confusion. 'You know I sometimes work in the college in Queens' Square?'

'Ah, I had forgotten.'

Swift was twisting his hands together. The arrival in the conversation of Sidney and Lucinda had, as she intended, punctured the disconcertingly febrile atmosphere. Now he was simply uncomfortable and a little wretched.

'I've tried to be strong for her,' he said. 'When her health improved, I suggested the college.'

'I hear she's a good student. You have had too much to bear. I hope I can still be of help.'

His hand had gone to his mouth and she was sorry for him. She patted the seat beside her, hoping to put him at his ease. He came and perched awkwardly next to her with none of his usual grace.

She shuffled the sheets of poems. She must bring this strange meeting to a close. 'These are very accomplished. Your writing is coming on in leaps and bounds,' then as an afterthought, a peace-offering, she said, 'Shall I pass them on to Mr Colvin? He might get them placed for you.'

He snatched the poems from her and stood up. 'No. Not Mr Colvin! I mean he has no need...' He was ready to leave, which was doubtless for the best.

Frances groped for a suitable farewell. 'Give my regards to your wife.'

'Thank you.'

He backed out of the door and she had to go after him. 'Don't forget your scarf!'

He turned to take it from her and they were momentarily united by strands of magenta and vermillion before he stepped out of the door to be enveloped by the night-time gloom.

When Matthew Swift had gone, she was oddly out of sorts, out of place even, in her own sitting-room. She had clearly misjudged his feelings and her attempt to put things back on an even keel by offering his work to Sidney was another error. Perhaps Sidney had already seen and dismissed the poems out of hand. Frances had no idea what she had done wrong. Suka would tell her she should never have taken on Matthew Swift and for once Suka would be right. He was not a suitable protégé.

She felt an urge to go to the museum and make things right with Sidney. She should stop avoiding the inevitable. To be married to Sidney, to live in his lofty rooms, what more could anyone wish for? But not tonight. She ate the cold supper left by Maddie, went to bed. Swift's poems had gone from the night stand and she could summon no desire to read anything else. She drew up the covers and waited for sleep.

31

December was not a good time to be alone but Sidney was always busy on weekday mornings. The Regent's Park, which she enjoyed so much in summer, was drab and robbed of any lingering colour by her melancholy. She sat there with a collected edition of Keats, desperate to find solace in the familiar and timeless, but the comfort she took from poetry was soon invaded by her surroundings. Chilled to the bone, she left and went home, the hem of her skirt soaking wet.

A few hours later, she took the omnibus to Westminster Bridge. From here she could walk to the museum and arrive at a more suitable time. The weather was damp but the cold had eased, and she lifted her face to catch the caress of a fine drizzle. Was it here she had stood with Louis all these years ago, watching the river, contemplating his future? She must write to him about her impending marriage. Her anxieties of yesterday were mis-placed and Louis loved Sidney's rooms at the museum. Was there a small chance that he and Fanny would come to London for the wedding? That would be the best possible celebration.

She turned from the river past Westminster Abbey and towards Whitehall. As keeper at the museum, Sidney regularly walked these pavements for meetings with MPs and government officials. Suka once asked what Sidney did all day, as if a major art collection would simply look after itself. Frances had to explain the enormous work involved in arranging exhibitions and acquiring new materials. With typical thoroughness Sidney had even devised an entirely new system of cataloguing alongside his necessary and frequent applications for additional funds.

On the corner of The Mall, there was a newsstand. The headline was flapping in the wind, the words illegible. It was only out of idle curiosity she went closer to see what was happening in the world. But the ugly black capitals defacing the white sheet made no sense. This must be some mistake. Or was she dreaming? But the heavy skies, the magisterial buildings, the clutter of sounds and smells were as before. Over everything the cry of the vendor proclaiming his news, a terrible dissonance on the air. Her stomach cramped. She laid her hand on it to stem the pain but it crept upwards, to her ribs, her heart, her throat.

Head reeling, she fumbled to find coppers which she then thrust at the vendor as she snatched a copy of the paper. Hurrying towards Bloomsbury, head down, she stopped twice to reread what she could not believe, not just the event but that news of it should be blowing so freely around London when not one of them knew. By the time she reached Great Russell Street, she was breathless and sobbing. She knew it was true. The weight of her knowledge pressed on her, cramping her neck and shoulders. The most onerous task of her life was to convey this to Sidney.

When Humphries answered the door, she brushed past him, knowing she had no words. From Sidney's study she heard voices. Behind her Humphries was pleading with her to wait, because Mr Colvin had a visitor. She turned and held up the paper to him. Humphries understood and stepped back, silenced.

Frances pushed open the door of the study, paper in hand, the terrible news on her lips, but was halted on the threshold by the scene in front of her. She swallowed down the words she had been struggling to find. She needn't say a thing, because Sidney already knew. Sidney's visitor was holding him in his arms, allowing him to weep against his outdoor coat, stroking his head and murmuring words of consolation. The bearer of the news was Matthew Swift, the devoted husband, the writer of questionable sonnets. He met Frances's gaze without embarrassment, as if to say *perhaps now you understand.*

Frances didn't care that Swift's desire was not for her but for Sidney. It was common, if unspoken, knowledge that some men preferred intimacy with their own kind. She cared only about Sidney and the unimaginable headline still in her outstretched hand.

Today it is our painful duty to announce the death in Samoa of Robert Louis Stevenson.

She strode across the carpet and pulled Swift away. Barely aware of his departure, she took Sidney in her arms and put her cheek to his. Their tears mingled as they clung to each other like sailors lashed to a mast.

They were soon exhausted by grief and agreed there was nothing to be done, not yet, except to mourn the passing of their dearest friend and a writer only just finding his peak.

In the carriage home, the London streets were obscured by its grimy windows, the stuffy interior, designed to protect her from the outdoors, simply suffocating. Her stomach churned with the movement of the coach and her thoughts skidded under its wheels as she recalled the strange prelude to her consoling Sidney. She supposed there were perfectly good reasons for Swift to have been at the museum that day, to have found himself in the unexpected role of comforter and to have snatched the opportunity for an embrace. Sidney hadn't even mentioned his name in the sorrowful aftermath and she guessed he never would.

She hurried from the carriage into her house. The immediate past, tiffs with Sidney, misunderstandings with Matthew Swift, were unimportant. What mattered was that Louis Stevenson, whom she had known as well as anyone, perhaps better, was no more.

In the alcove in the hall, she moved the pile of clothing from on top of her box and carried it through the front hall into her bedroom. The letters may have been light but the box was heavier than she remembered. She set it on the floor to catch her breath, then with a final effort lifted it onto her bed and opened the lid. It was packed with letters. She picked one out at random and the slope of his handwriting, from a time when his fingers were lithe and not worn out by countless essays and novels, carried the sound of his voice. Every page was peppered with alterations and marginal notes, reminding her of his eternal restlessness. Turning down the gas light, she fingered the pages in front of the bedroom fire and began to read them one by one, in order from the very beginning.

In the morning, she woke with a wrench in her gut to the knowledge of his death. The sky outside still stretched to the South Seas but there was no one there to shout at in exasperation, no one for Sidney to love and revere.

Days marched silently on and each evening she continued to read Louis's letters, replacing each of them in the box until she reached the last. She counted them, twenty, forty, eighty… Louis had written her one hundred and eight letters.

She took the box back to the dark hiding place where it belonged. Soon there would be public lamentations, obituaries, biographies even. A whole story was set to unfold and Louis would soon belong to the world. Her casket was a treasure trove of thoughts and fancies, dreams and nightmares, proof of Louis's tender and boyish affection. She would guard it jealously. It belonged only to her.

PART SIX

Enmity

I am quite miserable today – I have sent a wretched little note to Sidney, and I send a howl to you...this news has sickened me. For I wanted him to live forever.
E. Burne-Jones to Mrs Sitwell, December 1894[*]

* Lucas, E.V. The Colvins and their Friends. London: Methuen, 1928, p.238

32.

At Vailima, the home she and Louis had built in the jungle clearing, Fanny Stevenson kept to her room, preferring to face her widowhood alone. From behind the slatted doors, tightly closed, she could hear the family and the islanders weeping, tearing their hair, shrieking their grief in hysterical lamentations. She drew a curtain over the window, shutting out the intrusive glare of the sun, rejecting the fertile warmth that sustained their plantation, sustained it too well, so that she was forever cutting back the undergrowth to let the cocoa and the pineapples grow. Who would tend them now? Who or what would sustain her? She had come here over tumultuous stomach-churning seas for him, borne the heat, the work, the aggravations of jungle life, only for Louis, and he was gone.

He was buried on the day he died, carried to the mountain top and laid to rest in the spot he had chosen, *the sailor home from the sea.* That was two days ago, but the road, cut hastily by the villagers, was too steep for her to make a pilgrimage. She was robbed, not just of a husband but the chance to weep over the frail body she had tended, preserved and worshipped.

She needed to be alone, not out of grief but out of fury. He had keeled over while mixing a salad dressing, for goodness' sake. *What right did he have* to drop dead before her very eyes? She had lived to keep him safe and

226

he had abandoned her, or made his escape, as if death were preferable to life with her, his woman, his Tamaitai. She was embarrassed by her anger and worried she would lash out at the others. It was best to just sit here and let the storm run its course.

In her head the conversation with Louis continued. How could he die when she was the one who had been unwell? As he had found health and happiness, she had suddenly languished, taking to her bed with undiagnosed pains and the blackest depression. Lloyd was forced to take over the running of the household. Belle looked after Louis. Then just as she was emerging from illness, Louis left, without a word of warning.

On the third or maybe fourth day, Belle knocked timidly on her door, no doubt sent to test the waters. The natives called her Teuila, a flower. She had her son, Austen, with her. He was fidgeting next to his mother, confused by the maelstrom of emotions in his home. He had seen death amongst the islanders, and the bodies of animals rotting in the jungle, but this was different, the departure of his fondest teacher and the man he adored.

'Oh mother,' Belle said, 'please come and be with us.'

Fanny shifted herself reluctantly and let Austen take her hand down to the Great Hall where the local chief had come to pay his respects. She received him, thanked him for his help with Louis's burial, and dismissed him, claiming the need to see to family matters.

When he had gone, she asked the family to sit down with her. She had to face the realities. Lloyd, it turned out, had telegraphed London on the day of Louis's death. The news was printed and published. She imagined the hubbub amongst his old friends. 'Couldn't you have waited?'

Lloyd was taken aback. 'People needed to know.'

'But I need to think.' Besides, there were some she would like to have told herself. Wiring Frances and Colvin might have helped dispel the thunderous darkness of her grief. Now their letters, when they came, would be lost in the clamour of condolences.

Later, as the sun went down and the boys were cooking the evening meal, she went out to the porch where she found Belle, wearing a dark European dress instead of her usual shift. She had become Louis's secretary, his beloved amanuensis, taking dictation as his hands failed him. Then with Fanny indisposed, she had subsumed other tasks, cutting his hair, attempting to give him a shave. She loved the limelight, loved being Louis's chosen one, which of course she never had been. Fanny was his tiger and his tiger lily, his helpmeet and his wife.

Belle was leaning on the rail, staring into the distance, keening softly.

'Can't you pull yourself together,' Fanny asked her, 'for my sake?'

From behind the cloud of incomprehension, she was beginning to sense an itch, a need for activity. 'There's a lot to do,' she said. 'I need to write to Colvin.'

Years ago, Louis had appointed Colvin his literary executor. Colvin of the museum, the man she teasingly called The Monument. She needed to remind him of what was expected of him.

Belle turned round, her face puffy with weeping. 'Mother, he has only just died. It's as if you want him wrapped up, sent away, gone.'

'Don't you think I would bring him back if I could?' Fanny's voice was sharp with exasperation. 'Hanging around tearing our hair won't get anything done. If we love him, we need to put him where he belongs, in front of the whole world.'

Belle turned away, sobbing again, as if Fanny were being deliberately cruel.

Fanny sighed. 'Dry your eyes and make yourself respectable. Charles Baxter will be here in a day or two and we need to talk about that new edition. While you're parading your grief, you might like to think about where the money comes from.'

She didn't mean to be harsh but she had no choice other than to carry on. In all of her life and in so many places, she had faced and overcome adversity. But nothing had prepared her for this. No womanly skills or pioneering recklessness could bring Louis back. She sat down suddenly on a canvas chair and put her head in her hands. Did they think it was easy to be strong?

Belle knelt by her feet and Fanny rested her head on her daughter's shoulder.

'People think you're cold,' Belle said. 'I know that's not true.'

'What people think doesn't concern me. Only that they see Louis for what he was, a great writer, a good man.'

She was distantly aware not just of the hum of insects and the screech of a native starling, but of the voices of Austen and Lloyd coming back up the path from Apia, some clashing of pans by the kitchen boy, a command from the cook to take more care. Vailima, silent since Louis's death, was coming alive again. The world was carrying on without him. At last she felt the prick of tears, but she would save them for later, for when she was alone.

'Poor Graham,' Belle said, 'coming back to this terrible news.'

Louis's cousin, Graham Balfour, had visited from England for several months then left on a voyage to Honolulu. He was strong, handsome, liked by everyone. Fanny saw the direction of her daughter's thoughts. Belle had always been quick to move on from one love to the next.

'Leave me now.' Fanny said. She needed to gather her strength. She needed to weep.

Next day she steeled herself to go to Louis's room, to feel his lingering presence in the shadows, to catch the smell of his clothes and the bedsheets recently removed. At Vailima, in the strange climate and with new routines, they had decided to sleep separately. She didn't disturb him in the night with her maladies, he didn't wake her when he rose with the birds at dawn. Mostly they looked after each other at an arm's length. And so the joyous rough and tumble of a shared bed had gone, although those afternoons when they drew down the blinds and lay more quietly together were all the more appreciated for their rarity. She folded her arms around herself and dropped her head to her chest since this pleasure too was taken from her.

Downstairs Louis had a library and smoking room but most of his writing was done here, at the desk by the window. Fanny's eyes settled on the marks left on the room by Belle, her shawl flung over a chair, a note in her handwriting.

On the desk was a bundle of letters, sealed and ready to go. The boat that brought Baxter from England would take back the month's post. Fanny sat with the envelopes in her lap and imagined the recipients opening them, knowing that Louis had gone, then she flicked through them again, because one had caught her eye. It was addressed to 'Mrs F. Sitwell' to Frances, at her home in Marylebone.

Louis wrote assiduously to Colvin every month. If he or Fanny wanted to send a message to Frances in particular, it was simply tucked in the same envelope. She and Colvin were as good as man and wife, and things bundled up were less likely to get lost along the way. In fact, most of the London correspondence went to Colvin as a poste restante. Was this letter somehow different?

The envelope was bulky enough to contain more than a note. Frances had been given no editing tasks that Fanny knew of since Louis had asked for advice on his *Child's Garden*, and that was a long time ago. Fanny told herself this was of no consequence and yet she couldn't ignore the address, as if the thoughts contained in the letter required privacy of some kind. Frances, she recalled, had been 'like a mother to him'. Fanny had always taken that with a pinch of salt. They had written to each other freely and at length, but years ago, before Fanny's time. That history had never troubled her.

She went down to the Great Hall and called to Belle. 'Did Louis have a letter from Mrs Sitwell recently?'

Belle came in from the porch. Since the night before, she had regained some composure. 'There was something, a month or two ago. Shall I look for it?'

The envelope in Fanny's hand had been addressed by Louis. Belle was unaware he had replied.

'I'll look myself.' She, Fanny, was now the custodian of his possessions. If she found the original letter, she could add a reply to go with this one.

In the end, Belle insisted on helping, claiming to know exactly where to find such things, but a search of his desk, his bedside chest and the many pigeonholes in the library yielded nothing from Frances.

When Belle had gone, Fanny was left holding the reply to a letter that didn't exist. It had been lost or misplaced by Louis who filed everything carefully. Or had he preferred not to keep it? It was a mystery, but she had other more important things to think about.

Lloyd agreed there was no time to lose in giving Colvin his orders.

'We need a biography,' Lloyd said. 'Before letters and papers go astray, or others choose to give their own interpretation.'

Louis had no enemies, but some friends had fallen by the wayside. Speaking ill of the dead was easier than criticising the living. Fanny agreed with Lloyd and together they composed a letter to Colvin reminding him of his responsibilities. Louis had stipulated that, along with everything else, he should be the one to put together an account of his life.

The steamer docked a few days later and Baxter arrived for his sad pilgrimage to Vailima. He would stay a few weeks to help Fanny with paperwork. The boat left with Fanny's letter to Colvin and the rest of Louis's post on board. Except the letter to Frances Sitwell was somehow left behind. Fanny found it afterwards on her writing desk, where it had lain as she had considered its likely contents. Not that she would ever read it. That would be an invasion of privacy. It belonged to Frances. She would send it next month, if she remembered.

33.

During December, Frances and Sidney nursed their sadness separately, exchanging notes on the many obituaries of RLS, dulling the sharp edge of grief with daily concerns and seasonal duties. They celebrated Christmas apart, he with his mother, she with Suka who, for once, was attuned to Frances's mood and did her best to be kind. Soirees had been suspended indefinitely as London mourned.

Since Bertie's death, Frances had avoided church and the God who had failed to take pity on either of her children. She couldn't entirely be a rationalist like Sidney, but the act of praying had become a greater comfort than the hope of any outcome and she addressed her prayers to some nameless part of the sky. Louis, the confirmed agnostic she had known, had drifted back to a belief in some greater power, and professed a faith that was open to all-comers, regardless of creed or colour. Creeping into a pew near the back of the church they had visited together, she found no consolation for the loss of her sons but she gave thanks for the life Louis had led and her small part in it. Perhaps she too could drift back.

In January, a note arrived from Sidney, asking if he might call on a Saturday evening and she said yes immediately. In the aftermath of death, there was still a life to be lived. Her previous annoyance and the flurry of misunderstanding over Matthew Swift seemed ridiculous.

She imagined herself on the other side of some great divide, ready to journey on.

When Sidney arrived, she allowed him to embrace her. 'I've missed you,' she said.

He clasped her against him. 'I've missed you too. Very much.'

They ate supper together and he told her his mother was moving with her companion to Sussex. She would take only the most precious or needful of her belongings, the residue of a life that once delighted in fine things but was now limited in its requirements. Sidney had claimed a few pictures and ornaments for himself. This new situation would reduce his outgoings and he could take on the insurance contributions which formed his debt to Louis. He was confident he could provide for all of them; himself, his mother and his wife-to-be. He was answering Frances's previous misgivings. She had been mean-spirited to have doubted his loyalty.

Supper had been cleared. When they retired to the easy-chairs she stood behind him and laid her hands on his shoulders to ease the tension she knew was always there. She felt his anxieties dissolve as she stroked his head. He stretched back in the chair, reached for her hand and kissed it. 'I'm so happy we're to be married.'

It was like turning a page. This sad chapter could be brought to a close, there were better things to come.

'Stay with me,' she said.

In the morning they slept late, then lay awake, holding hands.

'I don't think I realised,' he said to the ceiling, 'how much I'm defined by Louis. These last few weeks, it's as if everything else has been erased: The museum, Cambridge, my own writing.'

'Your mother called him a thorn in your flesh.'

He squeezed her fingers. 'He was a joy. He will always be a joy. Things have just become rather overwhelming. So many letters of condolence to answer. Soon there will be Mrs RLS to contend with.' This was his latest name for Fanny. She claimed to have taken Sidney to her heart, but Sidney had never quite reciprocated.

Frances got up and rinsed her face with cold water, absorbing the shock of another day. 'Surely Fanny will be too distraught to cause problems.'

Sidney watched her as she examined the contents of her wardrobe, his hands behind his head. 'Baxter will bring back material from Vailima. I already have a pile of Louis's letters to look through, people are sending them to me every day, expecting they'll be published.'

Frances, in her petticoat, ignored a prick of disquiet as she picked a white blouse with a lace ruffle, pulled it on and fastened the buttons. 'You mean the Vailima journal?' Louis's monthly letters to Sidney had always been intended for publication.

Sidney sat up, warming to his theme. He was wearing the night shirt he kept at her house. It made him look both older and younger than his usual self. His eyes were shining. 'All his letters will be of interest, huge interest. They're what people want to read, and they can also form the basis of his life story. He wasn't especially in favour of a formal biography.' Sidney lay back and frowned. 'I'll start with the Vailima letters, certainly. They are easiest to tackle. Then the rest can be collected into chronological volumes.'

His curator's mind was in full flow. *Volumes of letters*, the prick became more intense, more like a wound.

Sidney rose and began to dress. If she had not moved

the box of letters back to its place, it would have been here now. The thought of Louis beside them, even in spirit, was oddly dislocating. What would he have made of the scene? Was this how he imagined her and Sidney, in the chill of the morning after, passion cooling in the watery early light?

The room was small and she and Sidney, always a little awkward at this juncture, moved around each other. As he washed and hopped into his trousers, she sat down in front of the cheval mirror to brush and pin her hair

'I've been rereading some of his letters to me,' he said, 'they're mostly business-like, but it's a comfort of sorts.' In the mirror she watched him lacing his shoes. 'I assume you've been reading yours.'

He hadn't forgotten that she had letters too. He stood up, a little red in the face and waited as she finished her hair, smiling at her in the mirror. 'I love watching you do that. Such a classic pose.'

The last pin was inserted but she remained seated. It wasn't that Sidney treated her like a decoration, this was just what his eye was trained to see. Still, it distracted her from saying something about Louis's letters until Sidney spoke to her through the mirror.

'You will let me have your letters, as soon as you're ready? You were such a significant influence on him.'

Here was the feeling of altered destiny. Sidney assumed she would hand them over. Her letters. At least it was aired, something to discuss rather than avoid. She raised her eyebrows. 'All of them?'

Sidney was blustering a little. 'It was such an important time in his development as a writer,' then more thoughtfully, 'I remember when I was with him in Menton, he wrote to you very often.'

Menton, yes, but so many other times and places too. She got up and walked around him. They were still not face to face. 'I was grateful for those letters. I was at a low ebb.'

Sidney softens. 'I know. I do remember.'

'But his letters to me were personal, not especially literary. Do they matter so much?'

He laughed. 'Goodness, Louis is always personal. That is the joy of him!' He corrected himself with a sigh – 'was, I mean.'

As they left the room, he stood aside to follow her. She felt uncomfortable with his weight so close behind.

'You will think about them?' he said. 'Perhaps take another look, remind yourself of their significance?'

She paused before answering. 'Of course. I'll look through them again.'

The letters were all she had left of Louis. Sidney, though, was in charge of his literary legacy. Had her promise to Louis somehow become a promise to Sidney?

34.

Two months later, Sidney was still in the throes of editing the Vailima letters and dealing with, as he put it, *a hundred and one things*. Frances called at the museum to find his study in the state of the organized chaos which had become habitual, the surface of his desk reduced to a small square by a border of letters, stacked in piles and bound with string. The labels bore names she recognised: Henley, *Gosse, Leslie Stephen, Bob S.* (Louis's artist cousin), *Minor Family*.

Sidney, however, had abandoned the desk and was kneeling on the floor next to it, in front of him a large trunk, left open to reveal a swathe of papers. Charles Baxter had returned from his ill-fated trip to Samoa.

'My goodness,' Frances said.

Sidney barely looked up. 'And there's more to come. Balfour is on his way with another batch.' Louis's cousin was returning after several months in the South Seas.

'Poor Baxter does not look well,' Sidney went on, 'exhausted and reliant on the bottle.' He went back to his sorting. 'He agrees an extended *Life* isn't required. He thinks Fanny will be content with a preface to the letters.'

Frances folded her legs under her skirt to sit beside him on the carpet. With the spring so cold, the fire was on and all of the windows closed. The room was airless.

Sidney's anxiety was palpable but she had to ask. 'Is a preface really enough?'

Sidney laid down the papers in his hand and sighed. 'A brief overview will suffice to accompany the letters. Maybe afterwards I can do a more substantial work.'

She laid her hand on his arm. 'That sounds ideal. You mustn't overtire yourself.'

He flashed her a smile and got up from the floor. 'Baxter forgot to bring the actual agreement, but the payment side is settled.'

'Yes, of course,' she said. He wanted her to know he was being careful in regard to money, but she had set aside that resentment. She peeked into the trunk, drawing out a bundle. 'Look, poetry.'

'Yes, more than I realised.'

They took the poems across the corridor to the dining table. Sidney lifted them one by one from the pile, passing them on to her to read.

'Sidney, what's wrong?'

His body was shaking. He couldn't stop the tears. Frances got up, put her arm around his shoulders and took the sheet from him. It was entitled 'For S.C.' They had read it before but now everything had changed and she read it aloud.

To other lands and nights my fancy turned –
To London first, and chiefly to your house,
The many-pillared and the well-beloved...
Most of all,
For your light foot I wearied, and your knock
That was the glad reveille of my day

Sidney turned his face against her. She stroked the top of

his head where his fine hair had given way to baldness and kissed the smooth dome. 'You see how very dearly he loved you.'

His voice was muffled against her blouse. 'And I loved him.'

She had never heard Sidney say so, not outright. She murmured reassurance. 'As did I. As did we all.' Love and friendship, where does one begin and the other end?

When they had tidied the poems as best they could, Sidney looked at her over the table. 'My dear, what you do with your letters is entirely up to you. I just thought you wouldn't want to be left out of Louis's history.'

She was grateful for the concession to her judgement. 'Mine was a small part compared to others. His life was filled with famous men.'

'You had a special place in his heart,' Sidey said. 'You should not be forgotten.'

Louis would not be forgotten, and others would bask in reflected glory. Sidney deserved recognition of course and many of Louis's other friends were established writers. She, on the other hand, had no obvious place in history. And yet without her, would Louis have found wings to fly? In her mind, her box of letters shifted in its dark corner. Was it retreating to the shadows, or begging for release? Perhaps she should not be left out, or consigned to one of Sidney's footnotes. She must offer something of herself and Louis, to Sidney, to the readers of Louis's life story, to future generations.

Some commotion outside, a *Stop thief,* a policeman's whistle and more scuffling and shouting penetrated the closed windows. To make the future right, Frances must deal with the present.

'I've been rereading the letters,' she told Sidney across

the table. 'I can pick out the very best, the wonderful anecdotes and descriptions. I'm sure these are what you want?'

'Yes, exactly those.'

He held her eyes for a moment, acknowledging there might be other things, things that didn't need to be divulged. He trusted her to show him only as much as he wanted to see. She took a moment to contemplate even parts of the letters let loose upon the world.

'I might write to Samoa,' she said. Fanny might not be aware of the frequency of Louis's letters. Not that it would be a problem. It was all long before Fanny and Louis met.

Oxford and Cambridge Mansions,
20th April, 1895
My Dear Fanny,
I feel the need to write beyond my first condolences and to tell you that Charles Baxter has returned safely and left a trunkful of papers at the museum. The other day I found SC on his hands and knees amongst them all. I told him he was in a 'sea of Louis' and at that moment he did look, poor dear as if he might drown. What could I do except get down beside him and we swam together in our memories. I can tell you our mighty Monument wept openly at seeing those lines Louis wrote for him. It was a sad afternoon in which we both found a kind of happiness. I too hold very dear those poems he wrote for me and for Bertie. If it is too soon for you to feel the same I hope you know you are blessed and will one day look back with joy on Louis's devotion and your part in his life.

I think SC will have written assuring you of his

intentions to carry out your wishes. Even before Charles's return, he had made a good start on collecting and sorting Louis's letters which arrive daily from all and sundry. They are piled on his desk, all carefully labelled, which I'm sure is no less than you would expect. However, I hope you will agree with him that a full biography can wait until the first slew of letters has gone to press. No one could be keener than Sidney to honour his lifelong friend in all possible ways but there is only so much one man can do and you know that his health is less than robust. I wonder if you knew that he was planning to visit you this year? I think the loss of that hoped-for meeting has made him even more downcast.

I don't know if you are aware, but with Albert gone we plan to marry as soon as time and circumstances allow. We are grateful for the commission to be paid to Sidney for his work. I hope he will feel stronger with me at his side.

One final thing I should mention. I think you know that I myself have many letters sent to me by Louis from the early days of our acquaintance. We plan to include some of these in the general collection, passages which exemplify some of his most fluid and entertaining prose. I consider myself blessed to have been party to these thoughts and hope you will come to enjoy them too.

You see how SC and I weep for Louis while celebrating his time on earth. Be assured all London is in tears. We think of you every day, my dear, and hope you are withstanding the loss of your soulmate.

With sympathy and affection,
Frances

Later that month, Sidney asked if she would like to accompany him to a play at the Haymarket. They had never gone to the theatre together, a concert occasionally, in a small auditorium, but not to see a play. This joint outing was a subtle change in her status, the woman who would soon be his wife. He called for her in a cab and they sat hand in hand through the lighted streets. Good weather had arrived from nowhere and London looked gay under the spring moon.

At the theatre they walked closer to each other than usual, shoring each other up on their first public outing since Louis's death. In the foyer they bumped into Edmund Gosse and his wife. Edmund, affable as always, grasped Sidney's hand as he greeted him and nodded to Frances. Nellie Gosse touched Frances on the arm. She was statuesque with the grace of an artist's model, although she herself was the artist.

'We did enjoy having Sidney the other evening,' Nellie said. 'Next time you must come too, Mrs Sitwell.'

The shock of Albert's name just as she was looking forward to shrugging it off, rendered her briefly mute. Sidney broke in. 'Edmund was very kind. We've been mourning Louis together.'

She pictured the men consoling each other, the men who loved Louis.

They met again in the interval and Sidney commented on the sparseness of the audience.

'Everyone's at the St James,' Nellie said. 'Have you seen *Earnest*? They say it's an absolute masterpiece.'

Sidney was tight-lipped. 'I'm sorry. I won't buy a ticket for anything from which Wilde stands to gain.'

Gosse gave Sidney an appraising look. 'I know he's a poseur but we all know men of his persuasion, don't we?'

In the pause, Sidney closed his eyes briefly and opened them again, as if he needed to readjust his vision. Would he mention Swift? No, that would be indelicate. Instead he shook his head. 'Wilde insulted me when he was in America. That's why I blocked his application to join the Savile. But it's not just that. It's his self-assurance, his swagger, his *green carnations*.' He lowered his voice, glancing around to ensure no one was listening. 'If he wants boys, so be it. But does he have to make such a song and dance?'

Edmund laughed and clapped him on the shoulder. 'The song and dance! I can see that wouldn't sit well with you, Colvin. It's a good play, nonetheless.' He drew his wife back into the group. 'We'll go, won't we, Nellie?'

Frances was curious about *Earnest* but to suggest attending was not worth Sidney's ire. She knew of his antipathy to Wilde but hadn't realised its intensity. No wonder he'd been so quick to forget Matthew Swift. But leaving aside Wilde and his like, Frances was struck most of all by the bond between all those who had fallen under Louis's spell. First her, then Sidney, Gosse, and so many others. In the end he had charmed the world.

35

The following week, Maud was at Frances's door for the first time since Louis's death. She had asked to stay for a week or more and Frances was happy to agree. In the hallway they took each other's hands.

'Come in, Maud, come in.'

They embraced and Frances took comfort in Maud's lean frame and the knowledge that she knew Louis before any of the acclaim. To Maud he was only ever Lou, the beloved if unpredictable cousin. Maud reached to unpin her hat. 'We have to be glad he didn't suffer,' Maud said, 'Or not at the end.'

In the drawing room, Frances showed Maud the recent photograph. 'He sent me this last year.'

Maud nodded. 'I have one similar. He did right, though, don't you think, in going to the South Seas? It was good for him.'

'Just hard for the rest of us.' But the sounds of a London afternoon, carriages on the road outside, the low hissing of the gaslights, brought a different comfort. Louis in the South Seas was easier to deal with than Louis close to home.

They sat for tea. 'And how is Sidney? He must be quite lost.'

'Actually, considering the work coming to him, he's quite galvanised. He has asked us to supper.' As Sidney emerged from mourning, he was regaining energy. Frances too was ready to move ahead. 'I'm sure he won't mind my telling you. We plan to marry. Not immediately, but...'

Maud put her arms around Frances and kissed her cheek. 'How wonderful! Such happiness in store for you at last.'

Frances hugged Maud in return. Sharing her news made it seem more real and Maud's company had always helped. They had seen too little of each other lately.

At the museum, Sidney and Maud greeted each other warmly.

'You were Lou's closest and wisest friend,' said Maud.

Sidney was clearly touched. 'But for you, I would never have met him,' he said, and there was a pause in which they were all transported to that hot summer in Suffolk.

At supper, John Humphries opened a bottle of claret and Sidney proposed a toast. 'To Louis—to his genius.'

This was the best company in which to celebrate Louis's life. His words were echoed by the women. Frances felt the astringency of the wine on her tongue and the warmth in her gullet. As they sat to the table, she was as happy as she had been since Louis's death. Sidney too was looking less drawn, ready to honour Louis as well as to mourn him. Perhaps he knew this was his chance to shine.

Over the meal, Maud asked, 'What will happen now? Is there more to be published?'

Frances explained, 'Sidney and Charles Baxter have *St Ives* and *Hermiston* to deal with. Then Louis's letters and eventually a biography.'

Sidney was composed. He had a plan in place. 'I hope to deal quickly with the Vailima correspondence, and by then I should have amassed the majority of the rest.'

'The rest?'

'Most of his letters will be published. He was in favour. I have quite a collection. Baxter brought instructions from the widow.' Avoiding referring to Fanny by name was becoming a habit. 'Did he write to you, Maud, in any substantive way?'

She shook her head. 'Just the odd "thank you" letter. His mother will be the one to help you on the family side.'

Margaret Stevenson had gone with Louis and Fanny to Samoa, another mother who outlived her son.

'Yes, I'm in touch with her, as are many of his friends,' Sidney said. 'And I've had hundreds from him through the years.'

'And so has Frances!' Maud turned to her. 'I remember you telling me how often Louis wrote to you, from wherever he happened to be.'

Sidney was pleased to have found an ally. 'Yes. Such a treasure trove. I've asked Frances to look through them.'

Maud paused then spoke down to the napkin which she was shaking out onto her lap. 'What a chance for you to be part of Louis's history. You were both so very important to him.'

Frances forced a smile. She was still uncertain of which letters or part of letters to give to Sidney. John brought in the main course. The subject could be changed. 'Maud envies you your museum house,' she told Sidney.

Maud objected, 'Oh not really. But it must be wonderful to be part of such a great institution.' She laid a finger on Sidney's sleeve. 'I hear it is soon to be Frances' home too. I'm so happy for you both.'

'Thank you.' With Maud, Sidney was unembarrassed. 'I look forward to sharing it,' he looked directly at Frances, 'very much.'

Frances appreciated the sentiment, even if she still couldn't think of this house as hers. 'Sidney calls it living over the shop.'

'Yes, but what a shop. And one he is building all the time.'

'I've been lucky,' he said. 'Some wonderful collections have come our way and I have excellent staff.' Sidney loved to be asked about his work and these rooms were part of that world. 'So much of our collection isn't on show,' he said to Maud. 'Next time you are in town, let me know.' He raised his eyebrows. 'I could show you behind the scenes, some of our best-kept secrets.'

'That would be wonderful, thank you!'

Sidney beamed. He was practically flirting and it suited him. Frances was reminded that this house occupied the tiniest part of an empire that stretched even farther than she had realised.

Next morning over breakfast, Maud stirred her tea, looking into the vortex created by her spoon. 'All these letters, what an undertaking! Have you decided which of yours to contribute?'

She had and she had not. Louis had asked her to keep his letters. Because she fully intended to, she had never asked him why. *When I'm gone,* he had said in Bournemouth, but there was too much in those letters that was private, and too much that could be misunderstood. Then there was Fanny. Frances's letter to Samoa had not been answered.

'Would you like to see my treasure chest?' she asked Maud.

'Your letters? Are you sure?'

'Let me show you.'

It was a test for herself to lead Maud to the back lobby, to drag the box from its alcove, to have it seen and touched by someone else.

'Help me take it through,' she said and they carried it between them into the breakfast room where the morning light slanted in.

She opened the lid. The letters were packed in furrows. Maud took a breath. 'Oh, my dear,' then knelt down and reached out a hand. 'May I?'

Maud's fingers stroked the rows of envelopes, some slim, others fat with many sheets. 'To think of him writing all of this.' She took her hand away, as if to go farther would be a liberty.

'We wrote for quite some time. Sometimes every day.'

'Every day?'

'A diary almost.'

'And you wrote back?'

'Of course. It was a difficult time and he was young. He needed a listening ear. If I'm honest it sustained me too through those last months with Albert.'

'I remember he was very attached to you for a while.'

Frances removed one letter, checked the date and handed it to Maud. 'Read it if you want to.'

Maud looked inside and hesitated.

'I didn't expect they would be made public. But I suppose they're significant. Sidney thinks they have their place, I should have my place.'

The sunlight showed up the lines around Maud's mouth. 'Sidney hasn't seen them?'

'He has skimmed through a few. He knows their style.' She sensed a need to defend herself. 'He had no objection to our corresponding.'

Maud sat back from the box and the silence hung

between them. 'So many letters, I had no idea. I hope there's nothing that could be... misinterpreted?' Maud had seen nothing at Cockfield, but something was making her pause and think back to the laughter in the shrubbery, the imaginary wood-finch.

'I suppose that's my worry. Anything can be misinterpreted, don't you think? But we were all close, the three of us. Sidney will recognise Louis's rhetoric for what it is.'

She put the letter back in the box, still unread, and thought of the first trespass of Sidney's fingers into her treasure trove. She told herself she had never fallen in love with Louis, but here was the clearest sign he had fallen in love with her.

36.

In the early evening, with Maud looking on, Frances sifted and sorted Louis's letters yet again. It was so much harder than she had expected. A single page could contain lyrical descriptions, scenes from his everyday life, then memories of times they'd spent together, all sprinkled with his usual endearments, my dear, my dearest, Madonna. Louis called those the happiest days of his life. She was proud of that and who could possibly take offence?

On Saturday, the very worst day for Maud to decide she needed some shopping, the two of them walked through the jostling streets and Frances reminded herself that if, or when, her letters were published, anyone in these milling crowds would be able to read what Louis had written to her, day by day, sometimes hour by hour. Her friends too: Maud, Henry James, Suka, college colleagues. All of them would be party to Louis's fine flourishes, the words he wrote for her.

'Frances, where are you going?'

Maud had stopped in front of Liberty's and Frances, daydreaming, was walking on unawares. She must attend to the present. When the letters were published, she would be Sidney's wife. Sidney was Louis's mentor, she his muse, no more than that. The history was clear. She'd had a note from Sidney asking if the letters were ready. She would like this matter settled before it wore her out.

'Couldn't you just give all of them to Sidney?' Maud asked in the evening, her eyes on Frances as she dithered over her bundles.

'I could. But he has far too much to do.'

Sidney had hinted he didn't want them all. This was a collusion between them, not to delve too deeply into the past.

It was after ten when Frances gave up. Letters over which she had no qualms stood at one end of her box, tied with an old blue ribbon. The others, an almost equal number, swam freely in the space that was left.

In the morning, after breakfast, Maud stood in the hall with her overnight bag. She was going to Suffolk for a few days before returning to London. 'I meant to ask,' she said, 'did you finish sorting your letters?'

Frances could look at the letters forever and still not be finished. 'Almost.'

They embraced. 'Enjoy your trip,' Frances said.

'I'll be back soon,' Maud replied, 'Take care of yourself. Take care of Sidney.'

This is exactly what Frances was trying to do.

When Maud had left, she thought of Georgie Burne-Jones, still a dear friend. Despite the many ups and downs in her marriage, *alarms and excursions* as Sidney called them, Georgie and Edward were together and always would be. Frances should be less anxious about Sidney's loyalty. But looking out on Marylebone Road she considered if Sidney's equanimity was an illusion that might shatter at any moment.

From the time of Louis's departure, she had maintained a friendship with Henry James who was currently downcast over a play which had been very poorly received. He might well need a listening ear, just as she did.

He replied to her note promptly. Tuesday morning would be an excellent time for him to call. In preparation she asked Maddie to bake shortbread and watched her measure the butter and flour. 'I should have learned to bake,' she said. 'It looks so satisfying.'

Maddie was now in her forties. 'Never too late to learn, Ma'am. Shortbread biscuits need only some patience and the right heat.'

She showed Frances how to knead the dough and sprinkle it with flour to stop it catching. Frances laid each biscuit on the tray and Maddie slid them into the oven.

'Thank you, Maddie. Next time I'll do it myself,' Frances said. This, she thought, would be out of the question when she married Sidney. Both he and the servants would be up in arms. Still, it did no harm to learn.

As Henry entered her sitting room, she remembered how much space the man took up amongst her dainty furniture. He had a high forehead and a good straight nose, the square jaw made squarer by the beard. His bulk could be reassuring or unsettling, depending on his mood which today hung in the balance as they greeted each other for the first time in months.

'Such a pretty sitting room,' he said. 'I've always admired it.'

She was pleased that at the last minute she had placed fresh flowers in a tall vase, and that Henry had improved enough in spirits to notice.

He was waiting for her to tell him why she'd summoned him. She invited him to sit and found herself comparing him to other recent visitors. He was more at ease than Swift, than Sidney, than Maud even.

'Tell me,' she asked him, 'how are you feeling in yourself?

We've all been worried about you. It has been such a difficult time.'

When he said he would never write drama again, she mollified him as best she could on the success of his novels.

'My dear Mrs Sitwell, if only everyone felt like you.'

'You can never please everyone, but you have a faithful following. I'm certainly not the only one to like *Washington Square*.'

It was her attempt at a joke. The book he liked least was his most popular so far. The hooded eyes were enlivened by laughter even if it was tinged with bitterness.

'That's better,' she told him.

'Dear lady, everyone and everything improves with your company. But something is troubling you, I think?'

'We've all been out of sorts with Louis's death.'

Henry heaved a great sigh. 'Dear Louis. We won't see his like again. I saw Colvin and Gosse weeping on each other's shoulders not so long ago.'

This was no more than Sidney told her, that he and Gosse had comforted one another. It was only Henry's choice of words that summoned up a different picture, Matthew Swift with his arms around her fiancé, their tears mingling. She chased it from her mind. She had asked Henry for a reason.

'You know I introduced Louis to Sidney? We began as a company of three. We were, both of us, Louis's critics and mentors. I was planning a writing career too.'

'And you have one! I read your piece on Blake and commended it to all and sundry.'

'At one time I had aspirations to do more, poetry, fiction even.'

Henry's look was appraising, 'Your efforts were lost in

the shadow of the great man.' He folded his hands. 'You want to re-establish yourself?'

The prospect of marriage had brought to mind her ambitions. To be part of Sidney's empire, his work, his house might not be enough, but her thoughts were vague and ill-formed. She hoped Henry might help solidify them. 'I will soon be Mrs Colvin. I think I may be reluctant to let go of Mrs Sitwell and what she might do or have done.'

He shifted in his chair. 'You and Colvin are to be married?' His surprise was obvious but he replaced it with a smile. 'Please accept my heart-felt congratulations.'

'My late husband's death has given me legal emancipation, but Sidney is not a man of means. No date has been set.'

Henry inclined his head. 'A very convenient union. And highly successful for all concerned I have no doubt.'

A convenient union is what the world would see, but it's not what she envisaged. Convenient to whom?

'I have a desire to preserve some independence, a life beyond what Sidney and I can accomplish together. Do you think that would be possible, to write more for myself, to be published?'

If she expected encouragement, she has misjudged the moment.

'I wish I could help,' Henry said, 'but a failed writer will be of little use to you. You must look for someone more attuned to what modern readers expect.'

She wished she could shake him out of his self-pity.

'And won't marriage enhance anything you do?' he goes on, 'You'll have a wider sphere of influence, surely.'

Or would she simply be subsumed? Not if she had true talent, like Georgie Burne-Jones or Nellie Gosse. The failing was in her.

Since Henry was disinclined to help she let him off the hook. 'Sidney will say the moment has passed and he's probably right. I'll be too busy at the museum to give my writing a moment's thought.'

'You and Colvin are very different and that is your strength. You will be more than the sum of your parts. As for writing, you must follow your instincts. I can't imagine he will stand in your way.'

Henry picked up a piece of shortbread, 'To be honest, I always thought of Colvin as rather like myself. He loves his club, his boyish trysts with Gosse and the others and your gracious presence when required. I thought he might not be the marrying kind.'

This time the disquiet had no real form, but it nudged at her, asking for attention. Henry crunched the biscuit and brushed crumbs from his waistcoat, fastidious as ever. He looked up with a smile. 'Of course, you will have changed all that. As I say, you two are quite a force to be reckoned with.'

All that, all what? An aversion to marriage? Sidney had never given any indication of such a thing.

When Henry left, she noted the crumbs on her carpet and sighed at the general ineptitude of men. She must face reality. Marriage was a matter of practicality; a shared home, a shared income, the status of *being a wife*. As Mrs Colvin (if only this didn't summon up the picture of her future mother-in-law) she would no longer work at the college. She would be free, with a new name and in a grander house, to pursue whatever writing took her fancy. While all this was still months away, she might write a few more essays, show them to Henry or to Edmund Gosse. Sidney was not the only editor in town.

37.

In the evening, she had a few hours' teaching and took an omnibus to college. From every news-stand the name of Oscar Wilde jumped out at her. She understood Sidney's antipathy to the man. Wilde despised the style of scholarship Sidney had learned principally from Ruskin. She grimaced to the window. If Ruskin and Wilde were anything to go by, the world of literature was peopled by some odd and unstable characters.

After her class, in the college office, she opened the accounts ledger, a habit from her days as superintendent. In the room next door, the secretary was struggling to master the recently installed typewriter. The stuttering of the keys and muttered imprecations made it difficult to concentrate. Frances's mind drifted back to Ruskin and Wilde. Artists and writers were allowed to be 'difficult' or outlandish and seemed to thrive on the attention it brought. Louis, even, stood out in his velveteen jacket and bohemian cloak. Sidney, thank goodness, was no attention-seeker, an editor and writer of a very different hue. Steady and unassuming, he'd completed a solid and well-regarded biography of Keats.

Not the marrying kind. Sidney had remained unmarried through circumstances. As for him and Gosse, didn't they say people were *united in grief?* A memory floated just out of reach. At the theatre, Edmund had come close to defending Oscar Wilde, despite those green carnations. Had Gosse ever been implicated in the accusations flying around London? Frances remembered how Fanny wrote years ago from Braemar that Edmund was going to meet a lover. At the time, Frances imagined a woman, but maybe not. *Inversion* was a word she recoiled from, but really, what business was it of hers? She knew what Fanny did say, that Edmund *adored* Louis, as did Sidney of course. What did she mean by *adored*?

The typewriter next door was giving her a headache. The room was stuffy and the horrible heat which, like her monthly bleeding, she hoped was behind her, rose through her body. She felt her face flush. Her neck chafed against her ruffled collar and perspiration was collecting between her breasts and under her arms.

In the scullery used by college staff, the heat departed as quickly as it came and she opened a window to keep it at bay. She abhorred pointless speculation but certain *what ifs* were becoming difficult to avoid. Sidney's tastes and abilities were shaped in lecture hall and common room. From there he graduated, like most of his friends, from college to club. Those invitations to house parties or visits to friends abroad were welcome alternatives to his string of London lodgings or the cold welcome of his mother's house. She didn't begrudge him his friends. She didn't dwell on the strength or nature of those friendships. That they were exclusively with men was hardly surprising.

The heat in her body was overlaid by a chill. She leaned against the window sill. Sidney and Edmund had been seen in each other's arms; simple affection, shared sadness. On the day of Louis's death, Sidney pushed Matthew Swift away, didn't he? She examined her recollections. No, she was the one who had ripped them apart.

On her way back down the short corridor to the office, she touched the wall for support, then lowered herself into a chair. Shivering gave way to mild nausea: a fainting fit was the last thing she needed. She blessed her colleague, Irene, for having left a bottle of sal volatile in the desk drawer.

Rather than take another grimy omnibus home, she walked to the Metropolitan line and felt the street firm beneath her feet, then on the rocking train the nausea returned. The dark windows cast back her pale reflection and behind, a blur of faces and conversations. Events from the past she had taken for granted were rearranging themselves into unsettling patterns.

She saw Sidney openly reviling Wilde, but did he protest too much? Was he battling some inner attraction? Then there was Davos. He'd come back energised, he said so himself, by the intellectual cut and thrust. When she asked him who had provided such stimulation, other than Louis, he had said Gosse, of course, and also John Addington Symonds, the academic, leaving unsaid that Symonds was a known uranist.

That night she slept, but had troubled dreams from which she woke sweating and shivering, trying to banish from her mind the pictures of men with other men, aware that amongst them, although she couldn't see his face, was the one she planned to marry. There was a bible by her bed but she wouldn't open it. She knew the judgement it would give.

Next day, she was relieved to be awake. It had only been a dream and she embraced the sounds of morning: the trundle of carriages out on the square, the shouts of early-morning hawkers and the distant rumble of the Northern

Line. She took breakfast, appreciating the familiarity of the small table with its embroidered cloth, Maddie's silent passage to and from the room. All was as it should be. She would speak to Sidney and put these wild imaginings behind her. She needed reassurance, that was all, and she wanted it resolved before she entrusted him with any of her letters.

In the meantime, she invited her sister to lunch. Frances was usually scornful of Suka's interest in gossip. Perhaps for once it would be useful.

Suka peered into her face. 'My dear, you don't look well.'

'I had a bad night. I just need some company.'

Suka sat down and kicked out her ankles. 'What happened to Louis's letters? I hope you're handing them over. People should know about you and him.'

Things felt so much less crucial over a plate of baked ham and chutney. Her time with Louis, so long ago, was a distant melody. By contrast, the threatening discord of Sidney's male friendships set her teeth on edge. 'Yes, I'll be handing them over, or some of them. Sidney's impatient to have them. I just need to talk to him first.'

'About a wedding date, I hope?'

Frances shrugged. Marriage had lost its relish. 'I'm used to my independence.'

Suka rolled her eyes. 'Please don't say you're staying single. I didn't have you down as one of those ghastly reforming types.'

Frances was going to object to the juxtaposition of *ghastly* and *reforming* then shook her head to dismiss the subject.

As Maddie cleared away the plates, Frances said, 'Henry said something the other day, that Sidney *is not the marrying kind*. Is that what you think?'

Suka threw back her head. 'Sidney is very much the marrying kind!' She leaned forward, as if someone might be eavesdropping. 'Unlike Henry, of course.'

Frances stayed silent, but if Henry had such predilections, it might taint his view of others.

Suka straightened. 'But we needn't worry about Sidney. He's much too dull.'

The 'dull' caught Frances off-balance, although it was, she supposed, a vote of confidence.

Suka continued with a sigh. 'So many rumours these days.' Rumours had clearly taken on a subtle change in meaning. 'Some justified of course.'

'You mean Wilde.'

Another roll of the eyes. 'He is well beyond rumours. Have you seen the latest?' Suka shuddered. 'But he is only saying what others keep private.' She reeled off several names which meant little to Frances until she came to the end, '... dear Gosse, of course.'

The name made a small explosion in Frances's head. 'But Edmund is happily married,' Frances said, knowing full well how little that might mean.

Suka raised her hands in a gesture of hopelessness. 'Oh, please! Don't be so naïve. For these inverts, marriage is *de rigueur.*'

Rumours had become inverts. Frances felt the pull of the dream she had recently escaped, of men, together, naked. She swallowed her distaste but Suka was unstoppable.

'You know Thornycroft, the sculptor? Gosse had a hopeless crush on him for years. They used to go cavorting around France together every summer.'

France and perhaps Inverness too? It hardly mattered. Frances's suspicions were correct. As to the cavorting, it was not in Sidney's nature to *cavort* but that didn't mean he never shared the pleasure men found in each other. As she felt the heat on her neck she struggled not to follow that train of thought.

With a shake of her napkin, Suka rose to go. 'I know Sidney and Edmund are two peas in a pod but don't worry. If Gosse ever had designs on anyone else, I'm sure it would have been Louis.'

Suka left, oblivious to the effect of her chance remarks. Frances remembered how Andrew Lang, the Oxford aesthete, had said Louis *possessed more than anyone else the power of making men fall in love with him.* Mentally she had agreed, assuming 'men' to mean mankind, people in general, or was he speaking more exclusively?

At least Suka, always inclined to think the worst of people, didn't brand 'dull' Sidney with any of those dreadful labels. It made no difference, though, a serpent's tail had coiled around Frances's heart, thinking of Gosse and Sidney in each other's arms. Both of them had loved Louis, had they desired him? Desired each other?

When Suka left, Frances's shock was gradually erased by sadness. She'd thought Sidney's old reluctance to indulge in intimacy was simple shyness. Since they'd been lovers, her pleasure, he said, was his happiness and she had accepted that and welcomed it. Then there was that sigh as he turned away to expend himself, a muted kind of ecstasy. Perhaps he had always wanted something, someone, else.

In the evening, she sat with the box of Louis's letters, still in two piles. She had spent so long deciding which letters to hold back and which to let go so that her privacy would be protected and to save Sidney from any possible hurt.

She poked the unyielding wood with her toe. Louis's words, the voice of a writer in the making, hers and Sidney's dearest friend, couldn't be tarnished by the insidious voices in her head. As for Sidney, the creeping shadow of doubt was draining her of energy. Did he have a secret cache of letters from Gosse, or a set of stanzas penned by Matthew Swift? If they came to light, would he protect her feelings as she had his? Perhaps it was time to let him know how much Louis loved her. She undid the ribbon that kept the piles separate, closed the lid of the box and secured it with a strap. In the morning, she wished to see it no longer. She had it sent to the Keeper's House before she could change her mind.

38.

Her box had gone and with it a lifetime of comfort and reassurance. The space it left was like a hole in her heart. This had been a terrible mistake. She had spent a long time selecting the least contentious letters then, in a moment of petulance, had let them loose, all of them, regardless of the consequences. It would have been better to have kept them all, to have told Sidney they were not his to read or publish than to have him face the most passionate of Louis's efforts. Sidney's love for her was not the whole truth but it was genuine. She accepted it, she always had. When she accustomed herself to the idea of Sidney's feelings for men, they could be put away again, out of sight and out of mind. Sidney loved her and would continue to do so. She would love him back.. Nothing had really changed.

She took a breath. Sidney probably hadn't even looked at the box since it was delivered. She could call on him and ask for it back. It was more difficult to decide whether she should mention her new understanding of him. He loved her and she believed in his love. She must ignore the thought of his indulging himself elsewhere.

By the time she arrived at the museum, her stomach was cramping. She put it down to the sudden and unbearable uncertainty of everything. Mind and body could not be entirely separate. Humphries answered as usual. Sidney, he said, was elsewhere but would be back shortly. He ushered her into the sitting-room and offered to bring tea but she declined and picked up the day's paper, glanced through it, laid it down and went to the window, expecting to see Sidney on his way back from his office.

She watched the people come and go, imagining their business, their lives. How often Sidney had stood here waiting for her, the regular visitor, but always a visitor. He wanted her here permanently, the lady of the house. With Sidney, respectability was all.

She was tempted to have tea after all, but she didn't want the palaver of cups and saucers to divert her from what she felt she must say, except she wasn't sure what that was. Did she want the truth, or just a version of events that would suffice, that would paper over the cracks?

Humphries hadn't mentioned the box of letters. She crossed into the study, feeling a little awkward at being alone there. *Lady of the house*, she reminded herself, and ran her finger along the tops of the books on one shelf to meet a fine layer of dust. Neither Humphries nor the housekeeper were allowed in here. Some things would have to change.

Still no sign of the box. She walked round Sidney's desk and sat in his chair. This was his view of the world, with the globe on his right, the revolving case of reference books to the left. The top of the desk was tooled leather, worn to a patina. Since she was last here, he had done some tidying. Baxter's Samoa papers were nowhere to be seen, sorted and filed no doubt. As she swung her feet, her shoe made heavy contact with solid wood; her rosewood box was under the desk. Despite the pain in her foot, its presence was reassuring.

Why was Sidney so late? His absence, on the other hand, could be a sign, a chance to complete her unfinished task. She dragged the box out to the side of the chair and lifted the lid, preparing to divide the letters once again.

She drew back. She was too late. The letters had been tampered with, taken from their envelopes, in some cases not put back, or inserted badly folded. She clicked her tongue. The sheets kept carefully for so many years would be damaged. She picked up the letters Sidney had disturbed to refold and tidy them. His study was not the place of safety she had imagined.

'Frances,' Sidney stood at the half-open door, watching her opening the box. 'What on earth…?'

She flushed at being discovered, even if she had every right to look into her own belongings. 'I'm sorry.' Should she be sorry? 'There was a mix-up. I didn't mean to send you all of them.'

'I daresay that's true.'

His tone was even but she heard an underlying brittleness, like porcelain with a hairline crack. The letters she had removed were sliding treacherously from her hands.

'Leave those now, please.' Sidney, the editor, the careful curator, was using his famous authority, but the voice couldn't sustain itself, and broke.

She glanced downwards and froze. The loose sheets on her lap, the lines containing Louis's dancing thoughts bore the heavy indentation of a blue pencil, words were underlined, sentences bracketed, several lines struck out completely.

It was inconceivable. She fumbled through the other sheets, finding everyone the same, gouged by Sidney's warped critique. She picked up another of the letters still in its envelope and slid the paper out, eager to know something had survived Sidney's butchery. A single line was drawn crosswise over the first sheet and at the top in block capitals the single word *NO*. She let the sheets fall from her lap to the floor. Louis's letters, her letters, were damaged beyond repair.

The clink of a tea-tray arrived from the other room and Humphries' voice, 'Mr Colvin?' Sidney went out, no doubt to send him away. Tea was the least of their concerns.

Time had come to a halt. The letters lay in a jumble on the floor. As she bent to retrieve them and smooth the crumpled sheets, she began to see a pattern to Sidney's revisions. Louis's descriptions of journeys, places and events were intact, his reflections on life and literature untouched. Any word of endearment to Frances, any mark of affection, had been struck out. She had been excised from the letters which belonged to her, hers and Louis's affection obliterated.

Sidney came back, peering around the door, diffident, hopeful nothing had gone too badly amiss. She was too angry to be gracious and saw his diffidence dissolve, replaced by petulance, as if his actions with her letters were entirely justified. After all, he had seen what he had never wished to see, Louis's youthful and ill-considered passion for her, the woman Sidney worshipped.

She tried to be lenient. Her breathing was easier but her voice was tight in her chest. 'My letters, Sidney. They are *spoiled*.'

He was caught off-guard, as if this was a small issue. 'I'm sorry. I can erase the marks, I think. I should have transcribed them first, but...'

'No, that's not what I mean. Everything is spoiled. Can't you see? I trusted you with these.'

He drew up an upright chair and sat down facing her. 'Judging from what I've read, you breached my trust long ago.'

Sidney thought she was guilty. She was hurt beyond measure. His redactions were aimed not at concealing Louis's passion but at covering up her wrong-doing, And yet anything she had felt for Louis was nothing compared to the years she had been faithful to *him*.

Something in his presence recalled the fear instilled by Albert. She tried not to recoil from him. 'I did not betray you. You just can't deal with it, with seeing how Louis loved me.'

He was bristling. 'I don't think that's quite true. I understood there was some... tenderness between you. But these,' he waved a hand at the letters, 'So many, so much...'

His fingers pressed the area between his eyebrows.

'So much what, Sidney?' If he wanted her to deny it, he must spell it out. Louis was never coarse, never referred directly to their moments of unconsummated desire.

Sidney reached into the box. 'Let's see, shall we?'

He extracted two letters, replaced them, then came to one that suited his purpose. As he read the lines, his throat worked. 'Look, here he talks of ardour. He wants to put his arms around your neck, and then sit down with his head on your knees!' He waved the sheet at her in accusation.

She took the letter from him. 'Don't stop there, Sidney. Read what comes next. He'll put his head on my knees and *have a long talk.*' It didn't matter how loudly she shouted, it was useless. Sidney was too prudish, or too corrupted by his own feelings, to take a more innocent view.

'And was it only Louis? Those tea parties you give to your poets, are they as innocent as I thought?'

She was flailing under his accusations when she had come here to ask questions of her own. 'There was no *carrying on*. With Louis or anyone else!'

He shook his head and reached into the box of letters, picking out phrases in order to misconstrue them. At the time she'd treasured them. She treasured them still but Sidney was using them as weapons against her. 'What about, *"Hold me to your breast"*! *"Christmas kiss"*?'

She stood her ground. 'Don't you know your Donne, Sidney? Kisses are letters.'

He ignored her sarcasm. 'I knew he desired you,' he said. 'I trusted you to be faithful to me.'

Louis's verbal ardour was as hard to resist as the man himself. She'd advised, remonstrated, asked him to be less florid, all the while bathing in his adoration, telling herself it was only words. But Sidney had no right to taunt her. '*You* said I should encourage him to write.' She could be caustic too. 'You will have to trust me, *as you always have done until now.*'

Sidney sighed, as if she was making everything too hard for him. The air was heavy with rancour. Frances's mouth was dry. She swallowed and took a breath, searching for some of their old affection 'My dear,' could they be dear to each other after this? 'I was faithful to you. You know when he threw himself at me, I rejected his advances. You agreed he should still write to me. These are the result. Can't you see the beauty in them?'

'I see he called you his *Madonna*, his mother, goodness knows what else. If these come to light, how will they make me look? We are very nearly married.'

She swallowed her exasperation. 'But we were not married then.'

His face worked in irritation. 'But you were married to Sitwell.'

This was too much. 'You wanted me to be faithful to an oaf?' She stepped out from behind the desk. 'I think I had better go.'

Sidney, still in the chair, was blocking her way. The stomach cramps were worsening and she needed to sit down but she would not give him the satisfaction. 'Excuse me, please.'

He stood up and gripped her arm to stop her. 'Frances…' His fingers were in her flesh. The violence made them both jump back. He had never laid a hand on her except in affection. She rubbed her arm, speechless.

He was undone by contrition. He rubbed his face. 'I'm sorry, I'm so sorry.'

She barged past him. 'It's too late for *sorry*.'

'Frances, *don't leave*.'

She was at the door. 'What else do you expect? I'm not staying for you to treat me as Albert did.'

'I would never…'

He had hurt her and she needed to hurt him back. 'As for Louis, you're right. He was a joy. I loved him with all my heart.' She searched for the final barb. 'More than I ever loved you.'

Sidney blanched. She had the power to wound him and had used it. She closed her eyes and when she opened them Sidney was dumb, not angry that she could see, but simply dumb. And in a bolt of blinding clarity, she knew why. He had known all along she loved Louis, because Sidney had loved him too. No, not Gosse or Symonds or Andrew Lang but Robert Louis Stevenson.

The knot in her abdomen unwound and warmth trickled between her legs. She fled the room. Perish the thought her woman's blood should leave its mark on the museum's polished floor.

39.

Sidney did not follow her and in the cramped closet she managed to tuck a handkerchief in her drawers despite her trembling hands. If she sat very still in the carriage, it might be enough to save her from the ultimate embarrassment.

Deposited close to her house, she mounted the steps, clutching her skirt. She wanted to reclaim the anger she had felt at Sidney for defiling her letters. Instead, she was reduced to helplessness. In the hall she let out a howl. Let the blood go where it would. There was no one to see or hear except Maddie, and she would bring towels and tea and provide a supporting arm.

'Frances! Whatever is the matter!'

It was Maud who caught her as she fell.

On her bed, a cover drawn up to her chin, Frances retched into a bowl placed by her head. Maud held the salts close to her face. 'There, there,' she said. 'There, there.'

The curtain was drawn and so Frances was uncertain of the time. She was wearing her nightdress. The thought of Maud undressing her and dealing with her undergarments... 'I'm so sorry. My dress. Is it...?'

'The stain is quite small and will come out in cold water. I gave it to Maddie to soak.'

'Thank you.'

Maud was just back from Suffolk. She bore the smell of the countryside, of freshly laundered cotton and of apples wrapped and laid in rows on the pantry shelf. She stroked Frances's hair and said nothing.

Later Frances gathered her strength, drew her silk kimono around her and sat with Maud by the fire. It had barely caught and the coals spat as they resisted the flame.

'Would our lives be easier without men, do you think?' Frances said.

'You're asking the wrong woman. I was very happy with Churchill. And hope to be again.'

Frances gave her a searching look.

'I told you about James, remember?' Maud said.

Frances recalled her mentioning a retired sea captain, a family friend. He had a large house and enjoyed Maud's company.

'You'll marry?'

'I hope so. He's very agreeable, and entertaining.'

She felt a pang of envy at Maud's good fortune. What stories might her husband have to tell? Had he been to the Pacific? Frances stopped herself. She must think of Maud and her happiness. 'Is he handsome?'

Maud allowed herself a roll of the eyes. 'Frances! He is in his sixties. His face is,' she stopped to think, 'weatherbeaten, with a friendly charm.'

They smiled at each other, falling back to their usual understanding. Maud deserved some explanation for Frances's distress, her flight from the museum, the argument with Sidney.

'I seem to have made everything worse. You know I was going to hold back some of Louis's letters to spare Sidney's feelings? Then in a moment of madness I sent them over wholesale.'

'And Sidney reacted as you feared?'

'Worse than that. He's written all over them, defaced them. I mean how could he?'

Maud looked at her narrowly. 'I suppose he drew the obvious conclusion. Letters are harmless enough, of course, if that's as far as it went.'

A shadow of doubt crept across the hearth-rug. During all this time Maud had suspected her. 'You think Louis and I were lovers?'

'I'm sorry, my dear, I never mentioned it because things seemed to settle down, but I worried what was going on that summer, those seductive looks of yours, the long walks, Louis's feverish gaiety. Even Sidney must have sensed the atmosphere, if not passion exactly, pent-up feelings at the very least.'

A coal burst loudly in the grate, nudging Frances to confession. 'All right. There were times he pressed himself on me.' A lift of the eyebrows from Maud. 'We understood each other in a very sudden and involved way. But I did resist.'

'And that led to all of those other letters.'

'Sidney encouraged me to write to him. Now he thinks I was betraying him. He will have to trust me.' She heard the petulance in her voice. She and Sidney were behaving like children. 'What can I do?' The question was to herself.

Maud answered. 'I'm very fond of Sidney. I hope you can make peace. I'm sure you can if you really want to.'

Maud was suggesting she should throw herself on Sidney's mercy, ask for forgiveness when she was guilty only of writing too often and too long. She shivered despite the fire. 'He will never publish the letters.'

'You'll have to decide how much that matters.'

The subject was closed. Maud would go back to

Portsmouth and marry her captain. Frances would miss her steady presence and her advice.

'Thank you for taking care of me,' she said, then to divert the conversation she told her about Henry James's visit, his continuing despondency and self-absorption.

'These literary types,' Maud said, 'I sometimes wonder how you put up with them.'

'This Wilde affair is unsettling. And according to Suka, Edmund Gosse has men friends, I mean he's an invert.'

The word was like a lazy wasp trapped inside the window glass. Maud frowned, no doubt wishing to coax it out before any damage was done. 'Please, must we...?'

'I'm sorry. I find it quite upsetting. He and Sidney are very close.'

Maud was guarded. 'What a strange thing to say. These things don't rub off, do they?' Her mouth pursed in distaste. 'You don't think Sidney is *unnatural*?'

Her face must have given her away.

'Frances, this is ridiculous. Sidney is devoted to you. Your mind is all over the place. You need to pull yourself together.'

Maud was too wholesome, too innately innocent.

'Of course. You're right. I just know how fond he is of Edmund, and both of them worshipped Louis.'

Another mistake. She hadn't meant to implicate Louis but Maud was quick to take offence. Maud, who had been her buttress and her bulwark, got up to leave.

'Please don't go!' Frances was pleading. 'I'm sorry I offended you. I'm just trying to explain how oddly Sidney has been behaving. He's in a lather over the Wilde affair. It's as if he feels threatened. And he was obsessed with Louis.'

Maud was still standing. In her soft grey eyes, Frances

saw shards of Suffolk flint. 'Obsessed? Just remind me where all of this started? With you and Louis I seem to recall. Sometimes I think you are too persuaded of your own virtue, Frances. I heard your laughter in shady corners. I caught him scribbling like a madman. He said he was writing to "Claire" but I knew who it was, then I looked at you and I didn't see a woman holding herself back.'

Frances blinked. Claire was a fiction, the rest couldn't be disputed. 'His imagination always outstripped reality. After that summer I was careful not to encourage him.'

Maud sat down. The sun had left the room and with it the flickering distraction of claim and counterclaim. If only she and Maud could start with a clean sheet, but no one was a bare palimpsest. Everyone carried their past lives just as she did when she went to Cockfield, looking for a safe haven, skidding onto the treacherous slope of Louis Stevenson's charm.

The fire had settled to an intermittent fizz and crackle. Maud spoke quietly, to herself as much as to Frances, as if she were regretting her self-righteousness. 'I suppose Louis was too young to understand the state you were in. And Sidney was either absent or oblivious.'

Frances accepted what seemed to be forgiveness. Maud's friendship meant too much to argue over what exactly she had or hadn't done with Louis.

When Maud had left, Frances went to her bedroom and sat on the bed. The smelling salts were on the nightstand. She wished for a moment she had some physic that would do the opposite of reviving her senses, something to allow her a few hours of oblivion rather than face up to the horrible fracas she seemed to have caused amongst those who were dearest to her.

She swung her feet up on the cover and lay on her back

examining the ceiling, contemplating a life without Sidney, whose love would be forever compromised, and Maud who still thought she was guilty. But then perhaps she was, since at Cockfield she had wanted everything Louis had offered.

That night, she dreamed she was in bed with Sidney. Louis looked on from the doorway, wide-eyed, turning in that languid pose, the cigarette trailing from his fingers. The triangle of love she had thought so perfect had come back to haunt her.

40.

Next day, from the window overlooking the back courtyard, she saw Maddie's freshly laundered pinnie hanging limply on the line, waiting for its next application of starch. Frances still felt wrung out and in need of some fresh energy to reassemble what was left of her life.

Her box of letters was back, returned by Sidney, whether in anger or sorrow she did not know. He had also sent several notes which she had not answered. Her fury at his mistreatment of the letters had subsided. With the past in shreds, she needed to set her mind to the future.

Then he was on her doorstep, his eyes cautiously penitent. She wished he hadn't come. She wasn't ready, and yet the sight of him gave her some comfort.

'I came to apologise,' he said. 'May I come in?'

In the sitting room, he said. 'You got your letters?'

The question was rhetorical. The box was in the corner of the room, neither hidden nor claiming pride of place. The letters were his apology and he wanted it acknowledged.

She nodded and they sat facing each other in the matching armchairs. He hung his head. Would he prostrate himself? She hoped not. They needed to cling on to some vestige of themselves.

When he raised his eyes, she recognised his sincerity. 'I am so sorry to have hurt you. I only wanted you not to leave. I should never ever have tried to restrain you. Please tell me there's no lasting injury.'

Instinctively she touched her arm. 'It's almost gone.' She would like the bruise not to heal, its yellow stain a reminder Sidney was not who she thought he was, the careful curator, the gallant husband to be. Under the skin were the hidden things, old hurts and festering desires.

He went on. 'I wish...I hope. Do you think we can put things right?' His discomfort was obvious in his quick look away, searching for something else to focus on, the coal dust escaping the hearth, a picture hung askew. The fading photograph of Louis still on her mantelpiece didn't help. 'Do you want to?' he added.

She had told him she loved Louis. If it was true, it was cruel to have used it against him. 'Louis and I were not lovers,' she said, 'I'm sorry if I implied otherwise, although we easily might have been.'

His eyes continued their journey around the room. 'Cockfield,' he swallowed. 'I had been of little use to you. I understand.' Was he going to forgive her for what she might have done? No, other things stuck in his craw. 'It's just those letters are hard to ignore.'

She sighed. 'Sidney, they were simply words. We each drew from them what we needed. The rest was mostly in Louis's mind. He promised to be good, remember? He mentions it more than once.'

Sidney's expression was sour. 'Yes, he promises, then in the next line contradicts himself. Did you check him? Remind him not to use these endearments? Did you use the same words back?'

Frances frowned. What she might have said was irrelevant. 'I said mostly inconsequential things, the weather, books I had read, encouragement to write.'

Sidney sighed. 'Well, perhaps we'll find out one day.'

'What do you mean?'

'I'm sure Louis kept your letters as you did his. Fanny may have them at Vailima.' He seemed to be considering this. 'Or perhaps she's disposed of them. She might not see them as significant.'

France opened her mouth to tell him why none of her letters would be at Vailima then saw this would be her final mistake. Admitting she had asked Louis to destroy them, a sensible precaution at the time, would be taken as proof that the contents were somehow incriminating.

'Who knows?' she said. 'If Fanny has them, she's most likely burned them by now.'

Sidney grunted, accepting this likelihood. 'An intriguing lacuna, then.'

Everything she'd done to protect herself and her reputation had gone against her but Sidney was pushing her when he had no right. In Paris, she had made her choice. It steadied her to think of Sidney then, his kindness and devotion when she had hoped for Louis to arrive.

She steered him back to the matter in hand. 'I can't deny that Louis and I had a close bond. He was charming, enticing, romantic, too romantic for me. Or just too young. And I was devoted to you. I told him not to expect my love, not even to ask for it.'

As the clock chimed, she thought of other days and other hours, the moment she first glimpsed Louis, the days in London when she thought she would faint with longing. Was that true love? More likely her love lay in the letters she wrote back, answering his pleas for consolation, comfort, understanding, the letters which had not survived.

'So, what will we do with his letters?' she asked, knowing the outcome.

'Well, we don't want them published,' he said, the royal *we*, or the *we* of a great publishing venture in which women did not play a part. 'Surely it's better to keep them private. As you always wanted.'

As she had once wanted, at some moments, not at others. 'But there will be a gap.'

He smiled. 'There are always gaps. It's the chance of history.'

It wasn't chance that would omit her from the record of Louis's life. It was Sidney, his cowardice and jealousy.

She got up and pulled out the baize-covered card table, a dainty thing on folding legs she suddenly wished to be sturdier. From the box of letters, she extracted an untidy pile and dealt them as if for a game of rummy.

'Now let me see. These have been kept carefully and despite some small defacements are in excellent condition. I think to hold them back would be no chance of history but an act of censorship, the choice of a steward who fails in his duty.'

Sidney was cut by the implication. 'But there are other considerations. Do you want your reputation...'

'To be maligned? That may be the case. Or I could be celebrated as the closest friend to a great writer, the woman who encouraged and guided him through a vital stage of his life.'

Sidney frowned, desperately looking for other reasons to deny her. 'What will Fanny say?'

'Sidney, these were written before Fanny and Louis met. You don't want to publish them because you cannot bear that Louis loved me.' He met her eyes and she saw his confusion at her sudden ferocity. 'Just as you loved him.'

He blinked and swallowed. His head fell to his chest. She thought he was weeping. It came to her then that they were equals in many ways. She had desired Louis Stevenson and resisted. Sidney had most likely done the same. What harm had come to anyone?

She touched his sleeve. 'Come, come. It's nothing to be ashamed of. Everyone loved him.'

She led him back to the armchair where he crumpled, his head on his hand. She sat down and let him collect himself.

'Frances, my life is nothing without you.'

She heard the humility: Colvin of the museum, previously Director of the Fitzwilliam, Stevenson's representative in London and on earth, a shy man with a surprising temper, a man with so much to offer who was always awkward around women.

She had nothing left to say. 'I think you should go. I'm very tired.'

She watched him from the window, straight-backed, a little less sure of himself than when he arrived. He had all the advantages, birth, education, a circle of famous friends, but she had brought him Louis Stevenson. While Sidney guided, directed, and applied his editor's pencil, she had tended to his inner life, free-flowing, unabridged. She tidied her letters back in the box and closed the lid. She knew the truth. Perhaps that was all that mattered.

PART SEVEN

Enlightenment

*Almost none know him; he has a husk; inside it is good
meat, but the husk is by most teeth invincible.*
RLS to Henry James of Sidney Colvin, August 1890[*]

[*] Booth, B.A. & Mehew, E. (eds.) (1994-5). The Letters of
Robert Louis Stevenson. New Haven/London: Yale University
Press. Vol.6, p.403

41.

Frances and Sidney were inhabiting an awkward truce. On the surface they accepted the apologies they had traded. It was more difficult to know how to proceed on a day-to-day basis. Frances reminded herself that she, Louis and Sidney had shared a close and nourishing friendship. They were a company of three, a tripod set on a solid base of affection and mutual respect. And then she would tell herself it had always been likely to collapse, its structure warped by secrets and misunderstandings.

Wilde lost his case and fled. She tried to draw Sidney out on the matter of Greek love, hoping it was best to have things aired, but he was sullen. There was no point of comparison between Platonic ideals and London rent boys, he said. She did not grasp where on that spectrum his feelings for Louis sat, but came to realise it was fruitless even to try. At the same time, her lack of understanding was an obstacle to simply moving on. A stalemate, perhaps, rather than a truce. When friends asked in whispered asides when the marriage would take place, it was easy to say she and Sidney were too busy to give it adequate thought.

They met, out of habit, on Sunday afternoons and talked over his various projects, principally the Edinburgh Edition and his *Letters* of which Louis's Vailima series had been published. For subsequent volumes he would write a biographical preface but the letters, arranged chronologically, were the bedrock on which it would be built. She didn't ask if she would be as much as mentioned.

Her post in college brought her less and less pleasure and so she gave it up. Surely she could eke out an existence on the family inheritance she'd received and the proceeds of her writing. If much of that had been won through Sidney's influence, she had had some book reviews accepted by two London magazines without his help. Still, she had no clear idea of where her future lay and hoped some hidden truth or a sign from the heavens would eventually arrive.

It was a year later when Sidney showed her a letter from Louis's cousin, Graham Balfour.

North Oxford,
14th June, 1897
My Dear Colvin,
I've recently returned from Samoa and would like to pass on those papers and documents which Mr Baxter was unable to bring back in the wake of Louis's death.

I will be in London for a few days next week and knowing how highly you stood in Louis's regard, I would cherish the opportunity to meet with you and Mrs Sitwell.

If you could reply by return of post that would be ideal.
Graham Balfour

You and Mrs Sitwell, it brought a flutter of regret, reminding Frances of how much closer they used to be. She was pleased Sidney invited her to the meeting. Perhaps he would have a letter from Fanny whose continued silence was troubling.

What was most striking about Graham Balfour was his complete dissimilarity to his cousin. Where Louis was willowy, Balfour was broad-shouldered with thick hair, a high forehead and strong nose. Tanned from his recent voyages, he bore all the physical hallmarks of a story-book adventurer. Sidney's narrow sitting room was charged with new energy as he shook Sidney by the hand and made a deep bow to Frances. 'Mrs Sitwell. I'm so honoured and so delighted to meet you, both of you. Louis spoke of you so much.'

She momentarily remembered Louis at Cockfield making his knightly bow.

'I know how much it meant to Louis to have you in Samoa,' Sidney said.

Frances recalled how Sidney had meant to visit. Would things have fallen out differently if he had? But then Louis might still have been alive. Everything would be different.

She arranged them around Sidney's small table and asked Balfour if he would take coffee or tea. He chose coffee with a deferential nod. Despite his physical presence, there was no hint of self-regard. If anything, he was too polite, too self-effacing. How did Sidney see him? Was he struck by his physical presence? All she saw was the polite attention he paid to all guests.

'You must have very fond memories of Vailima,' Sidney said.

Balfour relaxed into his chair and stretched his legs, transported to the place he'd recently left. Most of what he told them about Samoa they knew, but they allowed him to recount it again.

'Building Vailima took all of their energy,' Balfour concluded, 'but it repaid them with a wonderful life and a place in island society.'

She sensed Sidney muting his inclination to argue. He wouldn't go into island politics or the domestic arrangements he never saw. 'Some of his writing there was certainly of the best. Will Mrs Stevenson stay on in Samoa, do you think?'

Balfour's fingers were interlocked. 'Things are undecided. She would like to. I expect much will depend on what the others want to do, Loia, Lloyd I mean, and Teuila.' He used the native names given to Fanny's children and Frances saw Sidney bristle.

Frances leaned forward. 'How is Fanny, Mrs Stevenson? I wrote to her months ago and never received a reply. I've been concerned for her.'

Balfour's gaze didn't waver although his brown eyes darkened. Frances was reminded of a soulful St Bernard, faithful rather than heroic. 'She has been terribly busy and has struggled to cope with the number of letters to answer, as well as all of the business side.'

Frances felt herself reprimanded. 'Of course.' She couldn't argue the importance of women's friendship with this stranger.

Balfour shifted awkwardly. 'Please consider me her emissary, for the time being.'

He had a hefty suitcase which he had put on the floor and prodded, as he spoke, with the toe of his leather brogue. He'd told them of how he was happy to go barefoot in Vailima. London and the museum rooms must have felt like a constraint.

'And you, will you go back to Samoa?' Frances said.

He was bent over the case but looked up with frank

brown eyes. 'Exploring the South Seas was an absolute joy and I was lucky to have time with my cousin. I'm not sure that visit could ever be matched. Anyway, I'm to be married very soon. '

They congratulated him. Samoa without Louis, he was saying, would not be the same.

He was taking envelopes from the case. 'This is material Tamaitai thinks will be useful for the biography. I'll leave the bag with you. I can imagine how much you're collecting.' He extracted one document. 'This is a copy of Louis's letter of instruction which I believe Charles Baxter left behind.'

Instead of handing the envelope over, he laid it on top of the open case. *Read this first* was the message.

Sidney nodded. 'Baxter gave me the gist.'

Balfour was content. 'And how is your work coming on?'

Sidney said the *Letters* would be close to completion if it weren't for more turning up all the time. Balfour sat forward, shoulders hunched, more panther than faithful dog.

'And the *Life*? Have you given it much thought?'

'I thought it was to accompany the letters, as a preface?' Frances said.

Sidney flashed her a smile. 'It's quite usual to write a preface last. The principle turning points are in my mind: the problems of his health, the complications of his many journeys.'

Balfour was embarrassed. Frances glimpsed the edge of an argument.

'Yes, of course,' Balfour said, 'but although Louis proposed only a short account of his life, Mrs Stevenson does not regard this as satisfactory. I'm sure you agree with her that a full biography is required.'

Sidney frowned and folded his hands in front of him. 'But Louis was quite clear. The letters are to be the main thing.' He bent and took out the envelope Balfour had left on top of the case. 'Shall we check the instructions?'

'No, really, I understand what Louis proposed and what you had in mind.'

'But his widow is overriding him.'

'With her husband gone, she takes a different point of view. She wants the biography to be a priority.'

This could be why Fanny hadn't replied. She preferred not to accede to Frances's request to delay the writing of the *Life*. Now Fanny was speaking through Balfour. However uncomfortable her emissary felt, he would do his duty.

Sidney understood this. 'My preface to the letters will include a summary of his life, elegant I hope, as spare as Louis would have wanted. It will give me great pleasure to work up a full biography when other things have been dealt with.'

Balfour cleared his throat. 'We do realise how busy you are. If you feel the burden is too great, Mrs Stevenson wants you to know that another biographer could be found.'

Balfour, to give him his due, did not meet Sidney's eye. Sidney was too shocked to formulate a response.

Frances stepped in. 'But Sidney knew Louis for nearly all of his life. He was party to everything. Who else could possibly do the job?'

Balfour's bowed head admitted all of this, but he had his instructions. 'Mrs Stevenson is particularly keen for Louis's time in the Pacific to be given the importance it deserves.'

Sidney's opposition to Louis's departure, his failure to

go there himself, had finally counted against him. He was insulted, and rightly. 'I can give a very good account of the Vailima years. I have all of Louis's letters and can consult with his other correspondents, his visitors, *yourself*.'

Balfour accepted this with a nod. His hands were tied.

'Perhaps,' Frances says, 'I could write to Mrs Stevenson and assure her the work is in hand?'

In hand was an obfuscation, but one that might suffice.

Sidney was first to speak. 'That's a useful suggestion, my dear. Especially as you and she have always been good friends.'

Balfour was appeased. 'Thank you, Mrs Sitwell. There's no need for a letter. I'll tell her that exactly, that the work is in hand. I'm sure she will accept your assurance.'

'Oh,' he returned to the bag of papers and retrieved a package tied with hemp-like string, 'Just one more thing. These are letters which should have gone to the post the week of Louis's death and have recently emerged. You can imagine there was some confusion. I'm sorry they were delayed. Could you distribute them to the recipients?'

Balfour gathered his things and took his leave, thanking them for their hospitality, assuring them he would make clear to Fanny that Sidney was engaged in a biography.

When he had gone, Frances watched as Sidney flicked through the old letters, murmuring the names of the recipients, sighing over the circumstances. She imagined people receiving them so long after Louis's death. A little macabre, perhaps, but those people were lucky. There was nothing for her, but why would there be? Fanny was keeping her distance. Louis would write no more.

42.

1897

Vailima! How Fanny had loved the house they made, the people who visited, her family around her, but how she had come to hate the constant battle to tame the land and make it profitable. Without Louis, she did not have the heart to scrape at the earth and nor, it seemed, did the others.

Margaret Stevenson, Louis's mother and their beloved Aunt Maggie, who had always resisted old age, returned to Scotland. Lloyd and the others came and went as they pleased. Everyone expected that *she* would stay forever under the mountain where Louis lay, but it was a mountain she could not climb. She increasingly wished to be where the humidity didn't make her catch her breath, a reminder of her own mortality.

Out of necessity, she corresponded with Colvin over the *Letters*, the *Life* and the residue of Louis's work. She included Frances in her greetings but did not write directly to her. The gap between them had stretched. Everything was business, business; her requests to Colvin, his evasive replies. Friendship was pushed out and she lacked energy to reconstruct it. At the back of her mind was the letter from Louis to Frances she had never sent; the longer she defaulted on that duty, the harder it became to explain. She had it still, unread, a mysterious coda she preferred not to think about.

When the doctors recommended a change of air, she grasped the opportunity with both hands and moved with Lloyd to San Francisco. It was there that Lloyd met and married Katharine, and where, three years after Louis's death, they heard that Margaret Stevenson had gone to meet her maker. Fanny hoped she was reunited with her husband and her son. She, of course, must drag herself across the ocean, pay her respects and attend to the winding up of the estate which should have gone to Louis but now fell to her and her family.

She endured most of the voyage lying in her cabin, suffering the old nausea. Her sea-sickness was an excuse at least to avoid the surprising gaiety of Lloyd and his wife. He was returning to places of his youth, his wife keen to see Louis's home town and everything of the step-father revered by Lloyd.

On their last night on board, Fanny joined them for a light supper.

'Colvin is mighty slow with his biography,' Lloyd said. 'We need to gee him up. When will we start out for London? We should let him know.'

Having crossed the Atlantic, of course they should call on other friends and family. Graham Balfour would provide a London base. As for Colvin, the Vailima Letters had come out and been well-received. He was dragging his feet over the rest. The Monument was a hard man to hurry.

'First things first,' she told Lloyd. 'I'm here to honour Margaret and see to the sale of the house.'

Only a proportion of Louis's estate had fallen to her. She could do with the extra capital from the Edinburgh house, and with some extra time, to take in the magnitude of these changes, to plot the course of the years left to her. She had no appetite for arguing with Colvin, since that was likely to be on the cards.

'Tell Graham we might stay with him briefly. We'll see how things go.'

Katharine chimed in, 'If you're too tired we could go for you. I'd love to meet those folks.'

Her daughter-in-law was a dear girl but her desire to meddle was beginning to grate. 'No. I'll see to it myself. Don't bother me with it now.'

They docked in Glasgow and took the train east. In late summer, Scotland, so cold and bleak it had driven Louis away, was golden and benign. If they had had some good summers here, would they have left? Probably they would. Edinburgh, like London or Bournemouth, would have been just too confining.

At Waverley, Lloyd called for a carriage to the hotel but Fanny said they should walk. It was only a short distance and this might be her last visit, a last chance to see Louis's beloved hometown. Lloyd loaded the luggage and they set off up the carriage drive, to emerge, blinking, into the light, like creatures coming from hibernation.

Fanny was overwhelmed yet again by the stern castle glooming on its rock and the vertiginous effrontery of the monument to Scott. Directly opposite, a new department store hummed with the activity of a royal palace.

'America has nothing like this,' Fanny said to Katharine and for once the garrulous girl was silent. Fanny wished Belle had come too. She had missed all of this.

Next morning, the house on Heriot Row was opened for them by a lawyer, forewarned of their arrival. They would see him later to go over the details of Margaret's will. He left with a nod, handing Lloyd a spare key to lock up.

The house had been let out for several years, the best furniture shipped to Vailima. They ascended the stone staircase to the middle floor where the lovely sitting room was bare except for an empty bookcase and a cheap armchair left by the latest occupants. Lloyd was describing to Katharine how he had spent holidays here when he was a student, how it had been filled to overflowing with books, how Tom Stevenson had helped him with his studies before he became too ill.

Katharine was charmed. 'We could live here! It would be grand to bring up our family in Europe. Why don't we keep it? Oh Fanny, could we?'

The couple wandered from room to room, laughing and making plans. Their optimism offended her. She was shocked by the barren emptiness of the house. It could never be hers, it would never be theirs. And there was the money to think about.

Fanny left them, labouring up the spiral staircase with its pale distempered walls to the second floor. After their marriage they had been given the front room, reserved for guests, but Louis had shown her his old room, looking over Queen Street and the gardens, with the bookshelf and the desk where he had spent so many hours, not just as a child but as a student too, the writer struggling to emerge.

She pushed open the door and stood on the threshold. In the comings and goings at Heriot Row this room had been overlooked. There was the narrow bed just as she had seen it, still made up, as if his younger self might creep in after an evening's drinking in town and throw himself down for what remained of the night. The desk was bare and the bookshelf empty, but they were instantly recognisable, the clear north light casting them in sharp relief. She sat down on the bed and gripped the edge, feeling the cotton quilt, the same one that would have covered him, then covered her face. She didn't need to weep because he was here. She could practically smell him.

Lloyd's voice drifted upstairs, 'Ma, are you coming down?'

'Leave me be. I need a few minutes.'

There was nothing to see. The furniture, whatever its history, was cheap and could be disposed of. She would be clear in her instructions. The lawyer could do the rest. Nothing was to be left, here or anywhere else in the house.

In the corner, there was a wall-press. She had better make sure it was empty and pulled open the door which complained after so much time at rest. The cupboard inside was wider than the door and had a hanging rail along its width. A tremor ran through her when she saw two garments hanging at the back, a plain white shirt and a jacket of threadbare velveteen.

She removed them carefully, shaking out the shirt and laying it on the bed. The jacket was an older version of the one she had first seen him in at Grez, all those years ago. He had held on to it until it was falling apart, telling her it was 'part of him' and couldn't be thrown away, but it had clearly not been the first. This one was badly worn, faded on the edges of collar and cuffs where the chocolate brown gave out to pale camel.

She laid it next to the shirt and stroked the pile, not deep but still soft. Running her hand over the fabric, she felt the crackle of paper and pulled from the inside pocket an envelope addressed to *Mr. R. L. Stevenson care of the Speculative Society, Edinburgh University*. It made her smile. The club had been second home to the young Louis and his rakish friends. While at war with his disapproving parents, he used it as a post restante. She looked more closely. The postmark could still be made out. London, September 73. It was, she supposed, the summer he had visited the Babingtons and met the people who would be his life-long friends.

People changed over the years but some things stayed the same, and one of them was handwriting. She had identified so many letters not just by postmark but by the slope of the hand. And this was one she knew very well. It belonged to Frances Sitwell.

43.

Lloyd's footstep on the stairs shook Fanny into action. On the landing, she held out the shirt and jacket to him. 'Look what I found, do you want to keep them?'

He took the garments from her, peering in the half light. 'Let's go downstairs.'

In the drawing room, Katharine snatched the jacket and held the worn thing to her face, as if petting a kitten. 'It's like the one you told me about?' He smiled, nodding. He indulged her worship of Louis. 'How wonderful!'

Fanny would let the girl keep it. She didn't need Louis's old clothes to keep his memory alive.

It was later, alone in her room at The George Hotel, that she took out Frances's letter. She recalled her mantra. What belonged to Louis now belonged to her. Outside the lamps were being lit as they had been those years ago just a few streets away where Louis had first read it, tucked it into his jacket and neglected to take it out.

Chepstow Place,
September 5th, 1873
My Dearest,
Two letters already! I shall do my best to write to you as often and with equal sincerity.

I admit that I worried it would be the gravest error to bring you to London before you took the lang road hame (you see I am learning to love some of the Scots tongue!) but you are right. Cockfield was an awakening but the times we shared here were the most precious of all. To simply hold a hand while walking in the park, to hear and feel you laughing at my side, to know the joyful ecstasy of holding back. We shall never again find love in dark corners. Greater, more innocent happiness will continue here, in words on the page.

As for your muse, she has one request to make and one only. From this day on, if you wish me to be truly free in my thoughts and my words, promise not to keep a single one of my letters to you. Too much is at stake, I have the bishop's proctors to think about, my rancorous husband, your loving family, dear S.C., on whom both of us depend. I wonder if he could understand the sudden union of souls you and I have experienced? I think there is something in our natures, something deeper than is evident in our dear friend. My dear, you were not born for the slight or the somewhat and go wholeheartedly at everything.

I hear you make that promise and I imagine how you will mull over how to dispose of these letters, by casting them on the waters of the loch or into a stream in a fine romantic gesture at your beloved Swanston. But that won't be enough. Lochs may freeze and rivers run dry. Each may give up its secrets. Throw every letter on a fire, please, as soon as you have answered.

Be brave in your life and in your writing.
Your dearest friend,
FJS

Fanny dropped the letter onto the bed as if it might stain her fingers. This was no innocent gossip or literary exchange. Its insinuations were unmistakable. If Louis and Fanny had been, as he had written, *children venturing into a darkened room*, it turned out he was already acquainted with *love in dark corners*. Fanny's blood rose at the thought of their scrabbling in the dark. And Frances, always the height of respectability! The plea for destruction said it all. Innocent letters didn't need to be thrown on a fire. Nor had this letter been forgotten. It had been left behind, and for months, maybe years, he had kept it next to his heart.

The gravy at dinner had been too rich. She got up from the bed to ease the pain that nagged under her ribs, threatening the old agony caused by her gallbladder.

She slept fitfully, wading in waters muddier than the Forth, fishing for clues as to what the letter really meant. Louis would have obeyed Frances's command. There would be no other letters to discover, but Fanny was all too aware of that other envelope, still amongst her papers. And how much else had been written in between, across twenty years and two continents? What could it all signify, except a love-affair?

The realisation was almost a relief. Fanny was no fool. She could see exactly how it had been for her English friend. The husband was a brute, Colvin stand-offish. Who could resist Louis when his blood was up? And what young man would turn down a woman desperate for love, a woman of experience, and soft as a peach? Frances had been a young man's passion. What mattered was that he had turned to Fanny in the end.

She drifted into the haven of sleep to be woken by the early morning hubbub on the street outside. She gathered her fuzzy thoughts. Louis and Frances, an old affair, its remnants surviving in scraps of paper stumbled on by chance. The curtains were closed but morning light bled in around the edges. The room shifted into focus. What had Louis said? *We used to write to each other. Very often.* Fanny had one of those letters but Frances Sitwell had the rest, and what belonged to her was most certainly given over to Colvin. And if they were as fervent as this one?

Colvin had always been polite with her, sometimes too polite. He had never liked her and lately things had got worse. Was he at this moment sending Louis's letters to the typesetter, intent on giving Frances Sitwell the glory?

At breakfast, the letter was tucked in Fanny's reticule. She would do with it what Louis should have done before and throw it on a fire. Now she must attend to the rest.

'We will go to London,' she told Lloyd. 'Set up a meeting with Colvin.'

Lloyd was enthusiastic. 'Will we go to the museum? Or he could come to us at Oxford Place?'

Katharine was agog. 'The British Museum, I'd love to see it!'

'No, not the museum,' she said. Colvin was too at home there, too in charge of things. She could hardly impose on Graham Balfour's wife. 'We need to meet on neutral ground.'

Lloyd accepted this. He wished only to take Colvin to task for his sluggishness. Fanny knew exactly what was at stake, not just Colvin's intransigence but Frances Sitwell's hold on Louis, even her own status as Louis's wife.

44.

Frances felt a huge sense of relief that Fanny and Lloyd were coming to London. So much business had passed between them and Sidney, and yet there had been no message for her. Seeing Fanny again would lay to rest the feeling that something was amiss. Perhaps Frances could give her some comfort over Louis's death. It might have been three years ago but to Fanny, she was sure, he had barely gone. She had been thinking more and more of the afternoon they spent at Skerryvore, a day of such happiness and calm, and yet it had been the last they would spend together.

'Where are you meeting?' Frances asked Sidney. He had sent a note asking her to call and had the letter from Edinburgh in his hand. They were in his afternoon sitting room, a halo of light around him from the window behind but his face was in shadow.

'They want me to join them for tea at the Langham. You will come with me?'

He passed the letter to her. The hotel was unexpected, perhaps a celebration was planned? She read the note which was cursory and only Sidney was named. She wasn't included in any invitation. She sighed. 'If it's just business, maybe Fanny and I can meet some other time. I can invite her to Marylebone.'

'No. I would like you to be there.' His voice wavered. 'Please.'

She should have seen his anxiety straight away. At first, Fanny and Lloyd had accepted his assurances over the biography but lately they'd been pushing for him to begin. If he was behind, it wasn't through lack of effort. Each time she saw him he looked more drawn. 'How are the letters coming on? Nearing completion, surely?'

He shook his head. 'I'm too punctilious. I've been too slow.'

He needed cheering up. 'You know what you've told me. It's natural for publishers to be impatient, editors slow.'

He ran his hand over his forehead. 'But I more than most. Louis thought so too.'

'Surely not!'

He shook his head, left the room and came back with a sheet of paper. 'Look.'

She had forgotten about the document Balfour laid so prominently on top of all the rest, the actual instructions left by Louis in the event of his death. She took it from Sidney. It gave him custody of Louis's literary affairs without reservation. 'I don't understand.'

'Read it through.'

Close to the end Louis had added a note to the effect that Sidney was too prone to making endless alterations, a 'besetting sin' which would hold things up and add to the cost. The criticism was unequivocal.

Poor Sidney. He had been living with this for over a year. 'You should have told me,' Frances said. Of course, they no longer told each other everything. She searched for a crumb of encouragement. 'You always do your best. Louis gave you this responsibility, despite his reservations.'

'The fact remains,' he said, 'the letters aren't ready and

won't be for some time. Fanny and Lloyd won't be appeased.'

His face was sallow, his lips pale. Frailty wouldn't help him deal with the combined forces of Fanny and Lloyd. 'Your industry does you credit. There is a fine line between a besetting sin and necessary virtue.'

He managed a thin smile. 'They'll press for a *Life*, I'll just have to hold them off a bit longer.'

He needed her to prop up his confidence. 'Of course. Just make it clear what you can and can't do. Remember you have nothing to apologise for.'

By the time she left, he had collected himself, offered her tea and played a hand of cards.

'What would I do without you?' he said, as she made to go.

Frances patted his arm but said nothing. Her hopes for a sociable reunion with Fanny were looking less and less likely.

A week later, she met Sidney in the foyer of the Langham. From the tea-room, the sound of the palm court orchestra was interrupted by the rhythmic whump of the revolving outside door. Sidney nodded towards the interior. 'They're here, ready and waiting. I expect they're staying. They can afford it now.'

The couple at a table near the centre of the room were unmistakable, although Fanny's face, looking down to her plate, was in shadow and Lloyd Osbourne's thick glasses reflected blank light. He was known for treating Louis's old friends with condescending arrogance. Frances thought their behaviour to him might not have been so very different. She spoke under her breath. 'Don't be bitter, Sidney, not over Louis. Your name will always be paired with his.'

He smiled ruefully. 'You have always been the better part of me,' he said, and stood back to let her go inside.

If only Fanny and Lloyd had chosen somewhere other than the Langham on a Saturday afternoon. The accents in the restaurant were overwhelmingly transatlantic, the decoration gaudy. Now that she could hear the orchestra properly, Frances recognised the variety of light music Sidney called 'drivel.' It was as if the stage was set in Lloyd's favour.

Lloyd, The Boy, as the London set called him, stood up to greet them. Looming over Fanny (did they need to choose somewhere so exposing?) he was more handsome than Frances had expected and with a confidence that, yes, could spill over into arrogance.

Fanny stayed seated. Her face was puffy, the eyes hooded and her neck reduced to a fold under her chin. The expression in the face which had aged so dramatically was impossible to read, but Frances's heart went out to her. As the men went through the formalities, Frances took the seat next to her and touched her arm.

'Fanny dear, how are you? It's been far too long.'

Fanny's eyes rested on her briefly then she looked away, gesturing to the table. 'Help yourselves. We ordered the full tea.'

Fanny might be offering her bounty, but Frances felt rebuffed. 'How long will you be in London?' she asked. 'If you have time to call, we can catch up properly. Things must have been very hard, but I've really missed your letters.'

Fanny peered at her and retracted her head like a watchful tortoise. If she remembered Frances encouraging her to roll cigarettes in her pantry, or the steady arm she'd offered at Davos, she gave no sign of it. 'We're sailing back tomorrow. We have things to tie up in Samoa before it's sold.'

They had left Vailima for good. 'You must feel very sad.'

Fanny didn't answer but nudged the tiered cake-stand towards them. 'Since we're here, you might as well eat.' At last Fanny looked at her directly. 'Frances, I didn't think you would come. This is mostly book talk.'

Her expectation of friendship ready to blossom again shrivelled in this unexpected coldness. Had she and Sidney misconstrued the friendship she thought they all shared? From the cake-stand Frances chose a finger roll. 'I was looking forward to seeing you,' she said, and hoped Fanny would see the irony.

With perfect timing, the musicians launched into *After the Ball was Over*. People at other tables tapped their feet and sang along to the chorus, glancing round to smile at neighbours. It was a welcome break and a reminder of the need for civility. When the noise died down, Lloyd put his elbows on the table, his chin on his hands.

'Look here, Colvin,' he spoke in a whisper which contrived to be louder than many of the voices around them, 'you know the terms of the contract. Everything was to be finished within four years of Louis's death. I take it you're nowhere near.'

Sidney was irritated but composed. 'I don't remember a particular time being specified.'

'Not in his instructions, I know, but we were clear. You've had years and you haven't begun a biography. We need to use the tide of his fame. No point waiting until he's forgotten.'

The musicians laid down their instruments. Sidney's calm was icy. 'First,' he laid a finger on the tablecloth next to his plate, 'I have completed the Vailima letters and added,' he lowered another finger, '*five* volumes to the Edinburgh Edition, all of which are producing an income. The other letters are all but done and the biographical preface close to completion. The entire work can be out in time for the anniversary of Louis's death. *Thirdly*, as long as I and his friends walk this earth, his life and his work will be published and celebrated. Through our efforts, he will never be forgotten.'

This was a different Sidney, the man Louis had trusted with his life's work.

Fanny looked up from her millefeuilles and made a moue. 'Let's agree to that last one at least.'

Lloyd was not so easily placated. 'That's not the point. The *Life* needs to be done and you're refusing the job.'

'As I said, I am working on the biographical section.'

Lloyd was exasperated. 'You can't deny there should be a separate biography and it mustn't take another bunch of years.'

'That wasn't part of Louis' original instructions. I'd be happy to undertake a full *Life*, but not now. Not until I've finished what's begun, what Louis himself expressly asked for.'

Lloyd folded his arms but it was Fanny who spoke up. 'It doesn't matter what Louis asked for. We've decided. Since you're letting us down, we'll take it back. Lloyd can write the *Life* with my help.'

Frances hardly dared look at Sidney to see which part of this offended him the most, the *letting down* or the notion that Lloyd would take over. He already claimed joint authorship with Louis of several stories, something she and Sidney had never quite believed. His confidence, as far as Sidney was concerned, far out-ran his talent. She could feel his temperature rise. Fanny remained intent on her pastry.

Frances cleared her throat. If her friendship had been rejected, she could still act as peacemaker. 'Lloyd is very well placed, of course, especially for the later years, but not to write Louis's earlier life.'

Fanny sighed as if she had been expecting just this riposte. 'How much do we need to know about all that? He was a disgrace for most of his youth. He came into his real powers later. He wrote *Treasure Island* for Lloyd, you know.'

'But there was a great deal before *Treasure Island*, all the essays and travel books. All of his younger life fed into these.'

Fanny shrugged. 'Samoa was still the best of him. And he was happy. More so than anywhere else.'

Fanny had been infected by Lloyd's arrogance. It was hardly a good time for the band to strike up a boisterous march.

Sidney, ignoring the din, seemed better prepared. 'Vailima is very well covered in the volume of letters. Anyway, does a life-story celebrate only happiness? Surely it needs to show progress, development, and how the glorious ending was achieved. This is well-documented in his letters.'

It was a brave attempt and might have worked if it hadn't fallen at the last; Louis's end had come too soon to be glorious.

Fanny blinked and looked at Frances. 'I've been thinking about the letters. Are any he sent to you in this famous collection?'

Amongst the sentimental music and delicate clink of tea-cups, Frances saw a trap opening at her feet, the same one Sidney had lured her into. Louis had written to her, Fanny knew, most people knew. Nature abhors a vacuum. What reason could there be not to publish letters except one that incriminated them, incriminated her?

'They're still under consideration. Isn't that right, Sidney?' He avoided her eye. He wouldn't come to her rescue. To Fanny, 'Why do you ask?'

'Because if you were lovers, which I assume was the case, I'd rather it wasn't broadcast to the world.'

The silence which had descended on the table told Frances she had not misheard. *Lovers,* how on earth could Fanny think … and to mention it so casually. She forced out the words lodged in her throat. 'I don't know what you mean.'

'I know what went on, though I admit you had me duped. You acted more like his mother, and you were old enough to be just that.'

Frances's face burned with embarrassment, but she held on to her composure. She reminded herself Fanny had seen no letters. She sat as tall as she could, mimicking Sidney's previous calm. 'Louis and I corresponded for quite some time and at great length. We were connected in spirit. His letters to me reveal no more than that.'

Fanny grunted. Frances thought she spied a curve of amusement in the lower lip.

Fanny went on. 'Huh, more turgid reading, then, just words at the end of the day. Though folks will read between the lines, I have no doubt.'

Frances was more incensed. Did Fanny not see it was Louis she was insulting? She replaced the salmon roll on her plate with deliberation. 'As for the maternal role, I think you'll find there are those who think Louis's attachment to *you* was mostly that of son to mother.'

Fanny's reptile eyes were bright. 'As if I cared what people think!' She slurped her tea. 'I grant you age is nothing. But trust me, Louis and I had more fun in bed than you two could ever dream of.'

In this she included Sidney, who looked utterly aghast. His hand flew to his mouth. Talking of physical intimacy at the tea table, anywhere, was for him a special kind of hell. Frances cringed in sympathy. At least Fanny had dropped her voice so that the whole restaurant couldn't hear. Whatever had become of the understanding they had shared?

Frances spoke to no one in particular. 'I came here to meet an old friend. I don't know what has changed.'

Fanny's mouth crumpled into a grimace. 'I'm sorry, my dear. I won't be upstaged by your affair with him, whatever its nature. I have to think of Louis's reputation and my family.'

Frances had no family relying on her. Apparently, this deprived her of importance. She stood up. If people noticed, then let them. The woman was insufferable and needed to know it. '*Your* family has taken Louis for everything he is worth and Sidney has worked himself into the ground on their behalf. Do you want his life too?'

'Oh, my dear, calm yourself!' Fanny flapped at Lloyd the hand which was free of the pastry. 'This is no good. It's tiring me out.'

Frances would not sit down again. The afternoon of which she had such hopes was over. 'Sidney and I have only ever had Louis's interests at heart. Remember that before making any rash decisions. I think it's best we don't meet again.'

She walked around the table to stand at Sidney's side. 'Come along, my dear. It's time we left.'

45.

At the museum, Sidney asked John to bring tea and toast to the drawing room where they sat down at the small table. Frances was grateful for the buttery slices that soothed her empty stomach. She felt her energy return but Sidney's hands were trembling. He was smarting at Fanny's outrageous assertion. Her hostility was inexplicable. She had never demonstrated the slightest jealousy of Frances. What had happened to make things different? What did she know? Or was she suffering from psychosis? There had been rumours a few years ago which Frances had discounted as spiteful gossip.

She tried to focus on Sidney. 'You must win some time for the *Life*,' she said. 'You can start as soon as the letters are published. That's only a few months. They'll slake the public thirst for Louis and Lloyd's desire for money.'

Sidney's eyes were cast down. 'I wasn't entirely open about my progress.'

Disquiet stole over Frances. 'So not this year?'

He shook his head. No wonder he had been in such a state before the meeting. 'Sidney, forget Lloyd for a moment. Must you write the biography?'

He shook his head. 'I can't let it go. Not to Lloyd.'

There was no arguing with him in this state, maybe later she could win him round.

'Fanny was terribly rude to you,' Sidney said. He would

defend her in any circumstance, just as she defended him in front of Fanny and Lloyd.

'I don't know why. There were times when she was a true friend.'

He looked down at his hands, palms upwards, fingers interlaced. 'Why did you tell her your letters were "under consideration"? We agreed not to publish, as I recall?'

He had avoided her eye in the tea-room but wouldn't let it pass. Nor should he, they needed to tackle this. 'Don't you see, if I'd said no, she would have assumed the worst? I think we need to come clean, Sidney. We have to publish them. Anything else will only fuel suspicion.'

'But the letters themselves...'

She leaned towards him to make her point. '...can do no more harm than what people will conjecture. You said it yourself. Without them there will be a lacuna.'

Sidney was shaking his head, unable to comprehend such a shift in direction, and so she got up and went to the window, her favourite view of the museum entrance and the ever-changing pattern of people's lives as they criss-crossed on the steps. Louis had come here too, to Sidney's *many-pillared and well-beloved* house. She must ensure his wishes were fulfilled.

'I think it was what Louis wanted,' she said. 'At Skerryvore, he asked me if I had kept all his letters. I thought he was being sentimental. But he talked about *when he had gone*. Perhaps he was thinking not just of the past but of our joint futures, of posterity.' She rested her forehead against the glass. 'And it's the only way of refuting Fanny.'

'Wouldn't it play into her hand?'

'Not if we make a careful selection.'

'So, we choose what goes in the record?'

It would be a half-truth, but surely half a truth was better than none. 'Isn't that what a good editor does? Even without Fanny's enmity I don't want to be forgotten. I don't think Louis wanted that either.'

It was easier to ask because she knew Sidney's feelings for Louis were just as intense. All his letters from Louis would be published. Were hers so very different?

She reframed the question. 'Could you see your way to publishing some of them?'

She saw his frown of incomprehension or perhaps anxiety, but hurried on before he could raise objections. 'Louis asked me to save some passages for him to use elsewhere. They weren't just written for me, but for everyone.'

She lowered herself into the chair next to Sidney. His mouth worked as he considered her suggestion, and the weight of his responsibilities. She waited for him to come to his conclusion, to look up and meet her eye.

'Yes, you are right. Denying you was unreasonable.'

She felt like putting her arms around him but contented herself with a sigh. She rose and stood next to him, and he turned his face to her waist, a gesture of compliance, or possibly fatigue. There would still be obstacles to overcome. It would mean going through them again, all those *Madonnas,* all those protestations of love.

Her hand massaged his shoulder, an odd familiarity. 'They are all in the past, you know, all those words.'

He spoke into her skirt. 'But they have their place. You have your place.'

'Yes. Whatever Fanny may think.'

He sat up and studied the table, giving his full attention to what lay ahead. A final frown. 'You'll be reminded of my editing all over again.'

The memory of the pencil marks was not as hurtful as it once was. 'Editing has its place. You have... the wider view.'

They looked at each other, a little awestruck to have solved it so easily, as if the wall between them was no great feat of masonry, but jerry-built, ready to fall at the single blast of a trumpet.

'What if there are disagreements?' he asked.

'We can deal with disagreements. A joint stewardship, do you think?'

He looked down. They had both wanted to own Louis at different times and in different ways. 'Of course.'

He smiled and she sat down in the other chair. Every one of these last few hours had taken its toll. 'I need to go.'

She let Sidney lead her to the front door while John ran to the street for a cab.

'I'm curious. Will you have your letters published on account of Fanny?'

Fanny had insulted her but she had shown her the answer. 'Not just that. I wanted them published before. She made me see it was the right thing to do.'

She would not deliver the letters into his hands. He would have to come to her, spend time in her sitting room, reclaim his place at her table. She was pleased they had come this far, working together with Louis, the old threesome, even if one of them was gone. What had Henry said? They were more than the sum of their parts, a good team. She might hurry him over his editing.

'Promise me one thing,' she said, as he helped her into the carriage. 'Don't even think of taking on the biography.'

He hoisted her onto the seat and squeezed her arm. 'Don't worry. I'll write to Lloyd and tell him I can't do it.' He allowed himself a sigh. 'I could do with more time for other things. We could reinstate our soirees?'

They were taking small steps back to normality. As he moved away, he looked around the carriage door with the hint of a twinkle. 'I don't know if you're aware, but there are very few letters between Louis and his wife.'

The carriage moved off. Frances was not deceived. However many of Louis's letters she had in her keeping, Fanny had possessed much more of him.

A fog was coming down, rendering London invisible. She intuited the journey from the familiar bends in the road and the change in tone of the horses' hooves on cobbles old and new. It still pained her that Fanny had turned against her when really there was no need. She would not steal the limelight from Fanny, but her voice would be heard, speaking from the wings, saying exactly as much as she wanted to reveal.

46.

London, 1898

She and Sidney worked as she had imagined, in her sitting room, reading each letter and agreeing on which passages would be published. For Sidney, the familiarity of selecting and editing was calming. They could have been discussing letters between two strangers, the literary merit, the relevance to a wider picture. If most of Louis's tenderness had been removed, this was in the nature of the editorial process and the art of compromise. By the middle of 1898, the first volume of R. L. Stevenson's Letters *to his Family and Friends* was on its way to completion.

They were edging closer to each other, not physically but in the comfort of shared interests and like minds. In September, they embarked, after all, on a new season of soirees. It was another careful step to repairing what had been so badly fractured. 'Just our closest friends to start with,' Sidney suggested and Frances agreed.

On the first of these occasions, Frances was strangely apprehensive. So much had changed for her since Louis's death. She lingered on the edge of the company, concentrating on the practicalities, checking arrangements for tea and arranging the seating. But as the visitors arrived, all remarking on how well she looked and how much they had missed her conversation, she lost her hesitancy and threw herself into discussions. Her knowledge was respected. She felt like her old self. It was a pleasure to be in Sidney's house and at his side.

After the formal part of proceedings, Edmund Gosse and Leslie Stephen, the former editor of *Cornhill* magazine, came to offer their thanks. 'It's good to see Colvin back in action,' Stephen said, 'although he has a particularly lean and hungry look. He shouldn't let this business with Osbourne get under his skin.'

Gosse agreed. 'Sidney always gives too much of himself. I know how much he wants to write the *Life* but sometimes one has to be realistic.'

It was true that Sidney was in a perpetual state of exhaustion but Frances smiled and reassured them. 'Sidney is learning to admit his limitations and he is a lot happier for it.'

'I'm glad to hear it,' Stephen continued. 'It does no one any good to get caught up in a feud. But he looks like a man who is burning the midnight oil. Has there been any reply from the other camp? From The Boy?'

'I'm sorry?' Frances was unaware of any ongoing conversations with Lloyd or Fanny.

Stephen knew he had made a faux pas but declined to explain, 'Ah, no need to worry, I'm sure,' he said.

When the guests left, Frances completed her round of tidying up, just as she used to do, leaving Sidney to do his share. The conversation was turning in her mind and falling into a shape she did not like.

She had no energy for a new argument and so she left it until she was in the act of leaving, stopping in the hallway as she put on her hat. 'Leslie Stephen said something rather odd. As if you were still intending to write the *Life?* I hope he's mistaken.'

Next to her, Sidney inhabited an eloquent silence then toppled into a hurried confession. He wanted to gloss over it, to get it out of the way. 'The others persuaded me. Baxter, Henley, *and* Gosse,' as if Edmund must take the blame. 'We were at a dinner together a few months ago. They say it will be an outright flop if Lloyd takes over.' He paused, searching for further explanation. 'Louis's *Life* was always mine. It's the culmination of everything, the ultimate hope, the ultimate...'

'The ultimate prize?'

He was wringing his hands. 'It makes me sound very shallow, to need a reward.'

She disagreed. She sat down on the flimsy chair which stood in the hall. This couldn't be swept aside. 'Why shouldn't there be something to gain when you've worked so hard?'

'I had his friendship. I needed no more.' His forehead was knitted with the need to find the right words. 'But this would have been my gift to him.'

'Maybe you've given enough.'

He rubbed the wrinkled brow. 'Is it wrong to ask for recognition?'

Sidney had never craved the limelight. It made a change to see him standing his ground. She was glad that he knew his worth.

Sidney hurried on. 'They, the others, said if I could prove my intentions, Fanny would be prepared to wait. When I agreed to make another approach, they treated me like the hero of the hour.'

Men needed heroes. She thought of *Kidnapped* and David Balfour. William Henley reincarnated as a pirate. Sidney must have enjoyed his moment.

'You've started writing it?'

'Only a chapter or two, to give the feel of it. I sent it to the widow. I thought it might change her mind.'

'But how can you possibly manage with your other commitments? We agreed you would give up.'

He spread his hands, a plea for mercy, then couldn't hold back a smile. 'It comes so naturally it doesn't feel like work. Even if Fanny rejects it, I can publish it myself, one day.'

There was a fog in her brain she couldn't disperse. This had all been settled. 'I don't know what you were thinking. No wonder you're so tired.'

'It's a healthy tiredness. I have more energy.'

She thought of the hours she'd spent writing to Louis, descending into nervous fatigue.

'What have you written? May I read it?'

'Now?'

'Not necessarily. I'm just curious as to what you've said, what you chose to send to them.'

'I have a copy somewhere. Shall I send it to you?'

'Yes. Why not.'

She couldn't unpick the rights and wrongs. She might as well see how Sidney was framing Louis's life-story. Presumably he had chosen something of which Lloyd was relatively ignorant, his Edinburgh days – Suffolk even.

The following day an envelope arrived which Frances put aside until late afternoon. When she opened it, the top sheet, in Sidney's immaculate hand, was a note for her.

I've had no reply from Samoa where they are doubtless very busy. I hope you enjoy reading it.

I chose this period because although Lloyd and Fanny will have some knowledge, I can bring a wider

It took only a glance to see that Sidney had chosen to write about Davos, the time and the company he had enjoyed so much, the place where she had watched her son die. She threw the pages onto her desk with no intention of reading them.

47.

If Sidney was indecisive and occasionally intemperate, he was at heart a good man, but for him to have gone ahead with writing the biography felt like outright deception. Then to wax lyrical, as Frances imagined, about Switzerland, the delights of table talk and tobogganing, when he knew she'd left a good part of her heart in those bleak mountains. It was unforgivable.

Lately, she had pushed to the back of her mind her wilder imaginings about Sidney and other men. But wasn't that the attraction of Davos? To be amongst his own kind, those of scintillating mind but unfortunate habits,' as he once described Symonds. Only part of her believed Sidney was of their number, but it was enough to make her out of sorts.

She challenged him again. 'Do you really have to write the biography?'

'Anything written by Lloyd will be discredited in London,' he told her. 'I'll win this in the end.'

She was too tired for such belligerence. He was convinced, too, that Fanny would wreak some kind of vengeance for Frances's old intimacy with Louis. Frances tried to persuade him otherwise but he was immovable. Victory, she thought, would stop Lloyd from writing the *Life*, but at what cost to Sidney? She could not see an end to it until a letter arrived from San Francisco, Fanny Stevenson's new home.

San Francisco,
12th May, 1899
Dear Friend,
I would have written sooner to say I regretted our short and not too sweet exchanges at the Langham but sometimes the least said is soonest mended. At least that was my hope, but now things are going from bad to worse and where I once would have tackled Colvin directly (Louis once called him a husk, I prefer sea-urchin), I think I may only suffer a nasty sting for my efforts. So I'm appealing to you to rein him in if you have the power to do so.

I suppose it was only to be expected he would change his mind about handing over the Life and put up a new case for himself as biographer, but my son—Louis's chief executor as you may recall—is perfectly within his rights to refuse him. That the Monument (to think I once warmed to him) should refuse to hand over Louis's papers to Lloyd and generally obstruct him is unforgivable, and I know Louis would be turning in his grave.

I'm appealing—no, I'm demanding—this stops, before my husband's memory is tainted by such constant wrangling. Considering you and I were cut from very different cloth, we rubbed along well enough for a while. I hope you have the good sense to see this should come to an end.

I've been unwell and plan to be in England later this year for surgery. I don't want this difficulty with Colvin to add to my problems.

I am counting on you, for Louis's sake,
Fanny Van de Grift Stevenson

For once Frances welcomed Fanny's candour and her desire for a truce. She was ignorant of these 'legal obstructions,' but she had other reasons for wanting to talk to Fanny. It still pained her that they were completely estranged and not just over Sidney's behaviour.

Her reply to Fanny got no response, but she would not give up. Fanny was the last stumbling block to her peace of mind, and to Sidney's. As summer arrived, she got wind that Fanny was convalescing in Dorking, close to the home of George Meredith, another of Louis's circle of London friends. Rather than write in advance and risk a refusal, she stayed overnight in a local hotel from where she sent a note.

By morning no reply had arrived but she set out anyway. The weather was warm with a milky September sun, and so she went on foot, enjoying the lanes leading to the green edges of the town, keeping to the shade, drawing on an inner strength she had been saving for this moment. In the unlikely event Fanny was not at home, she would simply wait until she came back. She would not be sent away.

The cottage was set back from the road, faded stonework but with a pretty garden and hills visible to the rear. The air, poised on the tipping point of summer into autumn, was completely still. Frances wondered if everyone was out, then a maid answered her ring at the door.

'Mrs Stevenson is in the garden,' the girl said, 'you can go on through.'

From the French doors in a small morning room, the garden looked as deserted as the house. Frances took the only path, bordered by lupins and lavender, which branched two ways at the end. Fanny was on the right-hand path, on a low stool, digging with a trowel in the mulchy earth.

'Fanny, my dear,' it seemed best to start afresh, 'should you be doing that? Are you well enough?'

Fanny looked up briefly and carried on. 'This isn't real work, these are puny things.'

English weeds were clearly a poor substitute for the Samoan jungle. 'You must miss Vailima.'

'I loved it and I hated it. The struggle against nature was never ending. I had to leave and it cost too much to have the place looked after.' She flung down the trowel. 'I'll go back, though. I'll be with Louis in the end.' She tried to push herself off the stool and sat down again. She was talking like a woman close to death. 'If we're to talk, I suppose you'd better help me up.'

She was wearing a loose smock, of the kind seen in photographs from Samoa. Frances pulled her to her feet as gently as she could and Fanny, breathing heavily, responded to her unspoken thoughts. 'See? I'm not done yet.'

They were standing arm in arm. Before Fanny could detach herself, Frances guided her back up the path towards the house. 'Let's find somewhere to sit down.'

They went to a sitting room overlooking the street. Amongst the crumpled sofas, Fanny regained her old confidence, taking charge of the coffee brought in by the maid. 'Lloyd has gone into town for something,' she said. 'He'll be back in a while.' It was said in no particular tone of voice but Frances took it as a warning. If they were to achieve anything it had best be done quickly. 'You're staying at the hotel?'

'Last night, yes. I'm planning to go back today.'

Fanny nodded, approving the business-like brevity of Frances's visit. 'So, what are you going to do about the Monument?'

The pet name had become an insult and the pugnacious

tone set Frances's teeth on edge. 'He feels responsible for anything written about Louis. He worries that mistakes will be made.'

'You mean he doesn't trust my son.'

There was no point in denying the obvious. 'Lloyd hasn't exactly endeared himself.'

Fanny shrugged. 'That doesn't give Colvin the right to obstruct him. He's like a child deprived of his favourite toy. You know he's talking of court? As if he's ever going to win against us, Louis's family!'

Fanny was right. Sidney's annoyance had a child-like streak, but Frances wouldn't apologise for him. 'I'm not aware of everything he does. Only of how upset he is.'

'So, will you stop him acting like an ass? Can you?'

She braced herself to make a concession. 'I think Sidney's distrust of Lloyd is misplaced.'

Fanny raised her eyebrows. 'Don't tell me you're helping me out here. Why would you trust my son more than Colvin does?'

'Since our meeting in London...' Did Fanny even remember what she said that day? 'Sidney worries we'll be...'

Fanny put down her coffee cup and laughed out loud. 'Dragged through the dirt? By me and Lloyd?'

Frances flushed. 'Sidney has a real fear of any kind of disrespect or humiliation. I don't think that would be Lloyd's purpose.'

'That day at the Langham. I was only goading you, you know. I was ill and upset by something... I've apologised, haven't I?'

Frances nodded her acceptance. There was no point in prolonging bad feelings. 'There's no way we want you as a *cause celebre*.'

This is what Frances had finally deduced. To make public an affair between her and Louis was not in Fanny's interest any more than it was in Sidney's.

Fanny was settled into her chair. 'What I said in London. It began with something I found in Edinburgh, an old letter from you. I found it by chance.'

How and where had Fanny found a letter? Louis had assured her he'd got rid of every one.

'In it,' Fanny went on, 'you ask Louis to burn your letters, not even to throw them in a river, but to burn them. That told me all I needed to know.'

Frances's words came back to her. *Lochs may freeze…* Fanny had stumbled – somehow – on the single letter that incriminated her, the one with which she had hoped to preserve her good name for all time. She bit her lip to avoid laughing at the irony and the injustice.

Fanny was waiting for a response.

'So you have it then?' Frances said.

'I do not. I burned it myself.'

In the end it was Fanny, not Louis, who had carried out her wishes.

Fanny grimaced in satisfaction, whether from having found the evidence or having destroyed it, Frances couldn't tell. More than anything she was relieved. She had no wish to reread those words chosen by her younger self, in a different time and place, in a different world.

Frances was overwhelmed by a sense of finality. A moment of emotional connection years ago had carried her into the slipstream of Louis's eager correspondence and finally brought her here, to the jealousy of her old friend, Louis's devoted wife, now a sour-mouthed widow. It was time to bring it all to an end.

48.

Frances shook her head and gave a rueful laugh, but her mouth trembled.

Fanny was observing her with interest. 'It's funny?'

Funny and sad. Frances reached for a handkerchief and wiped her eyes to hide the tears. 'I'm sorry. I'm remembering how much I put into that letter. My separation was still in progress. I was anxious there should be no misunderstanding, but that's exactly what has happened.'

As for Louis, so upright, so insistent on honesty. He had broken his promise to burn all her letters, inadvertently perhaps, but broken it all the same. No one was perfect, not even Louis Stevenson. She tried to recall exactly what she'd said. Had she admitted to desire? 'We were never lovers,' she said, 'but I can't blame you for believing otherwise.'

Fanny gave her a long look. 'What he did before me doesn't matter. But I had to know if something more was going on, during all those years.'

The idea of a long-term affair was ridiculous. 'No nothing went on,' Frances said. Fanny was grieving, she reminded herself, and unwell. Lloyd's ill-will towards her and Sidney wouldn't help her state of mind.

'It doesn't matter now,' Fanny said. 'I have something for you. I meant to bring it down.' She heaved herself out of the chair and moved with reluctance towards the door and the stairs.

'Can I get it for you?'

'All right, thank you. It's in my bag, next to the bed.'

Mounting the narrow staircase, Frances wondered what this could be, some small memento, a photograph of Louis? She returned and gave the snakeskin bag to her hostess who opened it and handed Frances a letter. The envelope was addressed to her, in Louis's writing. It looked undamaged but the seal was broken, Frances frowned at it, not quite comprehending. One unexpected letter in a day was more than enough.

'It's from the week before he died. It should have come to you before.'

Frances sat down, the letter in her hand.

'You'll probably want to save it for later,' Fanny said.

Frances understood *for when you're alone.* 'Thank you.' Then. 'You've read it?'

'Yes, I'm sorry for that, but having read *your* letter, I thought it would answer my questions. And it did. Oh, it's full of romantic nonsense, but I can see you were never together, not really. And I was his wife.' Marriage, the ultimate prize, an act of possession.

'I just wish you'd told me how much Louis was in love with you,' Fanny went on. 'We were friends after all.'

What could she have told Fanny exactly? In London they had only just met. And if Louis himself had thought to explain his old feelings, all this could have been avoided.

'It feels like you were always holding something back.'

Frances considered this. *Holding back* had been the only way. Defending herself from Albert, her natural caution with Sidney. The only real letting go had been with Louis and that was confined to letters, letters she had guarded jealously. Yes, she had held them back, the only part of Louis that was hers.

Fanny leaned back. 'Do you know what a force you were, the three of you? From the start I had to put myself between you, prising you apart like a wedge.'

Frances found that hard to believe. 'When you and Louis arrived in London, he was…besotted. He danced attendance on you.' Quite literally, she remembered how he shifted from foot to foot in agitation.

Fanny shook her head. 'I would have to have been blind and deaf not to notice how close you all were, you and Colvin's cronies at that confounded club!'

Yes, the Savile had been a cabal. It still was. Frances knew how it was to be an outsider. 'We all wanted what was best for Louis.'

'As long as you could have a piece of him, I used to think.'

He'd complained of being divided up, but only in jest. 'He liked being fought over. He revelled in being the centre of attention.'

Fanny grunted an agreement. 'Louis gave his spirit, his friendship to them all, and to you. But after I came along, he belonged to me.'

Frances allowed Fanny her victory. *More fun in bed than you ever had.* She was probably right, but Frances had been offered the sparkling eyes and the fervent lips and turned them away. It was a loss she'd learned to bear.

'The letters really are finished,' she said. 'They'll go to press shortly. Mine are included, but not in their entirety. There's nothing to cause offence or hurt.'

Fanny nodded. 'Good. That's what he would have wanted.'

'Sidney would never invite scandal.'

'You say that, but folks will always wonder.'

Frances could say no more. Whatever people thought,

she had done her best not to feed speculation.

'Anyway,' Fanny went on with a hint of mischief, 'I got Louis away from you in the end, even if I had to take him to Samoa.'

Frances played along. 'You went to the South Seas for his health.'

'Yes, yes. And his happiness. When I saw him aboard ship, playing at being a sailor, he really was at home there. Not like me, always groaning on my bunk as soon as the wind picked up. His only sadness was in saying goodbye to Colvin. He knew the distance would be too much.' Fanny fell silent, then began again. 'There was something odd there, father and son, maybe. That's why I'm trying to avoid the all-out war he is hell-bent on starting.'

Fanny was still weak from surgery. It had lent her a streak of kindness. Frances was grateful for something she could take back to Sidney.

'You know Sidney loved him, not just Sidney, all his men friends.'

Fanny's eyes were half-closed but she was alert. 'Oh yes, I know. And some of them wanted him body and soul. He knew it too. I think, as much as anything, it amused him.'

'So he would never...?'

Fanny stopped her. 'Louis took everything life threw at him, for the sheer fun of it. He didn't run after men but who knows what might have happened along the way? If he had other adventures, I didn't need to know. I still don't. I was his Tamaitai.'

Fanny's generosity did her credit. Frances let it fall like a blanket over all the times Louis and Sidney had been together, the boyish capers, or nights when the comfort of chloral was required.

Despite this breaking out of peace, the problem of the *Life was* still to be solved. 'It's not just Sidney who's opposed to Lloyd writing a biography. The London crowd are just as much against him. Without their support it could easily fail.'

Fanny frowned. 'So who would you suggest?'

Frances was prepared for this. 'Gosse, Henry James, that young Scot, Barrie, any one of them.'

'All Colvin's friends?'

'In the main, yes.'

Fanny sat back with an air of triumph, as if she had some final card up her sleeve. 'And you think the Monument would want one of those names on the cover?'

Looking at it this way, Frances saw Fanny was right. It would be just as hard for Sidney to accept a friend, a rival for Louis's affection, as the man he saw as an enemy.

'I see what you mean.'

Fanny rang a small hand bell next to her chair. 'Let's have some tea,' she said, 'and see who else we can come up with.'

It was early afternoon by the time Frances left. She had had no luncheon but she had achieved what she had come for and would not outstay Fanny's cautious welcome. As she left, Fanny said, 'That letter I found in Heriot Row. It had some nice turns of phrase. I can see the writer in you.'

Faint praise from Fanny, perhaps deliberately so, but Frances was unperturbed. Her articles were competent and professional. The letter tucked in the pocket of her skirt would have more grace and elegance than anything she would ever write.

49.

Vailima,
29th November, 1894
My Dear,
You may blame this sudden desire to write on the weather. We are waiting for the rain. In December it will come in torrents, but the autumn months bring a sense of change, an unpredictability in the atmosphere that unsettles me. In a serious storm, we'll be cut off from the town as the road loses its fragile grip to the onslaught of water. Still, the anticipation of a minor catastrophe (the road will be mended in time) contributes to the piquancy of island life, always veering between static humidity and wild unrest.

This seasonal unpredictability puts me in mind of home, where no outing – a walk in the Pentlands, a stroll on Bournemouth's populated promenade— could be contemplated without scanning the skies in advance. There are days when I long to be setting out on foot amongst the purple hills and low-growing gorse instead of urging my stubborn pony through box-fruit and hibiscus. Bournemouth, though, is a town for which I felt little, despite its proximity to so many friends including your good self and your loyal consort.

I've been thinking of my last letter to you and what a poor fist I made of the death of The Vicar. I was grudging and mean-spirited as if none of that mattered any longer. You (I could say both of us) deserve better. One of my father's sayings springs to mind, "There are a lot of sudden deaths" and, having been so many times at death's door, I should know this better than most, and so here is what I think will be if not my last letter to you, my last attempt to sum up where you and I have been and where we have arrived. One cannot be forever turning over the past and so it is, if you like, my last embrace.

Something else made me think of you this particular morning and it was neither a letter from S.C. nor any remark by Fanny. No, as I sat down to work, I was distracted by a flash of feathers at the window and the cacophony of birdsong, but none of the native species sings quite like my birdie with the yellow bill, which is what turned my mind to Bournemouth and a conversation I had with our good friend Henry James. It must have been summer and near the end of the day because a single bird was singing to the dusk. I had been recently looking through The Portrait of A Lady *and I asked him if the bird's song didn't put him in mind of someone. After some to-ing and fro-ing he caught my drift and blinked those hooded eyes.*

'Ah, you mean my Madame Merle?'

'Beautiful, accomplished, not quite what she seems,' I prompted him, 'the name was picked for her singing voice, surely?'

Henry replied, this time with an even gaze. 'Dear boy, an author never reveals his sources of inspiration.'

We turned back to the house. 'By the way,' he went on, 'have you seen Mrs Sitwell lately?'

You see how easily you slide into all of our thoughts—sometimes even our books!— and you will understand how that memory disrupted my train of thought which should have been charging towards the next chapter of Hermiston. I'm proud to say I laid the thought of you aside as I went about my business because work (on which my family depends) comes first. Now the household is asleep, even Belle has stopped nagging me to write, and I have kept my promise to myself with this fresh sheet of paper and a full inkwell.

Henry James was right that day. You had recently been to Skerryvore and I remember how you chose Chant d'Amour to sing for us. Do you remember the melody? This is what turns in my head as I write, that and the need to tell you of the place you will always have in my heart, regardless of the infinite distance between us. If you think my heart is a crowded room, I hope you'll allow it is better to have one too full than too empty, and be content with the company you find there.

I must do the odious Sitwell justice too or his place in our history. What if there had been no Vicar? Or if I had pierced him through the heart with a dagger as I sometimes threatened to? Would we two have sealed the thing we started on that afternoon at Cockfield? You see, my dear, how we are entering the realms of fiction. I'm no swordsman and I've always thought it for the best by far that my youthful seed was spent too soon and too carelessly for it to sully your matronly beauty. I admit, as we walked back to Maud's demurely faded sitting room, I briefly imagined us as man and wife, something that had never crossed my mind until that day and so you were a great part of my growing up.

On the other hand, let's admit that we were never fated to grow old together. I can't see you here digging my garden amongst the flying foxes; your beauty is too refined and your constitution too frail for the tropics. Nor, however much I miss my London friends, could I sit out my days in drawing rooms and libraries. The sea, and the need to be on it or near it is in my blood.

We must be happy with who we are and who we are with. You will always miss Bert – I miss him myself—but I hope your life is more than a little consolation. You have the writers who have come after me and you have Colvin. He is a good man even if he keeps his tender heart well hidden. I love him and he loves you dearly. Surely with the vicar gone you two have your chance to seize the day.

I am writing as if you have regrets when I'm sure you have none. Who would want Fanny's job of spooning physic down my throat at all hours? I have only joyful gratitude for all you and Colvin have done for me. You raised me when I was at my lowest and gave me the wings I needed, if only by making sure I put pen to paper every day of my life. Because of you, I worked my full apprenticeship in the crafting of words and if my heroines were not acclaimed, it is only because none could match your beauty and intelligence.

The song, the song is still with me. I shall look out the music and write an arrangement for my flageolet, to capture your voice once and for all, even if I can never match its richness. Then I will rely as ever on the vagaries of ships and postal carriages to convey my letter out of this wild and magical place to the proud and gracious street where you now live. If it should be lost, will my thoughts somehow find their way to you, borne on the wings of memory or on a song of love? Now I am descending to the worst kind of cliché. I picture you frowning and your pencil hovering, considering striking it out!

The mail boat will come soon. This evening I'll be called upon to be the genial host. Fanny and Belle will be putting on their finery and my mother straightening her best white cap. My letter will be in the hands of good ships' captains and the horrendously, joyfully, unpredictable weather.

Good night, sleep well, take happiness where you can,

Ever your dear and faithful friend,
RLS

50.

Frances read the letter on the train, alone in the carriage and light-headed from lack of food. Outside, the summer greenery unspooled but she saw only a desk by a window overlooking a jungle clearing, where, in the cool of morning, Louis had taken up his pen to write. His voice rang in her head, as clear and mellifluous as ever, and she had to remind herself that this was written five years ago. As the train rolled through the drab outskirts of the city, she came back to the here and now, and wept anew for his untimely death.

She was glad to reach home, and, rather than call on Maddie, she went to the kitchen and scrambled herself an egg, letting the curd soothe her stomach. Then she used the hour before bed to reread the letter and give its contents her full attention. Louis said she and Sidney should marry and he was right. She should have stood her ground after Albert's death and hurried Sidney along. But then there was Louis, sitting in her heart like a book she had started to read and never finished.

She reminded herself that Fanny had read this letter too, but that was for the best. It had brought her peace and allowed her to put aside her jealousy of Frances. If they would never be friends in the way they once were, it was enough for Frances to be no longer at war. The letter was Louis's final gift to both of them. The book was closed.

336

She slept deeply and woke full of purpose. At nine-o'clock sharp she took the familiar route to the museum, heading not to Sidney's house but through the main entrance. Here she had no special privileges. 'I'm here to see Mr Colvin,' she told the uniformed attendant.

'You have an appointment?'

'I am Mrs Sitwell.'

If the man didn't recognise her name, her grey satin dress and implacable expression had the desired effect and he sent her on her way. Along dim corridors and after two false turns, she arrived at the row of rooms allotted to the Keepers, the heads of department of the museum, and at the end of the corridor, came to the door she was looking for. Like the others it bore no personal name, only the title of its occupant, Keeper of Prints and Drawings. She knocked, aware she was crossing more than one threshold.

Sidney answered her knock with a business-like 'Come!' Then rose to his feet in surprise. 'Frances, my dear, what brings you here?'

For an institution of such riches, the room was bleak. Sidney's desk was workmanlike and the cream distempered walls bore insipid landscapes and a row of dour portraits. She hadn't realised Sidney spent his time in such a stark and cheerless place. She thought of the other keepers, many of whom she had met. They were men of deep learning and high repute, scholars and archaeologists who spent long periods travelling. Perhaps they felt no need for creature comforts. Come to think of it, none of them had a wife.

Sidney was taking in her grey satin, her careful coiffure. He picked up one of the formal chairs ranged against the wall and brought it forward, inviting her to sit, then retired behind the desk.

Frances reminded herself she had not come here to feel sorry for Sidney. She was in the position of less authority but she was not a supplicant. She held herself erect. She would be business-like. 'I've been to Surrey to see Fanny.'

He sat back, regarding her with caution. 'You do surprise me. I know how much she upset you with her accusations at The Langham.'

Frances let this pass. Fanny had apologised. 'She told me how obstructive you've become. She's vexed by your quarrel with Lloyd, as am I.'

He shifted in his chair, eyes meandering to the papers he had been studying, his caution justified. How to deal with her, the woman he idolised but who had never presented herself in his inner sanctum and never challenged his authority.

Frances went on, 'Fanny knows there will be as many stories told about Louis as people who met him. She only wants something that will do Louis justice, a fair account, she called it.'

Frances watched Sidney pick up a pencil and roll it between his fingers. 'We, Fanny and I, have come up with a suggestion you would do well to consider.'

He raised his eyebrows at the *we*, transferring the pencil to both hands.

'We talked over the possibilities.' Sidney raised his eyes. She had caught his interest, 'Fanny has gone to visit Graham Balfour. She'll ask him if he will write the *Life*.'

Sidney sprang to full attention. '*Balfour?*' She thought for a moment he would break the pencil in two, but he drew back from such vandalism and laid it down.

She no longer felt the need to keep her distance. Despite the width of the desk, she was able to lean across and touch the back of his hand with her fingers. 'Think about it. Balfour is educated, cultured and devoted to Louis. He's not a gossip. You said it yourself; he is straight.'

'But loyal to the widow.'

Of course it was a compromise, but compromise was required. 'He is loyal to the family, not just Fanny. Because of Louis, he respects both of us. He won't show us in a bad light.'

'But he's not a writer!.'

So many of them pursued this Holy Grail. She was a writer, she could list her translations and her articles, but no-one would ask her to write Louis's biography, nor would she want to. Sidney had not withdrawn his hand but there was still a gulf to be crossed.

Then who would you suggest?' Frances asked. 'If the writer can't be you, whose name would you want on the cover?'

Sidney was about to reel off the names she had suggested to Fanny, people he trusted, people he could influence. He opened his mouth and closed it again, wracked by indecision. 'I don't know.' Fanny's final card had taken the trick.

'So, why not the cousin?'

He shook his head. 'All those letters and documents. I won't have him pawing…' He saw her look of reproach. Balfour showed them only deference. 'You think he will steer a path?'

'I think he will.'

His hand rubbed his face, anticipating the difficulty of explaining, of withdrawing from the position he had defended for so long. 'The others won't like it. What can I possibly say to them?' He shook his head not in refusal but realigning his thoughts, considering the unthinkable that Fanny might be right. 'I can't quite take this in.'

'You can find a way to defend your decision. And think of the time you will have for other things.'

As far as she was concerned, the decision was made. She stood to go. 'I'll let you get on with your day.' She took a final look around the room. 'I must say I expected something more ornate, or at least more comfortable.'

Sidney followed her gaze as if noticing his surroundings for the first time. 'I don't spend much time here. I'm mostly in the galleries or in meetings. This is just a place of work.'

His real life, he implied, was elsewhere. 'Yes, I dare say.' As well as the museum he had his house and his club. She hoped that she too was part of that elsewhere.

He rose to show her to the door then stopped and laid his hand on her shoulder. 'Did I say how elegant you look today?'

She accepted the compliment with a smile and left.

Hurrying back through the corridors, she barely felt the knotty floorboards under her feet. She was buoyed up by a sense of achievement. She had seen what was needed and brought Sidney to her way of thinking. As she emerged onto the museum steps, she inhaled deeply. Doubt and despondency were behind her. Unlike Fanny, she didn't have to contend with ill-health or loneliness. She had the society of the people she knew and loved. Louis might have gone but Sidney was very much alive. One day he would thank her for what she had done, for freeing him from a burden he could no longer carry. If not, she had done her best.

51.

A few months later, Louis's letters were published in an edition of four volumes. Some reviewers named it as the most important book of the year and Sidney's preface, a substantial review of Louis's life and work, was given the praise it deserved. Balfour's *Life* was under way but some way off from publication.

As the new century dawned, Frances found herself the object of some curiosity. Acquaintances remarked they had never realised it was she who had introduced Sidney to R.L.S. She was suddenly not just Sidney's companion, but also Louis's friend, supporter and early muse. Invitations arrived at her door to all the London gatherings. It was a matter of some surprise that they came addressed to *Mrs Sitwell*. Was she really that woman? One name, one life, she supposed, could encompass many people.

One evening, Sidney was at her home and on the point of leaving when he turned his hat in his hands and said, 'Frances, do you think ...?'

She could guess what was coming. *Will you sleep with me?* or *Will we marry?* But she wasn't ready to say yes to either. Given no encouragement, Sidney turned away, and so the question went unasked.

In April, she was invited for the very first time to the Gosses' Sunday tea, an institution more famous even than Sidney's soirees and more sociable in intent. It was

Frances's first visit to the house on Delamere Terrace which Sidney had so often spoken of.

He had walked from Bloomsbury to collect her and they had a longer walk ahead across the Regents Canal but he was brimming with energy. 'It's a wonderful house. You will love it.'

Gosse, Louis, Sidney: the importance of what they were to each other was fading and she didn't want to spoil the day by peering into past events.

In the Gosses' drawing room, there was much discussion of Browning, Edmund's close friend and neighbour, who had recently died. Frances gravitated towards Nellie, as tall and graceful as ever, and complimented her on her house. It had belonged previously to Nellie's brother-in-law, the artist Alma-Tadema. 'Such a wonderful position and fine proportions,' Frances said.

'We are very lucky,' Nellie agreed, 'and with the children growing up, we have more time to enjoy it.'

Frances said she had always been happy in her house in Marylebone, even if the neighbours were less illustrious.

'But just think,' Nellie said, dropping her voice, 'how wonderful it will be to live in the museum. I hear there's croquet on the lawn after hours, and the rooms are very gracious.'

Nellie assumed that she and Sidney would be married. Frances framed a reaction. 'I think it's too late to uproot myself.'

Nellie took her arm. 'Nonsense, it's never too late, and solitude is terribly overrated.'

Frances didn't consider herself solitary, but she remembered the bleak office that Sidney used and how the museum house lacked a woman's touch. He might be the one lacking company.

There was a ring at the door and the huddle of Edmund's men friends broke apart to admit the newcomers. A middle-aged man, a redhead with cherubic features, was accompanied by a woman of striking beauty and two equally angelic children, whose cotton jackets the mother was busy removing. Everyone seemed to know the family except Frances.

'Who is this?' she asked Nellie.

Nellie laughed. 'Don't tell me you haven't met the Thornycrofts!' Nellie crossed the room to take the man by the arm and steered him away from the others. 'Hammo, come here for a moment and meet someone new.'

Of course, it was Edmund's lover of old, of whom Frances had known nothing until Suka enlightened her. Hammo Thornycroft beamed at Frances and said how delighted he was to meet *the famous Mrs Sitwell*. She accepted his handshake, asked how his latest project was progressing, and then, feeling suddenly eclipsed by so many London celebrities, brought the conversation to a close. 'Go back to your friends and your lovely family. I am very dull today. We can talk some other time.'

His smile became impish. 'I think they have more fun without me!' he said, but she shook her head and gave him a gentle push so that he crossed the room to stand next to Gosse, who clapped him on the shoulder. They stood side by side, fair head next to dark, in an attitude of easy companionship, while Nellie took Frances to meet Agatha Thornycroft. The two families were clearly close.

Later, while tea was being served at the long dining table, Hammo regaled everyone with his new enthusiasm for cycling. Edmund immediately declared himself at least as proficient on a bicycle. There was nothing for it but the men should settle the matter with a race. Without more ado, what was left of tea was packed up in baskets and the entire company set off on the half-hour walk to The Regents Park, the guests forming a rough crocodile. Edmund and Hammo (who had agreed to push the bicycles rather than ride) took the lead. Agatha and Nellie followed with the children. Frances and Sidney came together at the rear of the meandering procession as it straggled along the canal.

'Isn't this a tonic?' Sidney said.

He was right. The glinting sun had worked magic on the impure water, creating a ribbon of light. The weather, the company, the moment were benign. Ahead of them the hair of Hammo Thornycroft, the tallest of the company, could be glimpsed bobbing golden in the light.

'Hammo is quite the Greek god,' Frances said.

Sidney's laugh was unselfconscious. 'Yes, he could be one of his own creations.'

'I didn't realise he and Edmund were still close.'

'Ah, you know about that? It's hardly a secret these days. Gosse used to worry dreadfully. When I went to visit Louis in Braemar, he was on his way to meet Hammo. He had a hopeless crush on him.'

Hopeless seemed to imply harmless. 'Did Nellie know about it?'

'I suppose she did, or some of it. Gosse and Hammo often holidayed together.'

Was Suka's *cavorting*, simply a holiday? Either way, Sidney did not see a problem.

At that moment Frances heard Gosse's wife and his former lover laughing at something the youngest child had said. On such an afternoon, what problem could there possibly be? If the men once indulged in something more intimate, that time had passed. Perhaps Frances needed to reconsider the many forms that love could take.

After the race, in which Edmund claimed a doubtful victory (Hammo's machine struck a stone and threw him off at the last gasp) the party headed back to Delamere Terrace, taking them farther from Marylebone. Sidney and Frances made their excuses and split off from the crowd.

'We've walked quite a way, today,' Sidney said, after they had walked nearly a mile.

'Sidney, I'm not in my dotage just yet.'

He was still entirely at ease and smiled into the sky before saying, 'You will never have a dotage. Not if I can help it.'

'I've rarely seen you look so happy. I'm going to start calling you Felix, as Louis did.' The name had stuck after that day in the orchard, a joke and a mark of affection.

Sidney's face creased in a grin. 'You do realise that strictly speaking *felix* means lucky rather than happy?'

The distinction was typical of Sidney. 'And you didn't correct him? I'm astonished!'

He shrugged. 'Between friends it hardly mattered. Besides,' he tucked her arm more firmly into his, 'With you I am most certainly both.'

52.

When they reached her home, she invited him in and he followed her into the kitchen, whose tendency to damp had rendered it pleasantly cool. Water from the tap splashed brightly into the jug which she carried into the sitting room with two glasses.

Sidney settled himself in the armchair, his legs stretched out on the rug.

'You know I've been thinking?' Sidney said.

'About my dotage?'

A wry smile from Sidney. 'Possibly about my own.'

She drew her chair close to his. The afterglow of the trip to the park suffused the space between them. 'I'm sorry we seem to have grown apart, compared to before.'

She let him choose from the possible 'befores' —Albert's death, then Louis, the furore over the letters.

'It has been a difficult period, and so terribly busy.'

She nodded agreement. The glasses of water were raised and lowered. The room faced west so she drew the blind down to remove the glare of the sun.

'Have you heard from Balfour?'

'Once or twice. I help where I feel I can. I've asked him to show me the passages where you or I are mentioned. I remind myself he's not Lloyd.'

She let these remaining annoyances glide by in the slipstream of the afternoon.

346

'Frances, do I recall we were going to be married?'

His smile was teasing. That morning she'd been determined to be single, or at least resigned to it. But solitude, as Nellie said, was overrated, and at the museum there was plenty of room. She might have her own sitting room, the small lounge overlooking the trees.

Sidney broke into her thoughts. 'What are you thinking?'

'I am thinking of how my cloisonne would enhance your mantlepiece.'

He looked at the dainty vases with their vibrant enamel and frowned. 'I would have to move the Wedgewood.' Then he caught her eye and laughed. 'But a change is always welcome.'

It was fun to have Sidney in this mood. A man in the moment of proposing did not want to be deflected, but she needed to be sure.

'Fanny talked about Louis. She accepts his other loves, as she put it, because she knows he was hers in all the important ways.'

Sidney met her gaze. 'I've forgiven you and Louis. We've crossed that bridge, have we not?'

She nodded. And she had subconsciously crossed another. 'Tell me, what's your happiest memory of Louis?'

He was at a loss. 'Happiest? With so many to choose from?'

'Something must stand out. The Riviera? Davos?' She no longer begrudged him happiness at a time when she had been downcast.

He nodded. 'Yes these, but shall I tell you another?' She motioned that he should go on. 'Do you remember the summer of '74, the evening you sent him packing?'

Frances suppressed a sigh. It was the one hour with

Louis she would rather not remember but she should hear Sidney's side.

Sidney went on, 'As you know he got back to Hampstead in a terrible state. I sent out for chloral.'

She had heard part of this story. Did she need to hear more? 'I know you looked after him.'

'I lay down and lulled him to sleep. The previous winter in Monte Carlo, after that awful suicide he had nursed me like a baby and I think I wanted to repay him.'

He left a pause for Frances to react but she was careful not to. Sidney must say what he had to say.

'Next morning,' he continued, 'I woke to see him propped on one elbow, smiling down at me. We were side by side, *like effigies on a tomb* as he put it. "Ye Gods," he said. "What did you give me? It could have brought down an elephant!"'

Frances smiled at the hyperbole, so typical of Louis.

'You know the girlish looks,' Sidney went on, 'the flamboyance, were just the part he liked to play, man of letters, aesthete even. The Whitman book he used to carry wasn't the signal people took it for. Anyway, it was obvious he was *madly in love* with you.'

Sidney was answering the question she had never asked outright. She was content. Like Fanny she wouldn't look any further. 'But was it his happiest memory?' she asked him.

'Let me finish!' Sidney gave a mock glower. 'There followed a most diverting breakfast in which he complained about the cold porridge, the unsuitable bowls and my irritatingly sincere character, admitting to an inexplicable love of my 'dry old bones.'

Sidney was only five years older than Louis but had always seemed very much wiser.

'He then threatened to throw me in the Thames until I spat bilge water, a threat he never carried out, although we laughed about it many a time afterwards. We were the only lodgers in the house that week. I promised to support him in his career. I remember his bony hands stretched across the breakfast table. "I believe you, Colvin," he said, "I'm relying on you to do just that. Introduce me to your friends, find me work, keep me to the task in hand. I'm a lucky beggar to have you."'

This was a glimpse of how Sidney and Louis were with each other. The breakfast with its verbal sparring meant as much as the night of consolation. Did she have a woman friend of the same kind? Maud was stalwart, Georgie could be diverting but never this close. She brought her attention back to Sidney.

'I believed absolutely in his talent.'

Sidney had been his most faithful servant. 'Take my hand,' Frances said, and when he did, she kissed his knuckles. 'He was the luckiest man alive.'

Sidney sat back and looked at her appraisingly. 'What about you? Will you tell me your fondest memory?'

Like Sidney she had very many. 'I think I would pick the orchard at Cockfield.'

'Your moment as Pomona? That was a long time ago.'

She recalled it as an age of innocence, and yet she was a married woman who had known both good and evil. It was only a year before the event Sidney had chosen, but so much had happened in between. For Sidney and Louis there had been adventures in London and Menton. Circumstances had kept her apart.

'There are others,' she allowed, 'but some of them were really only words.'

He stood up, took her by the hands and put his arms

around her. 'What a pair we are. Do you think we can manage without him?'

His summer jacket was smooth against her cheek. 'In some ways I think life might be easier.'

He was ready to leave, but hesitated. 'There's something I'd like you to think about.'

Some time ago he'd purchased a plot for himself in the churchyard at Hampstead. He wanted them to share their final resting place. He apologised for talking about death on such a happy day.

Frances was unperturbed. Death was inescapable and would make its presence felt all the more as they grew older. 'I'm glad you've thought of it,' she said. 'And where else would I want to be?'

His hands were on her shoulders, and for a moment she thought he was going to give her bad news. 'I thought you might like Freddie to be with us too.'

Her first born, and the first to be lost, was still shining in her memory, his body in exile in Albert's old parish. Sidney had barely known Freddie. This was for her, a gift that proved his love. 'He could be moved? Is that possible?'

'I've looked into it. There are certain regulations and some expense. Nothing I couldn't manage.'

If only Bertie could be transported from the snows of Davos, but one boy would be some comfort. 'Thank you, thank you, Sidney.'

He nodded, smiled and in the hallway picked up his hat to go, promising to come the following evening and stay. She was pleased to have a last evening to herself. They had the rest of their lives together, not the longest stretch, but who knew, possibly the best.

She looked around her sitting room, surveying the goods and chattels that would go with her to Bloomsbury. Her letters from Louis were back in their usual place, dissected, annotated, some sent to print. There was of course one more, given to her by Fanny, entirely different to the others. It linked the man she knew with the man he became; it talked of her past and her future and made sense of both of them.

She went to her bedroom, took it from her nightstand drawer and read it through once more, smiling at its well-meaning advice. She didn't need Louis's permission to marry Sidney. She had known it all along.

In the room no fire was laid but a box of matches was kept next to the kindling. The first one she struck burst into flame. There was no time for hesitation. She held it to the letter, the jagged lines of Louis's writing, the bond of friendship, the words of love. As the thin sheets curled and fell in a pale plume of smoke, she let go of sadness and remorse. He was gone and she was released from her side of the bargain. *Throw every letter on the fire.* Amongst the insubstantial ash she found a shard of satisfaction, that she had done to this last letter what he did to all of hers.

Outside, dusk had fallen but the sky was clear. She returned to the sitting room and lit the mantle but left the curtains open, savouring the previous afternoon, Edmund and Hammo charging pell-mell up the Broad Walk, just as Sidney and Louis once hurtled down the slope at Davos. *Take happiness where you can*, Louis had said. She must look to the future.

At the piano she opened the stool and rifled through the music then, in consternation, turned the pile upside down. *Chant d'Amour*, Louis's favourite, couldn't possibly be lost. The pile slid to the floor and she groped amongst the sheets until her fingers were grimy with dust. She stood up and smoothed her skirt. How foolish she was. She wiped her hands on a handkerchief then sat down at the instrument, closed her eyes, and played the piece from memory.

Afterword

The real Frances Sitwell (known as Fanny) married Sidney Colvin in a quiet ceremony at St Mary Marylebone in 1903, attended by a few close friends including Henry James and Maud Babington. They lived in the Keeper's House at the British Museum until 1912 when he retired and was knighted. Lady Colvin died in 1924 after an exceptionally happy and successful marriage.

The following, published in 1922, is Lady Colvin's only public statement about her relationship with Robert Louis Stevenson and the letters they exchanged.

MY FIRST MEETING WITH R. L. S.
LADY COLVIN.

ONE *summer many years ago I was staying with my friends the Rev. Prof, and Mrs Churchill Babington at Cockfield Rectory in Suffolk. Mrs Babington was a first cousin of Louis Stevenson, as he was always called then. I had come to rest and recuperate after a great sorrow and much illness, and one morning my hostess said to me, ' I am expecting a young cousin of mine to-day to come and stay here, I do hope you won't mind; he is a very clever, nice fellow, and I think you will like him.'*

That afternoon I was lying on a sofa near an open window when I saw a slim youth in a black velvet jacket and straw hat, with a knapsack on his back, walking up the avenue. 'Here is your cousin,' I said to Mrs Babington; and she went out through the open French window to meet him and bring him in. For a few minutes he talked rather shyly to us about his long walk out from Bury St Edmunds in the heat; and then my little boy, who was with me and had been staring with solemn eyes at Louis, suddenly went up to him and said, 'If you will come with me, I'll show you the moat; we fish there sometimes.' Louis rather jumped at this, and the two boys (for R. L. S. did not look anything like his twenty-three years) went out together hand in hand, and came back in a little while evidently fast friends. From that moment Louis was at his ease, and before twenty-four hours were over the little boy's mother was a fast friend too of R. L. S., and remained so to the end of his life.

Then the hours began to fly by as they had never flown before in that dear, quiet old Rectory. Laughter, and tears too, followed hard upon each other till late into the night, and his talk was like nothing I had ever heard before, though I knew some of our best talkers and writers. Before three days were over I wrote to Sidney Colvin, who was then Slade Professor and living at Cambridge, and begged him (with Mrs Babington's leave) not to delay his promised visit to Cockfield if he wanted to meet a brilliant and to my mind unmistakable young genius called Robert Louis Stevenson. He came very soon, and this was the beginning of that friendship which every one knows made so great a difference in the lives of both men, but more especially in that of R. L. S., since it came to him at the beginning, and at the very moment when he most needed sympathy and advice. For nearly three years after this Louis wrote me long letters almost daily, pouring out in them all the many difficulties and troubles of that time of his life. A number of these letters have been published, or part-published, in the volumes of letters edited by Sir Sidney Colvin, and a great many more, too sacred and intimate to print, are still in my possession.

Rosaline Masson (ed) 1922. *I Can Remember Robert Louis Stevenson*, Edinburgh: Chambers, p. 87-8.

Additional Notes

The real Frances Sitwell?
In the countless biographies of Robert Louis Stevenson, Frances Sitwell is allotted a few paragraphs or, at most, pages that combine verifiable facts with varying degrees of speculation. In these, opinions are divided as to what exactly happened between her and Robert Louis Stevenson in the summer of 1873 and its aftermath.

Few consider her life from then on, and I've assembled her story from many sources, trying to create a coherent whole from a jigsaw riddled with awkward edges and missing pieces. There are contradictions too, and in choosing one possibility over another, my version of events occasionally ignores, or embellishes, some details to present a believable character at the heart of a satisfying story. I hope readers will accept that the real Frances Sitwell (I apologise for using her more formal name – two Fannys in one novel wouldn't have worked!) is no longer available to us, and my version is just one of many that could be written.

As for the other characters, all are based on historical figures except for Matthew and Lucinda Swift.

Frances Sitwell's letters
When Lady Colvin died, aged eighty-five, her letters from Robert Louis Stevenson, which had been heavily edited

(some say butchered!) for publication by Sidney Colvin, became his property. They were then bequeathed, in a mahogany box, to the Advocates Library in Edinburgh, with the proviso they were not to be opened until 1949 i.e. twenty-five years after her death. Was this her idea or his? Or perhaps a decision by both of them? Again, we shall never know.

Having started this novel just before the lockdown of late 2020, I've never seen the original letters but they are now in the National Library of Scotland, although, according to their catalogue, the original box has gone missing. Ernest Mehew (in his introduction to the eight-volume edition of Stevenson's letters), thinks that Colvin is likely to have destroyed any letters he considered too personal, so even this collection may be incomplete.

Quotations from letters used and referenced in section headings are from the Booth and Mehew edition of the letters. In addition, these letters are alluded to in the text:

Chapter 6, p.115, Letter 343, Booth and Mehew, Vol 2, p. 93.

Chapter 26, p. 170, I imagine Frances replying to Booth & Mehew, Vol 8, Letter 2727.

Chapter 38 p. 247, Letter 354, Booth & Mehew, Vol. 2, p, 108.

All letters occurring in the novel, including the epistle from Louis to Frances in Chapter 49, are fictional.

As far as we can gather, Robert Louis Stevenson did destroy all of the letters sent to him by Frances Sitwell in the early years of their friendship, an act referred to in Letter 140 (Booth & Mehew, Vol. 1, p. 303):

"I...burnt all your letters but the first and the last; and these two I carry with me, my beautiful friend, as a sort of pledge of your existence."

And perhaps Letter 306 (Booth & Mehew, Vol. 2, p. 42):

"It shall be as you wish, dear friend, about your letters, only forgive me if I go about it slowly."

Some of Frances's letters from later years may have survived. One, for instance, is quoted in a note to Letter 2727 (Booth & Mehew Vol. 8) to which Frances replies (April 1894):

"In spite of what you say about old age (with which I deeply sympathise) we cannot but rejoice that the gods did not love you selfishly but have left you to us poor humans who can ill spare the like of you my dear...." (Booth & Mehew Vol. 8, p.283)

Frances and Fanny Stevenson
Letters from Fanny Stevenson to Fanny Sitwell and Sidney Colvin can be found in E.V. Lucas's *The Colvins and their Friends* (Methuen, 1928, also in online libraries).

The argument between Sidney Colvin and Fanny regarding Louis's biography is fully documented in two articles in the Times Literary Supplement (no. 3020, 15 Jan. 1960, p. 37 and no. 3021, 22 Jan. 1960, p. 52) by Graham Balfour's son, who reports that relationships between the Colvins and the Balfour family were eventually mended. According to Margaret McKay in *The Violent Friend*, (Abridged ed., Dent 1969, p. 347-8), Fanny Stevenson too was reconciled with the Colvins. She received them as visitors in 1907 in London, and after her death, they considered themselves "English god-parents" to Fanny's grandson, Austen Strong.

Lady Colvin
Descriptions of Frances Sitwell are nearly all from her twenty years as Lady Colvin when she was enough of a celebrity for Somerset Maugham to satirise her in the novel *Cakes and Ale.* According to E. V. Lucas (*Reading Writing and Remembering,* Harper, 1932), she made a very striking impression on those who met her and was famous for spotting new talent:

"With Lady Colvin there always had to be a young lion to nourish — that necessity was of the essence of her warm romantic heart — and nothing gave her greater satisfaction than to receive confidences from the unhappy and pour balm into their wounds."

And from the same source, quoting Hugh Walpole:

"...she had a deep understanding of the complexities of modern life; you could not tell Colvin everything, because to shock him was to hurt him too deeply; but there was nothing that you could not tell to her."

It was surely this ability to invite confidences, as well as her beauty, that attracted the young Robert Louis Stevenson.

Beyond the Book
Other research topics and sources are covered in *Beyond the Book,* a series of notes published by me over recent months. Early editions are available on my website https://alibacon.com where you can also subscribe to future issues.

The principal online source for the life and work of Robert Louis Stevenson is the website maintained by Edinburgh Napier University https://robert-louis-stevenson.org/

Here are a few more suggestions for those who would like to learn more.

The Letters

Booth, B.A. & Mehew, E. eds., *The Letters of Robert Louis Stevenson*. Yale University Press, 1994-5, Vols 1-8, is the definitive edition, but a very good impression can be gained from the either of following:

Mehew E. ed., *Selected Letters of Robert Louis Stevenson*. Yale University Press, 1997.

Stevenson's Letters (online) https://lettersofrobertlouis stevenson.wordpress.com/ a blog curated by Mafalda Cipollone containing Sidney Colvin's original edition with informative illustrations.

Biographies

Furnas, J.C., *Voyage to Windward*, Faber, 1952. The first biography to have accessed the uncensored version of the letters.

Harman, Claire, *Robert Louis Stevenson, a biography*. Harper, 2005.

Hodges, Jeremy, *Lamplit, Vicious Fairyland*, serialised online https://robert-louis-stevenson.org/lamplit-vicious-fairy-land/